Praise for
The Daughters of Edward Darley Boit

"Like Victoria, the heroine (novel, I have always been draw .mous portrait, but unlike her, I ystical boundary into the world of the painting. Shy, d, and encumbered by a back brace, Victoria's life begins to change when she befriends the Boit sisters and attempts to save them from the predations of a dangerous man."

—Mari Coates,
author of the award-winning novel *The Pelton Papers*

"Inventive, suspenseful and satisfying, *The Daughters of Edward Darley Boit* is a delightful read."

—Lisa Braver Moss,
author of the award-winning novel *Shrug*

"Part historical fiction, part time-travel fantasy, part psychological suspense story, *The Daughters of Edward Darley Boit* is a highly original coming-of-age novel whose themes include friendship, sexual identity, disability, and activism. This retro #MeToo novel—or rather, #NotOnMyWatch novel—follows fifteen-year-old Victoria Hubbard as she straddles two eras: the turmoil of the 1960s and the art world of the 1880s."

—Kate Brubeck,
writer and editor

Sara Loyster's imaginative and beautifully rendered journey into the past shows readers the importance of being courageous for others in the face of danger."

—S. Baer Lederman,
author and editor

"Victoria initially surrenders to the invisible pull from John Singer Sargent's famous painting of the Boit sisters out of curiosity. Traversing time through the portal of this grand and mysterious painting, she encounters a situation that sets off alarms in a twentieth-century girl's head. Art, art history, and the milieu of different time periods contribute complexity to the tale. Sara Loyster creates a vivid and admirable heroine, someone who acts swiftly and assuredly. It is a focused, fascinating reading experience."

—David Howd, children's librarian

The Daughters of
Edward Darley Boit

The Daughters of Edward Darley Boit

A NOVEL

SARA JANE LOYSTER

She Writes Press, a BookSparks imprint
A Division of SparkPointStudio, LLC.

Copyright © 2021, Sara Loyster

All rights reserved. No part of this publication may be reproduced, distributed, or transmitted in any form or by any means, including photocopying, recording, digital scanning, or other electronic or mechanical methods, without the prior written permission of the publisher, except in the case of brief quotations embodied in critical reviews and certain other noncommercial uses permitted by copyright law. For permission requests, please address She Writes Press.

Published 2021

Printed in the United States of America

Print ISBN: 978-1-64742-165-6
E-ISBN: 978-1-64742-166-3
Library of Congress Control Number: 2021904173

For information, address:
She Writes Press
1569 Solano Ave #546
Berkeley, CA 94707

She Writes Press is a division of SparkPoint Studio, LLC.

All company and/or product names may be trade names, logos, trademarks, and/or registered trademarks and are the property of their respective owners.

This is a work of fiction. Names, characters, places, and incidents either are the product of the author's imagination or are used fictitiously. Any resemblance to actual persons, living or dead, is entirely coincidental.

For Eugenia,
my inspiration always.

. . . he perceived that it was never fixed,
never arrested, that ignorance, at the instant one touched it,
was already flushing faintly into knowledge,
that there was nothing
that at a given moment you could say
a clever child didn't know.

—from "The Pupil" by Henry James

Chapter One

Four Sisters

April, 1963, Boston

"Victoria," her mother called through the door. "I hope you're getting dressed. I want to leave in thirty minutes." It was a Saturday morning in April, a couple of weeks before Victoria's fifteenth birthday, and she was in her room, still in her pajamas, as her mother had guessed.

Victoria didn't reply. She leaned over and turned up the volume on her record player. With the music this loud she could claim she hadn't heard her mother call. When her mother said nothing more, she leaned back on her bed and picked up her book again. She was reading *To Kill a Mockingbird* for the third time. Soon she'd know it by heart.

The song ended and the next one began, the voices spilling off the vinyl in perfect harmony as they did each time Victoria played this record. "If I had a hammer, I'd hammer in the mo-o-rning . . ." She loved Peter, Paul and Mary's version of this song, but it was starting to drive her nuts. *If I had a hammer,* she thought gloomily, *a really big sledgehammer, I'd bash down the walls of this house and get out of here.*

But, please, please, did it have to be with her mother? Her mother was insisting on taking her to the art museum today which was the last thing Victoria wanted to do. But what choice did she have? She had zero friends and a mother who refused to let her go anywhere alone. And she *had* to get out of the house.

A firm knock signaled that her mother was back. "Victoria!" Her mother entered without waiting for a reply. "You can't spend another weekend in your room. Please get dressed!"

Victoria groaned. "Just leave me alone," she mouthed, too softly for her mother to hear.

"Victoria!" her mother said again, and this time she was starting to sound angry.

"All right, all right," Victoria grumbled, putting the book aside and rising from the bed. "But don't rush me. I need to shower first."

"You need to hurry," her mother warned. "The museum gets crowded on Saturdays."

Victoria went into her bathroom and peered at herself in the mirror. Her dark hair, which was short and very curly like her dad's, needed a trim. She pushed back her bangs and leaned in close to study the constellation of small bumps that had taken up residence on her forehead. *This is only the beginning*, she thought. *Soon my whole face will be a moonscape of pimples.*

She took off her pajamas and began to remove the brace that encased her torso from shoulders to crotch, unfastening the complicated straps and buckles one by one. Acne was an imperfection everyone could see. Scoliosis, a curvature in her spine, was mostly an invisible deformity, but it meant having to wear this torture device twenty-three hours a day. Except for her parents and her old friend Pam, no one knew about her condition—and no one knew how itchy and uncomfortable the brace was, how heavy, how bulky, how hard it was to get the straps adjusted just right. Too tight and it pinched; too loose and it did no good. She'd managed to conceal it under her clothing since she'd started wearing it in January, but she didn't know if she'd be able to keep it a secret when summer arrived and she started wearing lighter clothes.

Once she was naked, she studied her reflection. She had no breasts to speak of and her hips were as slim as a boy's. It was hard to tell if her shoulders were leveling out or not. The tilt wasn't obvious to most people, but Victoria could see it. She'd been wearing the brace for three months now and hoped it was doing its job. She fingered the grooves on her flat stomach caused by the tight straps.

"You won't have to wear it once you stop growing," the doctor had said. "Hopefully not to your senior prom." His attempt at humor made Victoria want to snarl. What did he know about it? He wouldn't act so jolly if someone had forced him to wear a back brace to high school.

She turned from the mirror, sick of staring at her skinny, crooked body, and stepped into the shower. Thankfully, no one ever saw her naked. The doctor had written her an excuse to get out of gym class, and nobody invited her for sleepovers since Pam had moved away.

She finished her shower and toweled off. After the brace was back in place and all the straps were buckled, she pulled on a bulky sweater (one that did a halfway decent job of hiding the hideous contraption); a pair of comfortable corduroy slacks; and her mother's old riding boots, which felt as soft as butter on her feet. She grabbed a yellow scarf and used it to flatten her unruly hair.

"Okay. I'm ready," Victoria said to her mother, who was coming out of her own room down the hall. Her mother frowned at Victoria's sulky tone, but didn't comment.

At least she's not complaining about my clothes, Victoria thought as she followed her mother down the stairs. Her mother was dressed in her usual simple, sophisticated style—heels, stockings and a tailored wool suit, her smooth dark hair swept back from her forehead by a neat beret. Victoria felt scruffy by comparison, but so glad to be out of her school uniform—the pleated skirt, white blouse, and burgundy blazer she was required to wear all week. On weekends she insisted on dressing as she pleased. Her mother didn't like it, but Victoria didn't care. Since she'd started wearing the brace, she'd decided her mother had no right to tell her what she could and couldn't wear. Besides, pants were becoming more acceptable for girls—though never for school or parties. *Soon we'll be wearing them all the time*, Victoria thought, pleased to realize this was one battle her mother would never win.

"I want to see the new John Singer Sargent picture," her mother said over her shoulder. "It's a portrait of Mrs. Edward Darley Boit."

As if everyone would know who that was, Victoria thought.

"The museum's lucky to get it."

Blah, blah, blah.

Her mother, who'd majored in art history in college, had recently signed up to be a museum docent. She was full of inside information about the complicated workings of the art museum and loved passing it along to her daughter—in fact, it was all she ever talked about anymore.

On the cab ride to the museum, Victoria stared out the window, turning a deaf ear to her mother's description of the historical significance of the painting they were about to see. The young magnolia trees that lined Newbury Street were just beginning to show buds. Soon, Victoria knew, they'd break out in creamy white flowers that would sweeten the air and light up the entire street. She watched as two girls about her age stopped to admire something in the window of one of the shops. Victoria wished she knew someone she could invite to wander around downtown with her on a Saturday morning. *Even if I did,* she thought, *Mom would never let the two of us out of her sight.*

When they entered the vast Sargent gallery at the museum, Victoria's mother made a beeline for the new painting. Victoria looked at the portrait—a red-cheeked, middle-aged woman in a shiny polka dot dress, with an extravagant hair ornament poking out of the top of her head—and decided Mrs. Boit looked a little drunk. Victoria wasn't nearly as fascinated by art as her mother was, but she did find herself moved by certain paintings, especially portraits. She liked looking at people's faces and imagining what their lives might have been like. This portrait, however, left her cold.

Victoria scanned the rest of the gallery. The place was starting to fill up. It wasn't just the usual crowd, but also a bunch of teenagers with sketch pads who were making copies of some of the paintings. Victoria's eyes were drawn to an enormous painting on the far wall of the long room. From a distance, the odd arrangement of figures was hard to make out, but as she moved closer, details of the picture emerged. She was aware of people around her—a woman passed by wearing gardenia perfume, a man spoke of Sargent's brilliant use of light and shadow—but all of Victoria's attention was focused on the painting. It pulled her forward like a magnet, gathering her in. As she drew near, a girl about her own age moved to block her path. She planted herself and her huge sketchpad right in front of the picture and started to draw.

Stopping behind her, Victoria couldn't help noticing the girl's unusually long hair. She wore it in a thick braid that fell over one shoulder and brushed her drawing as she worked. These days, no one their age would be caught dead wearing braids. Most teenagers wore their hair short or shoulder length, sometimes teased into puffy beehives. Victoria's own hair was hardly fashionable, but at least it was short. This girl looked like a throwback to the 1950s, with her long hair and demure blue-and-white checked blouse.

The girl must have sensed Victoria's eyes on her and moved slightly to give Victoria more room. Victoria wished she had the painting to herself, but once she began studying it, she forgot about the girl beside her. If this was supposed to be a portrait of four girls, it was the most unusual portrait she'd ever seen.

The museum kept the galleries cool to preserve the paintings, but Victoria felt hot—the way she'd felt when she'd had the flu and a high fever had distorted her vision, making everything look like she was seeing it through a long tube. At the end of the tube were these painted images: four young girls and two enormous Japanese vases, each as tall as a man. The vases were positioned on either side of a large empty room, their white porcelain surfaces covered with fuzzy suggestions of blue birds and foliage.

In the background, nearly obscured by shadow, a tall, thin girl leaned against the side of one of these vases gazing at another girl, a slightly shorter version of herself, who peered out of the gloom at the rear of the hall and stared straight at the viewer.

By contrast, the two figures in the foreground were brightly lit. The youngest girl was seated on the floor with a doll in her lap, her eyes focused to the side. Beside her stood a fourth girl, with blonde hair and a pretty face. Like the older girl at the rear, she faced the viewer, wearing an expression that was both frank and appraising. It was this latter girl that held Victoria's gaze. She looked as if she had something important she wanted to say.

"There you are," the girl's eyes seemed to declare. "You've found us at last." Victoria could almost hear her speaking, and her voice and face were so familiar Victoria felt sure she'd seen her, the real girl, not just her painted image, somewhere before. But where? The memory was fleeting, but powerful, like a dream image floating just at the edge of her consciousness. She tried desperately to bring the vague impression into focus, but couldn't do it.

"What do you think she's about to say?"

A voice broke through Victoria's reverie, and she flinched with surprise. Her attention was so focused on the painting it took her a moment to realize the girl with the braid was speaking to her.

Victoria shrugged, annoyed by the intrusion, but also startled that the girl had so accurately read her thoughts.

"She looks like a person who always speaks her mind," the girl remarked.

"I guess," Victoria said.

"I don't think I've done her justice," the girl said. She held up her drawing to show a sketch of the girl's face.

It was amazingly good. "It looks just like her!" Victoria said, despite herself.

"Not really," the girl said, smiling. "But, thanks."

"What is this, anyway?" Victoria asked, indicating the other young people who were drawing nearby. "A class?"

The girl nodded. "The museum has classes on Saturdays for kids—drawing, art appreciation, stuff like that."

A slim, young Asian woman wearing an artist's smock approached, and Victoria realized it must be the teacher as she began signaling her students to follow her out.

"I've got to go," the girl said and, to Victoria's relief, left with the others, her braid swinging like a pendulum behind her back.

The crowd was thinning out and it appeared likely, for a moment at least, that Victoria would have the girls in the painting more or less to herself. Sargent's composition fascinated her. Why had he decided to paint the older girls in shadow and the younger ones in the light? Why had he positioned them so far apart? It was a crazy choice for a portrait, but she was sure the artist had his reasons and she wanted to know what they were.

The blonde girl in the painting, the one who looked so familiar to Victoria, was still the most arresting figure of the four. What was she thinking, this golden-haired child, as she stood there so brazenly, arms behind her back, looking intently into Victoria's eyes?

Victoria was now five feet from the painting. As she stared at the canvas, she thought she caught a flash of movement and the sound of other voices. There was a child's voice, a very young child, high and clear, and an answering voice, manly and deep. A feeling of vertigo made Victoria close her eyes. When she opened them, she took another step closer, the voices still echoing in her mind. Almost against her will, her hand reached out.

"Step away!" A museum guard, an older Black man in a jacket with the museum's insignia on its pocket, thrust himself between Victoria and the painting.

Victoria stared at him dumbly, her arm still raised.

The guard placed a hand lightly on her shoulder. "You can't touch the art, miss. These pictures are easily damaged."

The feel of his hand on her shoulder broke the spell. "Sorry," she mumbled, shrugging him off, hating, as always, to be touched, petrified someone might feel the brace under her clothing and wonder about it. Quickly, she backed away, confused by her own behavior and afraid that everyone in the gallery was looking at her.

An arm locked around her shoulder. She turned to see her mother beside her, her pretty face made ugly by the frown lines creasing her forehead. Victoria shrank under the weight of that arm.

"What's going on?" Her mother glared at the guard.

"Nothing, Mom." Victoria tried to twist out of her mother's grasp, but the grip on her shoulder intensified, so she waited, forcing herself to stand still.

"The young lady was getting too close," the guard said. "She—"

"You have no right to shove my daughter," Victoria's mother said, cutting him off. "I should report you."

"He didn't! Mom!" Victoria said, shocked, aware that several people had stopped to listen. "It was my fault. I wasn't thinking. I—"

"Why did you wander off without telling me?" Victoria's mother demanded. "I turned around and you weren't there."

"I didn't wander off," Victoria said, feeling her face flame with embarrassment. "I was here the whole time."

"I thought you were right behind me," her mother snapped.

The guard shot Victoria an apologetic glance, then moved away, leaving mother and daughter standing alone in front of the strange picture. Victoria succeeded in freeing herself from her mother's grip.

Her mother stared after the retreating guard, looking reluctant to let the matter drop. When she turned back to Victoria, the scolding tone intensified. "What were you thinking? You know better than to get that close to a painting."

Victoria said nothing, wanting the incident to be over and wishing her mother would calm down. It certainly wasn't out of character for her mother to act protective, but her reaction to the guard seemed extreme. Was it because he was Black? Victoria had never thought of her mother as prejudiced, but now the idea crossed her mind and made her feel doubly humiliated at having caused this scene.

Her mother scowled at the people who had stopped to watch the confrontation and they walked quickly away. Turning once more to Victoria, she waved a hand at the painting. "You must have seen this before," she said irritably. "The museum's owned it forever."

"I don't remember," Victoria said. "If I did see it before, I never really *looked* at it." She felt dazed, unsure of what had just happened. She stared fixedly at the painting for several seconds, but the voices and the impression of movement had evaporated. She moved to the side so she could read the title placard posted on the wall: *The Daughters of Edward Darley Boit*.

Apparently, these girls were the daughters of the woman in the portrait they'd come to see. If so, there was no resemblance between these pale creatures and their ruddy faced mama. Victoria willed her mother to go back to Mrs. Boit and leave her in peace with the daughters.

"What's going on?" her mother said, peering at Victoria's face. "You look like you've seen a ghost."

"Nothing," Victoria said. "This painting—" and she waved her hand toward it, unable to say more.

"It's not your usual sort of portrait," her mother commented, her voice softening to an almost reverential tone as she shifted her attention to the painting in front of them. "It has such an empty feeling. It was considered very daring for its time, very original. To think Sargent was only twenty-six years old when he painted it!" She pointed to the background of the picture. "And those vases! They were the prized possessions of the Boit family and, when Edward Darley Boit agreed to let his friend paint his daughters, he insisted the vases be included in the portrait."

Victoria finished reading the description on the placard, only half listening. The Boits were described as habitual travelers, always abroad, always moving from one great European capital to the next. In 1882, when the portrait was painted, they were living in a grand apartment in Paris. *What lucky girls*, she thought. Her own parents were reluctant travelers, so she'd never visited Europe even once. The Boits, by contrast, had crossed the Atlantic by ship sixteen times and always brought the vases with them when they did.

"Can you imagine?" Victoria's mother said, as she too read the description on the placard. "Hauling those huge vases around with them like that? You wonder why they didn't just put them in storage till they were ready to settle down."

Victoria shrugged. She wasn't interested in the vases. She studied the faces of the girls. As an only child, Victoria had always longed for sisters. When she was little, she'd begged for a baby brother or sister, even volunteering to care for the baby herself. But her mother said she was too old to have any more children. She'd tried for many years to get pregnant before Victoria was born, but hadn't succeeded until she was nearly forty.

Sometimes, Victoria thought, remembering the weight of her mother's arm on her shoulder, *being a miracle child is a heavy burden to bear.*

But these Boit sisters didn't look happy either, in spite of having each other. They didn't look at one another and none of them smiled. They looked alone—standing together in a room, but separated by too much space. It made Victoria sad, but, she supposed, it was foolish to assume that sisters would automatically be friends.

"What do you know about them?" she asked her mother. "The Boits?"

"I know the father was an artist. He and Sargent had a joint watercolor show here in Boston back in the early part of this century."

"What about the daughters?" Victoria asked.

"What about them?"

"I don't know. Anything! I'm curious about them. What happened to them after Sargent painted them?"

"Well, they didn't become famous or anything. I do vaguely recall reading that a couple of them had mental problems, but I'm not sure which ones." Victoria's mother took her arm and steered her to the other side of the room. "You should see some of these others. Look, here's one of my favorites," she said, pointing to a painting on the near wall.

Victoria wasn't ready to leave—she wanted to stay with these mysterious sisters for a bit longer. But, still burning from her mother's mortifying outburst and not wanting to risk setting her off again, she let herself be pulled along.

Her mother kept her tour of the rest of the Sargent gallery mercifully short. "I'm starving!" she said. "Let's head home for lunch." She glanced at her watch. "I just need to run to the office and ask where my docent class is being held next Saturday. They forgot to tell me. I'll just be a few minutes."

"Can I wait for you here?" Victoria said, indicating a bench they were passing.

Her mother looked concerned, but she said okay. "Stay right there till I get back."

As soon as her mother disappeared down the hall, Victoria hurried back across the gallery to the wall where the giant painting of the Boit sisters hung. She wanted to look at it one more time and luckily, this time, there was no one blocking her way.

Stepping close to the painting, she again felt its magnetic pull. Again, she heard the murmur of voices; a little louder this time, a little clearer. As before, she was unable to stop herself from lifting a hand, yearning to touch, even though she knew it was prohibited.

The guard had to be somewhere nearby, but she didn't look for him.

She moved another step closer, so close she could see every brushstroke in the surface of the paint. As she watched, the thin membrane of the canvas seemed to vanish. The voices grew more distinct and the painted room opened up before her like an unfurling umbrella.

Victoria's vision began to blur, then she was falling and everything went black.

Chapter Two

A Long Way

November, 1882, Paris

Victoria came quickly to her senses. Her first impression was pain: her head pulsed with it and her eyes refused to focus. She sat up and the objects around her took form. It was obvious that she was no longer in the museum. She was in a room that looked like the entry hall of a large apartment. Its parquet floor and thick Persian carpet looked old and elegant, as did the red, intricately carved screen standing to her right. The human figures appeared tiny in the hall's vast space; even the giant Japanese vases were dwarfed by the lofty dimensions of the room.

As unbelievable as it seemed, Victoria realized she had fallen *into* the painting. But it was no longer a painting. It was a real room containing real people—people who looked just like the ones Sargent had painted.

The two elder Boit daughters stood at the rear of the hall, their heads together, whispering excitedly. They didn't seem to notice as Victoria materialized in front of them, but the littlest sister, seated on the floor, stared up at her in astonishment. The blonde girl with the curls stepped forward, one hand raised in greeting.

A bearded man was standing beside a huge canvas on the other side of the room. The painting was turned with its back to the room, but Victoria knew at once that it had to be *The Daughters of Edward Darley Boit* and the man beside it was John Singer Sargent.

"We're finished for today, girls," the painter said, speaking in a booming voice that Victoria instantly recognized. It was one of the voices she'd heard earlier when staring at the painting. "We'll begin again tomorrow afternoon at our usual time." Sargent was bent over a small table cleaning his brushes and seemed unaware of Victoria's presence.

Victoria felt breathless and lightheaded. The waft of turpentine coming from Sargent's work area was making her sick. Glancing at the painter, the girl who had stepped toward Victoria darted to her side.

"This way!" she whispered, seizing Victoria's arm and helping her to stand. "They mustn't see you." She glanced nervously at her older sisters, who were still whispering to one another, then pulled Victoria into a small room on their left and closed the door. Light came from a high window and Victoria could make out racks of coats, shelves holding hatboxes, and a long bench with boots arranged in a row underneath. The smell of boot polish was strong in the close confines of the room. In one corner was an umbrella stand holding several black umbrellas with elaborately carved handles, and next to it a bin holding an assortment of wooden racquets. Victoria looked about, trying to take it all in. The strangeness of everything she was seeing was starting to overwhelm her.

"You're white as a sheet," the girl told her, guiding her to the bench and helping her to sit. "Are you going to faint?"

Victoria focused all her attention on the girl, trying to make sense of her simple question. The room was spinning. Victoria was sure she would throw up, but after taking several ragged breaths, the dizziness passed. Her back brace was pinching the soft flesh of her side and she had to straighten up to get the pain to stop.

"What happened?" she said. "How did I get here? I—" She started to breathe rapidly again, but the girl laid a calming hand on her arm. After a minute, Victoria was able to go on. "Where am I?" she asked. "Who are you?"

"I'm Mary Louisa," the girl answered, "and you're in my house." As she spoke, the girl studied Victoria, her head thrust forward, her long, honey-colored curls falling against her cheeks. "I know you," she said. "I've seen you before."

"I don't think so," Victoria answered. "I've never been here before. This isn't Boston, is it?"

"No," the girl told her. "We used to live Boston. This is Paris."

"But I . . ." Victoria stammered, "*I* live in Boston,"

"Then you've come a long way. It takes days and days on the ship."

"No!" Victoria said. Her voice was shrill and the feeling of panic threatened to close her throat altogether. "It took no time at all. I can't explain! One second I was there, and now I'm here." She was too upset to hold back the tears. They dripped from her eyes and nose, and she buried her face in her hands. This couldn't be happening! She wasn't in the museum; she wasn't even in Boston. Her mother would be looking for her—and would be wild with worry when she discovered her daughter wasn't waiting on the bench as she'd promised!

Mary Louisa's soft hand touched Victoria's arm once more. "I don't know how you got here," she said, "but I knew you would come. I dreamed it. I dreamed your face." Her voice was filled with certainty and her hand patted Victoria's arm the way Victoria's father had sometimes soothed her to sleep when she was a little girl.

"What do you mean?" Victoria asked through her tears. "How could you dream me?"

"I don't know," Mary Louisa said, her tone losing some of its confidence. "But, I did. I dreamed your face, and I knew you were coming."

"I must have dreamed you, too," Victoria said, "because I've seen you before! The real you, the alive you." She knew she was making no sense and shook her head violently to clear it, sending tears flying in all directions. Mary Louisa stepped back in confusion and fright.

Seeing Mary Louisa's expression, Victoria realized she had to get herself under control. She didn't want to scare the younger girl more than she could help, but her heart was thudding in her chest. It was hard to form a coherent thought.

"I'm Victoria," she said, as the tears finally stopped. Her voice was raspy, but she made herself speak slowly and with some pretense of calm. "Victoria Hubbard."

"Victoria," Mary Louisa repeated. "That's the name of the Queen of England."

"That's right. And you're the daughter of Edward Darley Boit," Victoria said, and took a gasping breath, the impossibility of the situation almost overpowering her again.

"How did you know?" Mary Louisa asked.

"Because I know about you," Victoria answered, struggling once more for composure. "You're famous."

"What nonsense," Mary Louisa said. "How could I be famous?"

"Because of the painting," Victoria said and nodded her head toward the closed door. "His painting."

"You saw the painting! Then you *have* been here before. I've never seen it," Mary Louisa said. "It's almost finished, but he doesn't want anyone to see it till it's done. He's very strict about that. How did you manage to see it without his knowing?"

"I didn't see it here," Victoria said. "I saw it in a museum."

She stopped, unsure how to proceed. "In Boston—in 1963."

Mary Louisa stared at her. "In a museum? In—? But, how?"

Horror flooded Victoria once more and she put a hand over her mouth. "What year is this?" she asked. She thought she remembered the painting was dated 1882, but her brain was so addled, she couldn't be sure. "What if I can't get back?"

"Get back where?" Mary Louisa said, her eyes huge.

"This is not my time," Victoria whispered numbly.

Mary Louisa gaped at her, speechless.

There was a knock on the door and both girls jumped in fright.

"Isa," a small voice called, "let me come in."

"Go away, Julia," Mary Louisa hissed. "You can't come in now."

"I want to see your friend," Julia answered, her voice getting louder. "Let me come in." Julia's was the other voice Victoria had heard that morning when she first saw the painting—she was sure of it.

"No, go away."

"Mama's looking for you," Julia said, her voice louder still.

Mary Louisa locked eyes with Victoria, then stood and cautiously opened the door.

"Come in," she said, "but be quiet. I don't want anyone to know we're here."

Julia, the youngest sister, entered. "I won't tell," Julia said, lowering her voice to a whisper. "Mama's feeling a little better—she got up to have tea with Mr. Sargent. They don't know where you are." She turned, and focused on Victoria. "I thought you were the surprise," she said solemnly.

"What surprise?" Mary Louisa asked. "What are you talking about, Julia?"

Julia turned to her big sister. "Mr. Sargent said he had a surprise for me, and I thought she was the surprise. But she wasn't. There was a big box on the table when we went in for tea, and he wanted me to open it. It was a doll, but I told him I don't like dolls," she said, her mouth turning down in a scowl. "I want a real baby to play with, not a doll."

"Did Mama tell you that was rude?" her sister scolded.

"Yes," Julia said, "but Mr. Sargent said it didn't matter. The doll is for the painting. He said I just have to hold it while he paints, I don't have to play with it. But, it's very pretty. And Mr. Sargent gave it to me—maybe I will like it." She stopped talking, her eyes stealing back to Victoria. Judging by her expression, she seemed to find this stranger more fascinating than frightening. "Why aren't you wearing a dress?" she asked.

Mary Louisa looked like she was about to correct Julia's manners once more, but as she, too, registered Victoria's outfit, her expression changed. Victoria's slacks, sweater, and boots were a far cry from Mary Louisa's starched white pinafore and Julia's ivory muslin dress. She suddenly looked nervous, as though Victoria might be some sort of alien, instead of the girl from her dream.

"Don't girls ever wear pants in your—house?" Victoria asked. She didn't want to say "in your time" in front of Julia. As disjointed as her own thoughts remained, Victoria felt the need to hide her confusion from Julia.

"Not in our house," Mary Louisa told her. "Once I saw a woman riding in the Bois de Boulogne wearing a man's suit, but Mama said she was an artist and liked to shock people."

"Are you an artist?" Julia said to Victoria.

"No, I just like wearing pants," Victoria said. "They're comfortable and warm—I'm always too cold. I'd like to wear them all the time."

"You're tall and thin like my sister Florence. She's always cold." Mary Louisa said. "She's fourteen. How old are you?"

"I'm fourteen, too, but I'll be fifteen soon," Victoria said. "Let me guess—your other sister is maybe twelve, and you're nine, and you, Julia, are—four."

"How did you know I was four?" Julia asked, clapping her hands. "Everybody thinks I'm five!"

"Because you talk so much," Mary Louisa said. "And I'm eight, not nine."

"I'm pretty good at guessing," Victoria said, "but I can't guess your other sister's name. I know you're Julia, and you're Mary Louisa." She looked at each of the girls in turn. She was glad to see that Mary Louisa's face had lost its anxious look. "You said your oldest sister is Florence, but your other sister is named . . .?"

"Jane!" Julia cried. "She's very mean. She tells me to go away. But I don't mind. She wants to be with Florence, and I want to be with Isa. That's how we are."

"And lately, Jane is being more horrid than usual," Mary Louisa said. "She doesn't like being painted and is always late to our sittings. Poor Mr. Sargent has to be very patient."

Julia was looking intently at Victoria again. "I've never seen a girl with short hair," she said.

Victoria reached up and retied her scarf more securely around her curls. "I have to keep it short or it flies all over the place and makes me look like I put my finger in the light socket."

"Put your finger where?" Mary Louisa asked.

It occurred to Victoria that she hadn't seen any electric lamps in her quick survey of the entry hall, and she guessed that light bulbs hadn't been invented yet. "I just meant I have really curly hair and it gets messy sometimes."

"I like dark hair," Julia said. She reached up and shyly touched a loose tendril of Victoria's hair. "I want my new baby brother to have dark, curly hair like yours—and blue eyes like mine."

Talking with Julia, who didn't seem to find anything remarkable about her sudden arrival in their midst, steadied Victoria and, as the pain in her head diminished, she was able to set her panic aside and study the faces of both girls. They looked just like their painted images: Julia with round cheeks and straight bangs, and Mary Louisa with delicate features, creamy skin and long, blonde ringlets. The dresses they wore were not exactly like the ones they wore in the finished painting, though Mary Louisa was wearing the familiar white pinafore. Their shoes were different, too—not black leather shoes with button closings, but soft slippers made of wool.

Mary Louisa was beautiful, but what was most striking about her at the moment was the expression of tenderness on her face which made her seem old for her age. She was gazing at her little sister now with almost parental concern.

"Julia wants a baby brother more than anything," she explained, "but we're worried because Mama's been sick. Our family lost a baby boy last year. His name was Elliot and he was only three weeks old when he died."

Perhaps it was relief that Victoria had stopped talking about the future or the pleasure of having a sympathetic listener, but Mary Louisa didn't seem able to stop talking.

"After Elliot died, Mama was so sad she didn't get out of bed for weeks. Next spring she's supposed to have another baby, but I don't think the doctor is happy about it. He has such a long face when he comes to see her."

"Why isn't the doctor happy?" Julia said. "Doesn't he like babies?"

"Of course, he likes babies, silly. But he says Mama's not very strong since her illness last winter."

Julia's blue eyes narrowed.

"Don't worry, darling," Mary Louisa said quickly. "She got up for tea, so she must be feeling better."

"I've always wanted a baby sister or brother," Victoria told Julia. "I'm an only child."

"I can't imagine what it would be like having no sisters," Mary Louisa said. "I don't know what I'd do without Julia." She stroked her little sister's hair, and Julia smiled up at her.

"I'd give anything for a sister," Victoria said. "Older, younger, I wouldn't care."

"I wish my big sisters were like you," Mary Louisa went on. "They treat us like babies. They're always whispering together and having secrets."

"Mary Louisa! Julia!" A woman's voice sounded through the closed door. "Mr. Sargent is leaving. Come and say goodbye."

"That's Mama," Julia whispered. "She must have heard us."

"They mustn't find you!" Mary Louisa said to Victoria. "Stay here. We'll get them to go away." Mary Louisa stepped to the door and opened it, beckoning Julia to follow. She pulled it closed behind her, but not all the way. Frightened of being discovered, Victoria crouched behind the door and listened intently to the conversation in the entry hall.

"There you are! Why are you hiding? Mr. Sargent wants to say goodbye." It was the light, sweet voice that the Boit sisters had identified as their mother's. Victoria remembered the portrait of the plump, red-faced woman at the museum and couldn't quite match that image to this melodious tone.

Then she heard the painter's deep rumble. "Julia, you'd better make friends with that doll. I want her in the painting, too. The composition needs something. I think adding the doll will help."

"I like him," Julia announced. "I'll name him Popau, like the man at the waxworks."

"So, it's a boy, is it?" asked the artist.

"Yes," Julia said. "I like boy babies best."

"Are you still planning to enter the painting in the Paris Salon?" Mrs. Boit asked.

"I haven't decided," Sargent replied. "I'll see how I feel when it's completed."

"I can't wait to see it!" Julia cried.

Sargent chuckled. "I know. It's cruel. Little girls of four should never have to wait for anything. But you won't be able to tell me what you really think, unless it's finished. And I need your opinion. You have to tell me whether I should take it to the Salon or not."

"Me?" Julia asked, her voice high with excitement.

"Yes. If you say it goes, it goes. But you have to be truthful. If you don't like it for any reason, you must say so," Sargent said with great seriousness. "I'm further behind with your portrait than I am with that of your sisters. I was waiting, saving the best for last. But I don't know if you'll be pleased with what I paint."

"John," Mrs. Boit protested, "you indulge the child too much."

"She has a fine eye, Louisa—you've seen her drawings. I think Julia has the makings of a real artist."

"You may be right. She's done nothing but draw since you gave her that set of pastels."

"I drew something today!" Julia said. "I'll get it and show you."

"Not now, little one," said her mother. "Mr. Sargent has an appointment. Mary Louisa, get Mr. Sargent's coat and hat for him. We've kept him long enough."

"I'll get them," Sargent said.

Before Victoria had time to react, the door to the room where she was hiding was pushed open by the great artist himself. She leapt back in alarm and tried frantically to bury herself in the coats that hung on the rack behind her. But it was too late; Sargent was framed in the doorway.

Terror overwhelmed her.

The light dimmed and the figure of the painter dissolved before her eyes. Her head spun and to keep from fainting, she dropped her eyes to the floor. It wasn't the floor of narrow, dark slats she'd just been standing on, but a broad expanse of polished oak planks. When Victoria raised her eyes, she realized why.

She was no longer in the Boit's cloakroom in Paris; she was back in the museum on a Saturday morning in April, in 1963.

Chapter Three

Saturday Class

April, 1963, Boston

Victoria's reappearance in the Sargent gallery caused no alarm; in fact, everything appeared just as it had before her sudden departure. New visitors flowed in through the doors, and the guard made his usual circuit of the big room. Sun slanted through the narrow window at exactly the same angle as it had when Victoria had watched her mother leave.

Nothing here had changed.

Victoria shook her head to clear it and, as fast as her rubbery legs could carry her, made it back to the bench where she had agreed to wait for her mother. Her mother was nowhere to be seen. Either she had come and gone and was at this moment alerting the authorities to search for her missing daughter, or, as Victoria suspected, she hadn't yet returned from her trip to the office. The journey to Paris felt like it had happened in some other dimension and that no time at all had passed in this world. She looked at her watch and realized her hunch was correct. Only minutes had passed since she last looked. By the time

Victoria saw her mother approaching along the corridor, she'd managed to slow her breathing and still her shaking hands.

"There you are," her mother said brightly, apparently noticing nothing odd about her daughter's appearance. "Let's go." She walked briskly toward the exit. Victoria followed. "Your father will be wondering where we are."

On the ride home, Victoria let her mother chatter on about her docent class, while her own thoughts flip flopped like a fish out of water. Exiting the taxi, Victoria trailed her mother up the front steps to the massive oak door of their three-story brick house. The day had turned cloudy with a gusting wind, which matched Victoria's mood. The house loomed over her. All the curtains were open, but the windows seemed to resist, rather than welcome the light. Exhausted and disoriented, Victoria was glad to creep into her home's dark interior and hide from the world.

"Put your boots in the closet," her mother reminded her. Wearily, Victoria picked up her boots from the floor where she'd dropped them and put them away. The sound of Rose, the housekeeper, vacuuming in the back of the house, drove her upstairs to her room.

Victoria pulled back the covers to get into bed and lay there, trying to make sense of what had happened to her at the museum. Her head still ached, but otherwise she felt fine. Mentally, it was another story. *I must be losing my mind*, she decided. Was it really possible she'd traveled back in time—and to Paris, of all places? It was a city she'd always dreamed of visiting, but in this century, not in 1882.

"Your father's looking for you," Victoria's mother called through her bedroom door. When Victoria didn't respond right away, she cracked the door and looked in. "What are you doing in bed?" she asked.

"I have a headache," Victoria told her. "It's making me sick to my stomach. I think I'll try to sleep a little."

"So, no lunch? Rose will be disappointed." Her mother's brows lowered. "Shall I bring you some aspirin?"

"I took some already," Victoria lied. "I'm just going to rest and see if it goes away." She lay still and waited, every muscle tense. Her mother was being her usual hypervigilant self and she couldn't stand it; she needed to be alone with her thoughts.

"How's your back today?" her mother asked.

"Okay," Victoria answered, closing her eyes and steeling herself to be patient. "But I need to take off my brace for a while. It's pinching worse than ever today."

"All right," her mother said. "Just for an hour or so."

Victoria could feel her mother studying her, probably wondering if this was the start of her first menstrual cycle. They'd talked about the headaches and cramps and the heavy, listless feeling she could expect, and Victoria, though she was desperate for her period to begin, wasn't looking forward to any of it.

"Let me know if there's anything I can get you," her mother said finally. She hesitated, then withdrew, closing the door behind her.

Victoria let out a sigh. As soon as her mother was gone, she shed her sweater and fumbled her way out of the brace. When it was off, she breathed deeply for the first time that day and her headache eased, but she still felt half mad. Wouldn't it be funny if she really was getting her period, today of all days? All the girls she knew had started their periods ages ago—Pam when she was barely thirteen. And Victoria was nearly fifteen! She was sure it was abnormal and worried she might never be able to have children—that her body would stay boyish forever. But her doctor wasn't concerned and her mother said delayed puberty ran in the family, so she tried not to obsess about it.

She put on a loose T-shirt, climbed back into bed, and lay on her back, taking long, slow breaths as her mother had suggested she do when she got upset. She looked around her room.

It looked the same: neat and clean, no clothes on the floor, no posters on the wall. She'd hung up some of her father's framed photographs, but otherwise the walls were bare. It was furnished with heavy old furniture, tall bookshelves, and an antique captain's chest that held her turntable and a small collection of records. Nothing was different, but the feeling of sanctuary was gone; today it felt too perfect, too safe.

When Victoria closed her eyes, the image of Mary Louisa's unhappy face swam beneath her closed eyelids. She couldn't get the girl out of her head. Bizarre as it seemed, she was convinced Mary Louisa needed her in some inexplicable way. She thought about walking into the painting again and wasn't sure she was brave enough to try. Her attraction to it—her desire to get as close to it as possible—was now at war with a strong wish to stay far, far away. Her thoughts grew fuzzier and fuzzier, and finally she slept.

She woke when the day was almost over, the sun getting ready to set. She struggled out of bed, still tired, put on the brace with a groan of protest, and went downstairs to tell her parents she didn't really feel well enough to eat dinner; maybe she'd have a little soup. While her mother was heating it, she went into the study and found a book on Sargent among her mother's art books.

After she ate, she took the book to her room and read a long time, fascinated by the description of the Boit girls' portrait having an *"Alice in Wonderland* feel." Victoria knew what the author meant. She'd always found Alice's story about falling down the rabbit hole very disturbing. That business of Alice getting smaller, then larger, and the Queen of Hearts shouting "Off with her head!" had frightened her as a child. She realized there was something slightly creepy about the painting as well.

That night, Victoria dreamed that Mary Louisa was being chased by a giant rabbit. She called imploringly to Victoria as she ran past, but it was impossible to make out her words. Victoria woke the next morning feeling like she'd had this dream, or some variation of it, before, and it left her with a strong sense of foreboding. There was something really important Mary Louisa needed to tell her.

She *had* to go back. She had to enter the painting again and return to the Boit girls' apartment. It was terrifying to think she might get stuck there, in Paris in 1882, but somehow that didn't seem very likely. She'd bounced back quickly enough the first time and felt sure she would again. And though there was nothing pleasant about the nausea and disorientation that went along with the experience, all that was better than not going back at all.

There was something dark hanging over the Boit sisters, or at least over the older girls if Sargent's painting was a clue. What had her mother said about two of the girls being mentally ill? Perhaps it was the two older girls, and that was why Sargent had placed them in the shadows—perhaps he had some inkling of their mental state. Having met Mary Louisa and Julia, Victoria refused to believe they were the ones who were unstable; they seemed like the most level-headed children she'd ever known. But they were still little kids and needed a big sister to look out for them. If Jane and Florence weren't up to the task, why not her? Conquering her fear would be hard, but the more she thought about it, the more she realized she was excited, even eager, to return to Paris and see what she could do to help the younger Boits.

If only she could think of a good excuse to visit the museum again soon. Then, she remembered the girl with the pendulum braid.

"I was thinking," Victoria said at dinner that night, careful to keep her tone casual, "I need something to do on the weekends. What if I enroll in an art class at the museum? I could go with you, Mom, when you take your docent class. Didn't you say you'd be there every Saturday?"

"What a wonderful idea," her mother said, her voice full of pleasure. "What did you have in mind?"

"They have a young people's drawing class then," Victoria said. "Yesterday I talked to one of the girls who's taking it. She showed me her drawing. It was really good."

"Why don't we phone tomorrow and see if there's room in the class?" her mother said, patting her lips with a cloth napkin. "It's fortunate the time coincides with my docent training."

"Great!" Victoria said, trying to keep her excitement from showing. If the schedule worked out, she was sure she could get a few minutes before or after the class to visit the painting. With luck, she'd be able to get to Paris and back without being missed.

"So," Victoria's father said, leaning back in his chair, "your birthday's coming soon. Have you decided what you want?"

"I still want a camera," Victoria said. "I know the Nikon I asked for is expensive, but I could chip in some of my own money."

Her mother frowned. "I was hoping you'd decided to take up drawing instead of photography." She sat up even straighter. "Otherwise what's the point of enrolling in this class?"

Victoria paused before answering. She was so tired of her mother's decrees about what she should and should not like. There were no photographs on the walls of their home, though there were plenty of paintings on display. All of her dad's art photographs had been relegated to the attic except for the few that Victoria had rescued to hang in her room. Otherwise they were banished from the house. *Mom, I know you painted when you were young*, she grumbled to herself, *but does that mean I have to do it, too?* But all she said was, "Taking a drawing class doesn't mean I don't want a camera."

"Photography's not real art," her mother said. "It puts too many limits on your creativity." She threw her napkin onto her plate and continued, sounding more and more agitated. "And it—it exploits its subjects. I don't see why you want to involve yourself with something so sordid!"

Victoria stared at her mother. She knew her mother didn't like photography, but she'd never heard her get angry about it.

"Dad asked me what I want," she muttered, ready to let the subject drop. She glanced at her father and thought he looked as startled as she was by her mother's outburst.

"Well," her mother said, making a visible effort to speak more calmly, "if you insist on getting a camera, you should start with an inexpensive one—to make sure this is not just a whim." She picked up her napkin, folded it carefully, and placed it next to her plate.

"You can't call it a whim," said her father, coming to his daughter's defense. "Victoria's been talking about the Nikon for months."

"It's out of the question to buy a camera like that for a child," her mother snapped.

"I'm not a child!" Victoria burst out, unable to contain herself any longer. "I'm almost fifteen!"

"Well," said her mother, "not a *child*, a *young person*. You know what I mean." With that, she stood abruptly, took her plate, and walked out of the room.

Her father caught Victoria's eye and grimaced. She knew he'd gotten his first good camera when he was her age and probably thought it was just fine for Victoria to have one. But he didn't like arguments, never had. He was much more likely to retreat than to engage when her mother got mad. It made Victoria furious. Why did her mother always have to have things her way? And when was she going to stop treating Victoria like a baby?

Back in the privacy of her room, Victoria grabbed the pillow off her bed, threw it on the floor, and gave it a few good kicks. Then she yanked open the middle drawer of her desk and pulled an envelope from its hiding place at the very back. In it was a black-and-white photograph she'd discovered weeks ago when she was looking through some boxes of clothing in the attic. She'd found it in the pocket of one of her mother's old beach robes.

She held the photograph up to the light and examined it. She was convinced it was a picture of her mother taken when she was about Victoria's age. Looking in the mirror, Victoria could see the resemblance. It was a beautiful photograph—with its moody lighting and soft focus—but unsettling, too. It was a head shot with only a bit of throat showing. The way the light fell on her mother's face made her pale skin glow. It was her expression that was odd. Her head was tipped to one side, and she looked at the camera with an uneasy smile.

Looking at it, Victoria wondered what her mother was like as a teenager. Was she as uptight then as she was now? This photograph made her look more anxious than controlling, but the picture was so obviously posed, it was hard to tell. Victoria was dying to know more about her mother's early life, but every time she brought it up, her mother changed the subject. For whatever reason, she didn't want to share that part of herself with her daughter, or with anyone as far as Victoria could tell.

Victoria had other questions about the photograph, too. Where was the picture taken? By whom? Someday she'd get up the nerve to ask, but for now, feeling less indignant, she slid it back into the envelope, shoved it to the back of the drawer, and went to bed.

Victoria woke up the next morning consumed with questions about the Boit girls and full of doubts about her experience at the museum. Had any of it really happened? She hadn't found out much about the Boits in her mother's collection of art books, so after school she stopped at the Public Library to look for more books about Sargent. She found several, one that included a page or two about the Boit family, and took them to a table to read.

Edward Darley Boit, the father, she learned, came from a wealthy family and never worked, but did have some success as a watercolor painter, as her mother had suggested.

As for the daughters, contrary to the conventions of the time, none of them ever married. Julia, the youngest, became an artist, and she and Mary Louisa had remained close for their entire lives.

The book confirmed that it was the two older girls who were mentally unstable. Jane's illness started a short time after Sargent painted her and was serious enough that the family had to send her away for treatment. Florence, or Florie as she was called, was described as eccentric. She suffered a mental breakdown in middle age and died soon after. So, Victoria's suspicions were confirmed. Florence and Jane were indeed living under a shadow at the time Sargent painted them.

Victoria walked home slowly from the library. She'd found death dates for all the sisters, except Julia. Could she still be alive? Still living in Paris? If so, she'd be in her mid-eighties, by Victoria's calculation. It was chilling, having just seen these girls as youngsters, to read about them as people who were already dead or else very, very old.

She passed a playground, and, still thinking about the Boit girls, stopped and sat in an empty swing, idly watching as three little kids dug holes in the sandbox nearby. If she had a camera and took a photograph of those kids over there, she'd want it to be something like Sargent's painting of the Boits—something unexpected and revealing. For the rest of her walk, she slowed her pace to study the buildings and trees she passed, thinking about shapes and shadows, and got home well past her usual time.

"Victoria?" her mother called from the living room as Victoria walked through the front door. She came out into the hall, a sherry glass in her hand. "Where have you been? I've been worried sick."

"Sorry, Mom. I stopped at the library," Victoria said, holding up the books she'd checked out. "I didn't notice the time." She hoped her mother wouldn't insist on driving her home from school from now on. The doctor said it was good for her to walk. In fact, it made her back feel better when she did, and she relished being out on her own for those few precious minutes.

"I need you to come straight home," her mother said.

"I do," Victoria said and dumped her school bag on the hall table, then started toward the living room to greet her father.

"And don't leave your school bag there. Take it to your room."

Victoria bit back a retort. When her mother was in one of her moods, there was no point in arguing.

"Hey, kiddo," her father called. "There's a letter out there for you from Pam."

"Hi, Dad," Victoria called back. She grabbed her school bag and Pam's letter, opening the envelope as she walked upstairs, not really wanting to read it. Letters from Pam, her closest friend since kindergarten, used to be cause for celebration, but lately they were only short notes, more dutiful than sincere. This letter contained only a clipping from Pam's school newspaper with three scribbled words at the top—"I got it!"—meaning Pam had scored the leading role in the school play.

Victoria frowned. Was that it? Her friendship with Pam felt over. It had started to unravel last fall, when Victoria's parents had pulled her out of the public-school system and enrolled her at the Winslow Academy for Girls, the same private high school her mother had attended as a girl. Then, just before Christmas, Pam's family had moved to North Hampton and now their only contact was through the mail—if this could be called contact.

Victoria crumpled the article and tossed it into the waste bin in her room.

It wasn't easy making new friends, especially now when she felt like such a freak because of her back brace. It was only a matter of time before someone discovered it and teased her about it. She could just hear the cruel nicknames they'd throw at her—Gimpy Girl, Crooked Creep. Better to spend the rest of high school alone in her room.

Registering for the drawing class was easy, but Victoria found it tough to wait until the weekend to get back to the museum. She woke up the next Saturday with twitchy legs and a shivery feeling in the pit of her stomach. She tried to eat breakfast, but could only manage a couple of bites before pushing her plate aside. Her mind was filled with misgivings. What would happen when she tried to enter the painting? Maybe nothing—maybe she'd dreamed it all.

Her mother took forever getting ready. Through great good fortune, her docent class was scheduled at more or less the same time as Victoria's class, but for an hour longer. Her mother had given her daughter permission to wait for her outside her docent classroom door, but Victoria had no intention of doing that. She had a visit to the Sargent gallery in mind instead.

"Come on, mom," Victoria called up the stairs. "I'm going to be late for class."

"You're more nervous than I am!" her mother remarked, but she hurried on their way to the car. They drove from their house in Back Bay and parked the big Pontiac in the lot next to the art museum.

Victoria's classroom turned out to be just down the hall from where her mother's class was being held, and when Victoria peered in, there was no one there. She was early, so she sat down and pulled out her book on Sargent to read while she waited for the others to arrive. The first person who walked in was the girl with the braid.

"I know you," the girl said, seating herself in the chair next to Victoria's.

Victoria nodded. "I saw you in the Sargent gallery last Saturday."

Today the girl was dressed in a slightly rumpled skirt and sweater set in a peculiar shade of green that did nothing for her complexion. *I guess she doesn't care about clothes*, Victoria thought, *or else she's colorblind.* If Victoria were honest, though, her own baggy getup was not going to win any fashion awards.

"So, you've joined the class?"

"It wasn't full," Victoria responded. "I only missed the first one, so they said it was okay."

"I'm Hillary," the girl said. "I'm in ninth grade at St. Catherine's."

"I'm Victoria," Victoria said. "I'm in ninth, too—at Winslow." She felt embarrassed naming her school. St. Catherine's was a Catholic school in one of the shabbier neighborhoods of Boston. Winslow Academy, on the other hand, was an expensive private school in a section of town dominated by large mansions. But, if Hillary had a reaction to the Winslow name, she didn't show it. She just smiled and leaned across to peer at the title of Victoria's book.

"John Singer Sargent," she said. "You like him?"

"I really like his early paintings," Victoria answered cautiously, "the ones he did while he was still in Paris." She wanted to say more, but it felt risky saying too much about her interest in Sargent and his painting of the Boit girls. Not that she didn't *want* to talk about it, but it felt vital to keep her special connection to the painting a secret. Who would believe her, anyway? Anyone she told would be more likely to ship her off to the loony bin than believe such a far-fetched tale.

"Have you seen his *El Jaleo* at the Gardner?" Hillary asked.

"I don't remember," Victoria said. The Isabella Stewart Gardner Museum was just two blocks from the Museum of Fine Arts. Victoria remembered a lot of dark, gloomy paintings and the blister she got from wearing brand new shoes. "I haven't been to the Gardner in years."

"You should go, if you like Sargent's early work," Hillary said. "I love the Gardner. It's more like a haunted house than a museum."

Victoria's interest was piqued, but their teacher came in and the girls stopped talking.

The teacher arranged five pears in a ceramic bowl on a table at front of the room and took her students through a lesson on still-life drawing. Victoria did her best to follow the teacher's instructions but was aware that her attempt was pitiful—the fruit she drew looked more like potatoes than pears. But she didn't really care; learning to draw was not her real goal.

"You need to finish up," the teacher told them. "Then we'll go on a brief tour of some of the museum's most famous still-life paintings." She smiled and pushed her glossy black hair behind her ears. "Does anyone here have a favorite?"

Hillary's hand shot up, and the teacher called on her. "Cezanne's *Fruit and a Jug*," she said. There was no doubt Hillary knew the collection, but Victoria couldn't help thinking she sounded like a know-it-all.

The teacher nodded her approval. "That's one of my favorites, too."

They got down to work finishing their pears and then brought them up to the front of the room to display. Victoria saw immediately that Hillary's still-life was the best. Victoria studied her as Hillary listened to the teacher's praise. Other than her obvious artistic talent and her knowledge of art history, Hillary didn't seem to have much to recommend her. She was scrawny, even

even thinner than Victoria. *Maybe, like me,* Victoria thought, *she hasn't even gotten her period yet.* Many of the girls in Victoria's class at school, with their full figures and polished, fast-talking ways, seemed much older than she was. Hillary, on the other hand, looked younger. She acted fearless but appeared almost mousy in her hand-me-down clothes. *If the girls at Winslow think of me as an odd duck,* Victoria mused, *what on earth would they make of Hillary?*

When they left the classroom for their tour, Hillary gave Victoria a quick preview of some of the pictures they might see. "I hope she takes us to see Sisley's *Grapes and Walnuts,*" she said to Victoria.

"Why do they always paint food?" Victoria asked, then flushed, thinking how stupid that sounded. "I mean, people are so much more interesting."

"I guess cause food doesn't move. *Still*-life, you know. People move. They blink and scratch and have to pee. Food is way easier to paint." Hillary laughed and Victoria was glad. She'd been starting to think Hillary had no sense of humor.

Their teacher led them to a painting called *Plate of Peaches* by Henri Fantin-Latour and they both giggled.

"More food," Hillary intoned in Victoria's ear.

As soon as class was over, Victoria gathered her things, ready to make a dash to the Sargent gallery.

"So," Hillary asked, "do you want to go to the Gardner sometime?"

Truthfully, Victoria just wanted to get away—she only had so much time to get to the Boit girls before she had to meet her mother. But it felt rude to rush away when Hillary was being so friendly. "Sure," she said, with as much enthusiasm as she could muster.

"We could go together," Hillary said, writing her phone number on a slip of paper. "Call me."

Nodding, Victoria took Hillary's number. "I've got to go,"

she mumbled and bolted toward the door. She glanced back and saw a flash of puzzlement cross Hillary's face, but it was too late to say anything more. She gave her a quick wave and sped off down the hall.

When Victoria stood, at last, before the painting, she knew it would welcome her in. The look on Mary Louisa's face was less intent, more distracted than before, but Victoria paid it no mind. She felt an electric charge in the air and a keen sense of satisfaction flooded her brain. All her worries that she'd be shut out were forgotten. She rejoiced as the feeling of vertigo took hold. There was a rush of movement, then darkness, and she was gone.

Chapter Four

Fly on the Wall

November 1882, Paris

Victoria landed with an imperceptible thump in front of the red screen in the entry hall of the Boit's apartment. Her head felt fuzzy, but the extreme dizziness she'd experienced on the last trip was absent. She quickly pulled herself together and slipped into hiding behind the screen. Peeking through a crack between the panels, she could see the entire room. It still looked immense, but its size was not such a shock as last time. She was getting used to the high ceilings and lack of furniture. The warm, earthy colors in the rug softened the effect of too much emptiness, and the tall Japanese vases helped define the space.

Julia was seated on the rug playing with the big doll in her lap. Mary Louisa was there, too, standing near Sargent, who was staring at the canvas in front of him. There was no one else in the hall, and none of them saw Victoria arrive.

The two girls were wearing the clothes they wore in the finished painting—Mary Louisa in a burgundy colored dress with her blindingly white pinafore tied over it, the same as the ones Jane and Florence wore in the portrait that hung in the Museum of Fine Arts. Julia was dressed in a white, long sleeved dress with smocking on the collar and cuffs. Both girls wore black leggings and black shoes with dainty button closings. Sargent could have chosen to paint them dressed in colorful silks or satins like some of his other child subjects but, peering out, Victoria realized that the stark white of the pinafores and Julia's dress worked well to heighten the drama of the scene.

Mary Louisa was speaking. "Tell me about your sister," she said.

Sargent stepped out from behind the canvas to study Julia on the floor and asked, "You mean my sister Emily or my sister Violet? I have two sisters."

"I mean the younger one," Mary Louisa said.

"Violet," Sargent said, moving closer to the canvas to make a quick dab with his brush. "I've been meaning to bring Violet over to meet you. She's just a little older than you—twelve, the same age as Jane. She's been asking about you."

"Oh, would you?" Mary Louisa clapped her hands together in delight, then, looking chagrined, resumed her dignified expression. "We don't get to see many children."

"Why is that?" Sargent asked, stepping back to study what he had just done. "Doesn't your mother take you to see friends?"

"We don't have any friends," Julia piped up, "except Popau." She patted her doll's big head with great tenderness as she spoke. The doll wore what looked like an infant's christening gown covered by a short pink shawl and looked nothing like a boy.

"That's not true," Mary Louisa said. "We have our cousins, but they live in Boston and we don't get to see them very often. Most of Papa and Mama's Paris friends don't have children."

Sargent looked over at Mary Louisa. "Well, I think you'll like Violet. She's very lively. There's nothing she enjoys more than a good romp in the park." His eyes strayed back to the painting. "Maybe we could all take a walk in the Jardin des Tuileries, if it's not too cold."

"When?" Mary Louisa asked, sounding thrilled. "We haven't been to the park since summer."

"Soon," Sargent said. "I'll check with Violet today."

"Maybe Mama can come, too," Mary Louisa said. "If she's feeling well enough."

"And your father?" Sargent asked. "Is he still traveling?"

"Yes," Mary Louisa sighed. "He's always away. We never see him."

"Oh, come now," Sargent said. "I've seen him several times in the past month."

"But he's going to be gone for weeks this time," Mary Louisa said, frowning. "And even when he's here, he never plays with us." She rubbed her forehead distractedly. "He used to play with us when we were little."

Sargent laughed. "Maybe he thinks you're too old to play."

"I'm not," Julia scoffed. "I'm only four."

"Well," Sargent said, "your father's busy trying to arrange a buyer for his paintings."

"I know," said Mary Louisa, looking glum. "He wants to be a big success—like you."

As Mary Louisa finished speaking, Mrs. Boit came into the entry hall, calling to Sargent as she approached. "John, you're still here. Good. I wanted to ask if you'd stay for tea."

Though her costume was cleverly designed to hide her pregnancy, as Mrs. Boit drew near Victoria could see, especially when she turned to the side, that her baby bump was beginning to show. The dress was made of cornflower blue silk and had tiny buttons from the neckline to just above the waist. In the midsection, where the buttons stopped, were several loose swaths of fabric, and below that wide pleats fell to the floor. She wasn't a big woman, only slightly plump in the face, yet Mrs.

Boit moved with a heavy tread, one hand on her back as though it gave her pain. Her face wasn't nearly as red or jolly as it was in the portrait Sargent would later paint. In fact, she looked pale and drawn and not at all well.

Sargent smiled warmly. "I'd like that. I'm dining with Paul Helleu this evening, but I have no appointments till then."

"Such a British custom—tea," Mrs. Boit remarked. "But, we seem to have adopted it. It's become our nursery supper for the girls, until they're old enough to dine with us."

"Surely Florence is old enough now," Sargent said.

Mrs. Boit frowned. "But she has no interest in dining, unless your friend Mr. Graham is invited. Both she and Jane have taken a great shine to him."

"Oh well," said Sargent, moving in to dab at the canvas once more. "She'll soon be begging to join you."

"I doubt it," said her mother. "I've tried bribing her with pretty frocks, but it does no good. She hates dressing up."

"That's odd," said Sargent. "I thought all girls loved pretty clothes."

Mrs. Boit waved her hand dismissively. "I'm glad you'll stay for tea. I've been feeling so poorly and haven't seen anyone for ages. It will give me a chance to ask about your time in Venice. Did you see much of your cousin Ralph?"

"Yes," said Sargent. "I stayed with the Curtises in Palazzo Barbaro. I was able to complete a portrait of Mrs. Curtis while I was there."

"You promised to paint me, John," said Mrs. Boit, smiling coquettishly. "Don't forget."

Sargent smiled back. "Of course, my dear. When you're feeling perfectly well and have rosy cheeks again."

"Is Mrs. Curtis still in Venice?"

"She is. I wrote to tell her how I envy her, staying in Venice so late in the year. The city looks so beautiful with the snow clinging to the roofs and balconies. And the canals turn the most gorgeous shade of green."

"But most of our friends have left, I'm sure. There would be no one to visit, no parties to attend." As she spoke, Mrs. Boit fingered the tiny buttons at her throat.

"That's true," Sargent agreed, "but I can do without parties every night."

"As I've been forced to." Mrs. Boit sighed. "But, as soon as I'm well, we must plan a grand supper to celebrate."

"We will," Sargent said.

"I want to hear everything—what you did, whom you saw," said Mrs. Boit, turning to leave. "Come along as soon as you're finished here."

"Before you go?" Sargent said, taking a few steps after her.
"Yes?"

"I wanted to ask if I might bring my sister Violet by to see the girls? They say they haven't seen any children for some time, and I think Violet would cheer them up enormously."

Mrs. Boit looked surprised and then her face took on an expression of regret. "I feel so ashamed. Poor things. They must be missing company as much as I am."

"I think they are," Sargent replied. "So, you approve? Violet may come with me to a sitting?"

"Of course, John," Mrs. Boit said. "Your sister is welcome here anytime." She gave Sargent a last smile and left the room.

Victoria allowed herself to shift slightly behind the screen, careful to make no sound. Her back was aching, her legs were full of pins and needles from holding one position for too long, plus the conversation was making her seriously uncomfortable. Was Sargent the only adult in the house who thought the Boit children were in need of attention? Mrs. Boit was preoccupied by a difficult pregnancy and Mr. Boit was gone. So, who was looking after them?

A forgotten memory came to Victoria's mind. She was seven years old and attending the funeral of her maternal grandmother, whom she barely knew. The occasion felt sad, and she was puzzled by the fact that her mother didn't cry. Weren't you supposed to cry if your mother died? Had her mother and two aunts been poor little rich girls like these Boit daughters, pampered, but unnoticed and unloved?

Julia, who had been quiet this whole time, was starting to squirm. Sargent noticed immediately. "Oh, you poor thing. I must mind my business, or you'll get a cramp."

Tell me about it, Victoria thought.

"And Popau, too," Julia said. "He says his foot has gone to sleep."

"Poor Popau," Sargent said. "Shall I tell him a story?" As he spoke, Sargent made several quick stabs at the canvas with his brush, working quickly now that he was refocused on his task.

"Please," said both Julia and Mary Louisa in unison.

"Once there was a little boy named Popau," Sargent began. "And his mother, Julia, loved him very much. Popau loved turtles, and one day a wishing turtle came to his house and asked if there was anything he wanted. Popau said he wanted a friend. 'I'll be your friend,' said the turtle. He was a sea turtle, so he took Popau on an adventure under the sea. They dove down into the azure sea and saw amazing rainbow fish and corals the color of blood."

Sargent paused to stare at his painting, and Julia asked, "How could he breathe underwater?"

"Magic," Sargent said. "The turtle was magic."

"Then what?" Julia demanded.

"Then they all had tea with the King of the Sea, who was a tuna," Sargent said. "And then they went home."

"Is that all?" Julia said, sounding disappointed.

"That's all for now," Sargent replied, studying his handiwork.

"If I do anything more today, I'll ruin it." He busied himself putting away his brushes and pallet. "Aren't you two hungry? I know I am. It's time for our tea."

Taking the girls by the hand, Sargent led them away.

It was deathly quiet in the large hall. Victoria crept out from behind the screen, rubbing her back and flexing her stiff legs. She wondered how the Boit sisters managed it, posing for long stretches without moving. It must be challenging for Sargent, painting children, and he painted them often judging by the number of child portraits she'd seen in her Sargent books. She guessed his child subjects hadn't all been as cooperative as the Boit girls.

Victoria looked about, wondering what she should do. The younger Boits had disappeared into the recesses of the apartment, and she had no clue how to search them out without alerting the others. She should probably wait here and hope they would return, but she felt far too impatient for that. She started to creep down the long hall after them, but had only taken a few steps when she saw two figures emerge from a room to her left and start toward her. Victoria moved back into the entry hall and ducked into her hiding place just in time to avoid being spotted by Jane and Florence.

"Good," Jane said, "he's gone." She was wearing a long, loose gown of lavender silk with lace at the collar. The color gave her face a wan, washed out look.

"Or maybe he's having tea with us." Florence replied. "Mama always begs him to stay when he's finished painting for the day." The older girl was dressed more plainly than her sister, in gray muslin with a white sash at her slender waist.

"I wish she'd invite Mr. Graham to stay for tea," Jane said.

"I'll tell her she must," Florence declared, "next time he comes."

"But Miss Bossyboots will protest," Jane said.

"Let her," Florence said. "Mary Louisa finds fault with everyone and everything we like. If she doesn't enjoy Mr. Graham's company, she can eat in the kitchen with the servants."

Jane covered her mouth with both hands and let out a small squeal.

Victoria was appalled—Jane and Florence sounded like the two evil stepsisters in Cinderella. She needed to ask Mary Louisa why her older sisters disliked Sargent so much. And who was this Mr. Graham, and why would Mary Louisa object to his staying to tea?

"I wonder when Mr. Graham will want us for the special sitting?" Florence went on.

"You mean dressed as orphans?" Jane asked.

Florence nodded. "Remember he asked if he could choose our costumes," she said and smiled to herself. "We have to go to his studio for those pictures. It's not far. We can walk there quite easily."

"I hope it's soon," Jane breathed. "I can't wait to see his studio. I'm sure it's quite grand."

"He asked me if we could come without Madame Fouche," Florence said. "Since I'm fourteen now he wondered if we were old enough to come alone."

"Oh," Jane exclaimed, "What did you say?"

"I said we'd try," said Florence. "He explained he finds most adults, but especially Madame Fouche, so very tedious. He much prefers young people to old." Giggling, the two girls swept out of the room, arm in arm, following in the footsteps of Sargent and their younger sisters.

Once more, Victoria stepped out from her hiding place and started down the hall. Maybe she could find Mary Louisa's bedroom and wait for her there. Mary Louisa had sounded so lonely, and Victoria wanted badly to try to cheer her up. And she had so many questions she needed to ask the younger girl!

She'd gotten halfway down the hall, when a tall woman dressed all in black came out of a door at the end of the hall and walked toward her. Victoria searched wildly for a place to hide, but all the doors in the corridor were closed. There was nothing between herself and the approaching woman but a flowered carpet.

In that instant, Victoria's vision darkened and she vanished back to her own time.

Chapter Five

The Gardner

When Victoria left the Sargent gallery to join her mother, she was seething with frustration. Her mother met her with a barrage of questions about the drawing class, which she answered as best she could through gritted teeth. Finally, her mother gave up. Victoria spent the ride home fuming in silence.

Incredibly, she'd had no trouble entering the painting and arriving in the Boit's apartment for a second time, but she hadn't managed to speak to Mary Louisa or learn anything to alleviate her fears for the Boit girls. It was clear they were lonely and bored and no one but Sargent seemed to care—and that Jane and Florence were mean as snakes! Victoria wondered what the Boit parents would think of the older girls' plan to go to Mr. Graham's studio alone—would they even care? Perhaps this Mr. Graham was a trusted family friend, a stand-in uncle like Sargent, but still . . . . Victoria had absorbed enough of her mother's paranoia to hear alarm bells sounding.

It drove her up the wall. She'd gone to Paris with so many

questions and come back with no real answers, only more questions. The whole trip felt like a complete waste of time, and she had another headache to boot.

After grabbing a quick lunch at home, she went to her bedroom to sulk. It was all so complicated! Getting to Paris wasn't the only hurdle; getting there when Mary Louisa could spend time with her was also vital. But, what could she do? It was out of her control. Her feeling of helplessness was giving her a stomachache on top of her headache.

Her birthday was the next day. Her parents had promised to take her out to lunch—the last thing she wanted to do. She considered pleading an upset stomach, but Hillary had given her a better idea. Maybe she'd ask her parents to take her and Hillary to the Gardner instead, as a birthday treat. If she couldn't control anything else, maybe she could at least control what she got to do on her birthday. She'd much rather go to the Gardner than eat lunch at a stuffy restaurant, and she was eager to see the Sargent painting Hillary had mentioned.

That night, during dinner, Victoria laid out her plan, describing Hillary to her parents by emphasizing her love of art and her amazing drawing talent.

"But I already made reservations at the Lenox," her mother huffed. "It's all arranged."

Victoria didn't argue, but she let her disappointment show. *Nothing is easy*, she thought, as she pushed food around on her plate.

Her father laid down his fork and looked at his daughter. "Is that what you'd really like to do on your birthday?" he asked.

Victoria nodded, not willing to trust her voice. She felt ridiculously close to tears.

Victoria's father looked at his wife. "What if we skipped the lunch?" he asked. "I know Rose is planning one of her fancy birthday dinners, and I can't see us eating two big meals in one day."

Victoria's mother reached for her sherry glass, frowning. "I suppose I could call and cancel the reservation," she said.

"And didn't you say you have a lot of homework for your docent class?" her husband continued. "I can take the girls, and you can have the afternoon to yourself."

"Oh, Dad!" Victoria said. "Would you?"

"I'd be honored," her father said. "But," he said, smiling somewhat sheepishly, "I'll bring a book."

His daughter, who was well acquainted with his dislike of art museums, laughed; surprisingly, his wife joined in.

"Why don't you invite Hillary to join us for your supper?" her mother said, sounding much less upset than Victoria had expected she would be over the sudden change in plans. Maybe her mother was curious about this art prodigy friend and wanted to meet her. "Rose is making your favorite chocolate cake."

"Call Hillary now," her father said. "See if she's free."

The next day, Victoria and Hillary stood side by side before *El Jaleo*. The date on the painting said 1882, the same year Sargent painted the Boit girls. This canvas was even bigger than the portrait of the Boit sisters and, unlike that painting which was static and somber in tone, *El Jaleo* was all movement and bravado.

The foreground was dominated by a bold flamenco dancer, her arms raised, her body leaning back at an impossible angle (*Try that wearing a back brace!*), her skirts awhirl. In the shadows behind her, flamenco guitarists strummed furiously or lifted their hands to clap along. Victoria could almost hear the wild rhythms of stamping feet and clacking castanets.

"Isabella Gardner wanted this to be the first thing everyone saw when they entered her museum," Hillary said.

"It's amazing," Victoria murmured, feeling a bit breathless looking at it. "Did she and Sargent know each other?"

"They were friends. You know about the portraits he did of her, right?"

Victoria shook her head. Was there no end to the things Hillary knew? In spite of all Victoria's reading about Sargent, she still made Victoria feel like a complete dunce.

"Come on!" Hillary said. "There's one upstairs you have to see."

Victoria followed Hillary up the grand stone staircase, grateful that today the girl was dressed in a floral print dress that fit her reasonably well, even if the style was a little out of date. *I'll bet it's her best dress*, Victoria thought. Victoria had worn a dress herself, in honor of the occasion, and just prayed it was doing a good job of hiding her brace. It was brand new, a birthday present from her mother's sister, Aunt Margaret, and Victoria had instructed her aunt to get a size larger than what she normally wore. Plus, it was one of the new A-line dresses that fell from the shoulders in a sweeping line that bypassed her waist and was surprisingly comfortable. It was bright orange with yellow spots. Her mother had shuddered when she unwrapped the package, but Victoria didn't mind it at all.

Leaning over the staircase wall, the two girls peered into the inner courtyard and waved to Victoria's father, who was seated on a bench under a giant fan palm reading his book. This month, the indoor garden featured spring bulbs. Masses of yellow and white tulips in terra cotta pots had been placed under the tree ferns and palms that bordered the vast open space. Water from a fountain played softly, and the whole effect—the flowers, the benches, the soft pink stone made golden by sunlight streaming through the skylights four stories above—was mesmerizing. Victoria felt as though she'd been transported to the interior of an old Italian villa owned by some fabulously wealthy duke, or, as in this case, his fabulously wealthy widow.

If she'd had a camera along, Victoria would have photographed the scene. She felt a rush of anger at her mother's refusal to buy her one, but she put it out of her mind, unwilling to let anything spoil her enjoyment of the day.

By now, Hillary was almost to the third floor. Victoria hurried after her. As she followed Hillary through the galleries, Victoria couldn't believe how much there was to see: walls crowded with paintings and tapestries, cases full of gold ornaments and delicate Chinese ceramics, illuminated manuscripts from medieval times, first editions of rare books, letters from famous people, and old sepia photographs. Everywhere she turned there were treasures—delicate hand-painted chairs and inlaid cabinets next to ancient Chinese carvings and life-sized marble statues.

Hillary led her straight to Sargent's portrait of Isabella Stewart Gardner, painted, Victoria saw from the placard, in 1886, only four years after he'd painted the Boit girls.

"Not bad, eh?" Hillary said.

"Not bad at all," Victoria agreed. Again, it was an unusual portrait. Mrs. Gardner wasn't beautiful, but she had a lovely figure. In the painting, she was dressed in a simple black gown, cut into a deep V over her ample bosom, with ropes of pearls circling her tiny waist. Sargent had painted her against a background of golden tapestry, the pattern creating an odd halo effect around her head. She looked a bit like an angel, though her exaggerated cleavage left a somewhat different impression.

After admiring Isabella's portrait, the girls wandered slowly through the museum's upstairs rooms, staring at paintings by old masters—among them Titian, Rembrandt, Vermeer, and, Hillary's favorite, Velazquez, ". . . who," she told Victoria, "was a great influence on Sargent."

Soon, Victoria began to feel strangely uneasy. "I see what you mean about haunted," she said. "It feels like there's a ghost ready to pop out around every corner."

"Yeah," Hillary agreed, "I suspect Isabella is still hanging around making sure nobody touches her stuff."

"I can't believe all of this belonged to one woman."

"Well, it's true—and she was very possessive about all of it. When she died, she wanted her mansion turned into a museum, but her will stated that nothing in it could be altered or moved or else the museum would have to be shut down and all the art sold at auction."

"Wow," Victoria said. "No wonder it feels like it's stuck in a time warp." She consulted her watch. "Oops! We need to check in with my dad."

"Wait," Hillary said, "I want to show you one more painting." On the ground floor, in a small side chapel near the entrance, Hillary pointed out a Zurbaran painting of the Madonna holding the baby Jesus.

"Look at him," Hillary whispered.

Victoria, feeling the solemn mood in this enclosed space, whispered back. "The baby?"

"Yes. I don't know if it's true, but one of the old docents told me that after Isabella Gardner's son Jackie died—he was only two—she had the face of baby Jesus repainted to look like him. He said Isabella visited the chapel every night before going to bed."

"Did she have any other children?"

"No, only Jackie."

Victoria could picture Isabella Stewart Gardner sitting here in the dark, weeping. She felt a tug of sorrow, remembering Mary Louisa's description of Mrs. Boit's grief over baby Elliot, who had died so young. And, surprisingly, she thought of her own mother. *Did she ever lose a baby in those years before I was born?* she wondered. Victoria had never thought to ask. It might help explain why she held on so tight to the one child she had.

"Do you have brothers and sisters?" she asked Hillary, once they were back out in the hallway.

"Yes," Hillary said, "five."

Victoria gasped. "So many!"

"We O'Briens are good Catholics. There's lots of us, but we all get along, so that's a blessing." This last was said with an Irish lilt that made Victoria laugh.

"Six children! How many boys and how many girls?"

"I have two younger sisters and three older brothers. My parents said they wanted to have a girl after having three boys, but when they had me, they decided girls were so much fun, they needed two more." Hillary laughed unselfconsciously. Victoria could imagine her at home, surrounded by her many siblings, behaving more like a goofy kid and less like the teacher's pet.

"And you? " Hillary asked. "Do you have any brothers or sisters?"

Victoria shook her head. "No, I'm the only one."

"You'll have to come meet my family," Hillary said as they entered the courtyard. "My oldest brother James wants to be an artist—he's going to New York to study art next fall."

Victoria's father saw them coming and rose. "There you are," he said, and yawned. "I was starting to nod off."

"Dad!" Victoria said. "You've got to see Sargent's painting of the flamenco dancer."

"You know I'm not much of an art connoisseur—" her father said, but Hillary seized him by the hand and pulled him toward the hallway.

"It's so dramatic," Hillary said. "You can't miss it!"

Victoria was surprised by Hillary's familiarity, but her father didn't seem to mind. He let himself be tugged along, a grin on his face.

Dinner was the usual five-course extravaganza Rose always prepared for birthdays. After tasting the soup, Hillary said, "You're a wonderful cook, Mrs. Hubbard. This soup is delicious. What do you call it?"

"It's called vichyssoise," Victoria's mother said, "but I didn't make it. Rose, our housekeeper, made everything. You wouldn't want to eat my soup. I'm a horrible cook."

"Oh, I wouldn't say that," her husband said gallantly. "Back when we were first dating, you made a mean BLT."

"When I didn't burn the bacon," his wife said.

"My brother Patrick won't eat bacon," Hillary said. "He won't eat any meat. It drives my mother crazy. She worries he's not getting enough protein."

Hillary blushed a little as she said this, and Victoria wondered if she were feeling insecure. She probably wasn't used to eating such fancy meals. Looking around, Victoria realized that her family's dining room, with its extravagant chandelier and lovely, antique tableware and furnishings, was enough to make anyone used to a simpler way of life a little uncomfortable.

"Is he a vegetarian?" Victoria asked, curious about all of Hillary's many siblings.

"Now he is. He's always been an animal lover, but lately he's been volunteering at the Humane Society. They have a pot-bellied pig there that's Patrick's favorite, and now he refuses to eat bacon or meat of any kind."

"Having a vegetarian in the family must make it awkward to plan family meals," Victoria's mother murmured, as she passed the leg of lamb.

After the cake and candles, they all moved to the living room to open presents. Hillary handed Victoria a package, a book by the feel of it. "I'm sorry," Hillary said. "It's a used copy."

"That's okay," Victoria muttered, surprised that this girl she barely knew had thought to bring a gift on such short notice. "I like used books." It turned out to be a slightly worn paperback edition of *Wings of the Dove* by Henry James.

"They were friends, you know," Hillary said. Victoria knew Hillary was referring to Sargent's longstanding friendship with the author. "The palace that's described in the book is the one Sargent and Henry James used to stay in in Venice. It belonged to Sargent's cousin."

Victoria felt a shock of recognition. She remembered Sargent telling Mrs. Boit he'd stayed with his cousin's family at a palace in Venice.

"Not only that," Hillary went on, "but Isabella Gardner based the design for her museum on that same palace in Venice—the Pallazo Barbaro."

Victoria was speechless. So, she and Hillary had just spent the day in a replica of the Venetian palace she had overheard Sargent mentioning the day before? No, it was even spookier than that—it wasn't a day ago at all; it was more like a day and eighty some years ago! She hoped no one could tell her heart was pounding too fast.

"I'm amazed you've read Henry James at your age," Victoria's mother was saying to Hillary. "I never made it through any of his longer novels, though I did read *Turn of the Screw* in high school. I quite liked it. A good ghost story."

"My parents read us Dickens and Robert Louis Stevenson when we were little," Hillary explained, "so I got used to the classics."

"Sweetheart?" Victoria's dad said, studying his daughter.

Victoria turned to him. Had he noticed anything odd about her expression?

Still eyeing her, Victoria's father handed her a large package. Victoria took it, smiling uncertainly, but when she pulled away the wrapping and saw the Nikon label on the box, she shrieked with real delight. From the look of surprise on her mother's face, Victoria could tell her father had bought the camera without her knowledge. But she was so happy with the present, she didn't care if it caused a row. At the moment, none of it mattered. Victoria could hardly wait for morning, when she'd sneak out into the backyard and take her first shots.

Victoria's mother presented her gift next, which turned out to be a set of beautiful drawing pencils and a heavy drawing pad. Victoria tried to thank her sincerely, but her mother didn't look convinced. Hillary, on the other hand, obviously found the art supplies more thrilling than the camera and couldn't stop picking up the pencils and running her fingers over the pad.

Victoria sat in the back seat while her father drove Hillary home, listening to her new friend chatter away. Hillary lived in a tall brownstone, one of a long row of similar houses on West Brookline Street in the South End. As Hillary let herself in, Victoria found herself wondering about the large family that lived behind that door. She hoped Hillary would follow through on her invitation and she'd get to meet them someday.

Her mother was in bed when they got home, so Victoria said good night to her dad and headed straight to her room, happy to lay on the bed and review the day. She placed her new Nikon on her stomach, balanced on her brace, admiring the weight of the camera.

It'd been an eventful birthday. Hillary had turned out to be good company. They'd had a good time together at the Gardner and she'd loved seeing more of Sargent's work. It made her feel closer to the painter, and, by extension, to the Boits—all the people she fervently hoped to see again. She was grateful to Hillary for giving her *Wings of a Dove*. She planned to read it right away, if only to learn more about the place Sargent had visited in Venice.

Best of all, Victoria was finally fifteen—old enough by any normal parents' standards to venture out into the world on her own. She decided it was time to insist on more independence. Smiling to herself, she imagined marching up and down in front of her house carrying a sign that read "Freedom Now!" like the signs she's seen on the news carried by civil rights demonstrators down South.

She got up off the bed to put her camera away on a shelf beside her desk. Then she pulled out the desk drawer and retrieved the photograph of her mother as a teenage girl. Someday she'd like to take a picture as good as this one, but more candid—her mother's pose was too contrived for her taste. Once again, she wondered who had taken it. She decided to get up the nerve to ask her mom about it soon. It seemed to hold some clue to her mother's early life, and Victoria was starting to think of her mother's girlhood as a mystery she wanted to solve. Perhaps it wasn't really all that interesting, but in Victoria's experience, when people kept things secret it only served to make other people more curious about them.

School on Monday was more tedious than usual. At lunch, Victoria sat with Jill and Angela, the only girls who had gone out of their way to be nice to her since she'd started at Winslow in September. Their conversation was almost enough to make her wish she was eating alone.

"You should have seen how that creep at the bus stop was staring at Angela this morning," Jill said, banging her soda can on the table.

"Yeah," Angela said. "He's so weird. He tried to talk to me, but I just ignored him." She gave an exaggerated sigh and pushed her too-long bangs out of her eyes. "We should probably walk on the other side of the street from now on."

Victoria didn't reply. They'd been talking about the same boy for a week, and she was sick of it. She couldn't figure out why they were so fixated on him—by their own description he had bad breath and bad skin. Were they that desperate to be noticed by *any* boy? She was being unkind, but these two were so boring. The three of them had nothing in common. They only cared about boys and their own appearance. They listened to Elvis Presley and the Beach Boys, and she liked Joan Baez, for heaven's sake!

She was convinced she'd never find a real friend at this wretched school. Most of the girls thought she was stuck-up and teased her about her ramrod posture. "Got a broom up your butt?" one of the older girls had asked on her first day. Because of the brace, Victoria couldn't slouch even if she'd wanted to. She liked to think, with her long neck and straightened back, she moved carefully, but gracefully, like the swans in the pond at the Public Garden. *But really*, she thought, *I probably look more like a deer in the headlights than a swan.* It was hard feeling so isolated, but she supposed she brought it on herself. As much as she hated it here, she should try harder to fit in.

"So, did you guys get what Mrs. Barnes was talking about in algebra?" she asked, determined to move the conversation away from Blackhead Boy, her secret nickname for the boy who had a crush on Angela.

"What?" said Angela, looking startled. Jill merely stared at Victoria as though she had suddenly started spouting Greek.

On Tuesday, Hillary called to say she would miss the next art class. She and her oldest brother, James, were going to ride the train to New York City on Saturday morning to visit their uncle. They'd be away until late Sunday night. "We're going to spend all day Sunday at the Metropolitan Museum of Art," she said.

"I'm so jealous," Victoria said. "I'd love to go to the Met."

"Why don't you come?" Hillary asked, sounding excited. "James won't mind, and my uncle has lots of room."

"My mother wouldn't even let us go to the Gardner alone," Victoria said glumly. "She'd never let me go to New York with just you and James."

"Well, ask her anyway," Hillary said, "and let me know."

Victoria knew it was hopeless, but went immediately to find her mother, who was in the study with her father, watching the evening news on their small black-and-white television. Victoria told her about Hillary's invitation, and her mother, of course, said no.

"It's not fair!" Victoria cried. "I'm fifteen. And James is eighteen."

But no matter what she said, it was useless to argue; her mother would never relent and her father kept his focus on the television, refusing to be drawn into the argument.

Art class on Saturday was dull without Hillary there. Afterwards, Victoria went directly to the Sargent gallery. The Black guard, who recognized her as a regular, smiled at her on his way to the adjoining gallery.

How lucky Hillary is, she thought, *to be in New York with James, able to stroll the halls of the Met, no parents along to tell them what to do.* She stopped in front of the *Daughters of Edward Darley Boit,* not really seeing it, her mind elsewhere.

It was oddly quiet. She realized why when she saw that the gallery was nearly empty. Her eyes locked onto Mary Louisa's painted face. The girl was regarding her with more than her usual urgency. Victoria stepped forward and immediately entered the scene.

Chapter Six

Lost Child

November, 1882, Paris

This time, Mary Louisa was alone with the painter. John Singer Sargent, busy daubing paint on the canvas, was again unaware of Victoria's arrival. Mary Louisa, standing in the center of the room, saw Victoria right away and broke her pose long enough to nod toward the red screen, which stood only inches away from where Victoria had landed. Her heart racing, Victoria made it to her hiding place behind the screen just as the painter looked up.

"Mary Louisa," said Sargent, "please don't move, my dear. Not even your eyes. Your position is perfect." He picked up a different brush, but held it motionless in the air, studying the patch of canvas he had just painted.

Scarcely breathing, Victoria was again able to watch the scene unfold through the gap in the screen's panels. Her head ached a little, but she had no trouble focusing her attention on what was happening in the hall. Mary Louisa was dressed in her portrait clothes and looked perfectly composed, but Victoria noticed she had dark circles under her eyes that stood out starkly against her pale cheeks.

For long minutes, Sargent went on silently with his work. He laid down the brush at last and came out from behind the canvas to stand near Mary Louisa. "Your mama's getting better, I think," he said, as he wiped his hands on a rag. He regarded Mary Louisa with concern. "She told me about losing the baby. I was very sorry to hear it."

Mary Louisa nodded and averted her gaze.

"I told her I wouldn't come today, under the circumstances, but she insisted," Sargent went on. "She thought it might do you good to have me here."

"Oh yes," Mary Louisa said. "Mama says you're like one of the family. I'm glad you came."

"So, how are you doing?" Sargent asked. "How is Julia? I know how much she wanted a baby brother."

"Julia's taking it hard," Mary Louisa said. "She cries herself to sleep at night, and there's nothing I can do to comfort her."

"My mother lost three children," Sargent said, "one before I was born, and two more when I was a boy. I thought I had to be strong to help my parents bear it, but it was very sad for me, too." The painter gave Mary Louisa's shoulder a reassuring squeeze as he spoke.

"Were they boys?" Mary Louisa asked.

"Two of them were boys," Sargent said.

"So, now it's just you and Violet—and one other sister?"

"Yes, I have two sisters who lived. My sister Emily had a terrible illness as a young child, which affected her spine, so she's never been strong. But my youngest sister, Violet, the one I'm going to bring over to meet you, is healthy as a horse and wants to have lots of children of her own someday."

Victoria's attention was caught by the mention of Emily's damaged spine. *I wonder if she has to wear a brace like me,* she thought. Victoria felt sorry for Emily, but Mary Louisa didn't react to Sargent's comment about his sister's illness.

"I'm so worried about Mama," Mary Louisa said, bringing her hand up to the front of her pinafore and holding it there as though her chest hurt. "She lies in bed all day just like last year and when baby John died. She only gets better when she knows she'll have another child. This time though I heard the doctor say she mustn't try again."

Sargent glanced up in surprise. "Baby John? Wasn't the baby who died last year named Elliot?"

"I'm talking about a baby who was born before Florie. John died when he was six months old. We don't mention him in front of Julia. I only know about him because I heard Florence telling Jane about him."

"So, your family has lost three children as well," Sargent said, shaking his head at the sad coincidence. "How wretched for everyone."

Mary Louisa nodded forlornly.

"When does your father return from Boston?" Sargent asked.

"Next week. He booked his passage as soon as Mama wired the bad news."

A banging sounded at the front door. Victoria caught a glimpse of a tiny woman dressed in an old-fashioned maid's costume rush across the room to answer it and, just behind her, Mary Louisa's two older sisters.

"Who is it?" Jane cried, bumping into Florence, who had stopped abruptly in the doorway to the entry hall. "Is it Mr. Graham? Has he come?"

All eyes turned to the front door. The little maid pulled it wide, and a young man with long, pale hair and a floppy hat came in carrying a huge box camera and other photographic gear. He set the camera down and swept off his hat, bowing to the two older girls, who smiled their greetings and hurried to help him with his equipment.

So, this was the Mr. Graham Victoria had heard Florence and Jane discussing. He wore a brightly colored neck scarf and a long, velvet-trimmed jacket that made Sargent's dark wool suit look almost shabby by comparison. *He makes quite the show-stopping entrance*, Victoria thought, wondering if he were there to take photographs of the girls.

While the others bustled around her, Mary Louisa stood frozen in place, holding her pose, though Sargent was clearly finished with her for now.

Sargent stepped forward and held out his hand. "We meet again, Clifford. I see you've come to make good on your wager."

"Yes, yes, I meant what I said," the young man replied. "When we're both finished with these girls, we'll let the world judge whose portrait has more artistic merit."

Sargent took the heavy camera from Jane, watching as the blonde man unstrapped the rest of his camera equipment and set the cases on the floor. "Did Mrs. Boit know you were coming today?" he asked. "I understand she's feeling quite unwell."

"Oh, no!" The photographer looked crestfallen. "We made this appointment several days ago, the girls and I. I didn't think to inquire about their mother's health."

Sargent seemed surprised. "You made an appointment with the girls? Mary Louisa," he said, turning to her, "you never mentioned it to me."

"He made no appointment with me," Mary Louisa said, her voice tight with disapproval. "You must ask Jane and Florence. I think they're the ones who are meant to pose."

"But Mary Louisa," the photographer protested, smiling. "It's not that I haven't asked you to pose—begged you, in fact. You've refused. And I believe you've instructed Julia to refuse as well, which puzzles me very much. I was especially keen to photograph Julia this time." He spoke plaintively, but Mary Louisa appeared unmoved. "I'm desperate!" he went on. "I don't know what I can do to persuade you." He reached out as if to ruffle Mary Louisa's hair, but she stepped away and came to stand stiffly in front of the red screen, her little back just inches from Victoria's face.

"Come, come, Mary Louisa," the photographer went on, "I need the cooperation of all four of you, if I'm to have a chance of winning this wager."

Mary Louisa did not reply, and the photographer turned aside with a frown.

Sargent was studying Mary Louisa. Then he looked at the older girls, who had picked up the rest of the photographer's equipment and were moving toward the hall. "Clifford," he said decisively, "perhaps you would do best to come back another day. Mrs. Boit is really quite indisposed."

Florence turned. "But you came," she said pointedly to Sargent. "Mr. Graham will create no more disturbance with his camera than you have caused with your brush."

"Florence!" Mary Louisa gasped. "Mama would not like to hear you speak to Mr. Sargent that way."

Florence glared at her. "Mama is asleep and doesn't care what we do, as long as we don't wake her."

The maid stepped between them. "*Pardonnez moi*, sir," she said to the photographer, her English mixed with French. "*Attendez*—please wait *un moment*."

The maid left the room. The photographer strode over to the huge painting, which was still turned toward the wall. Sargent moved just as quickly to block his path. "No one sees it till it's finished," he said, "not even the girls."

"Well, well, so you're particular about work in progress." The photographer chuckled. "But then, so am I. I've been known to make a hundred prints before I'm satisfied. And I destroy the ones I reject. I can't bear anyone to see a less-than-perfect product from my studio."

"How was your show at Vivienne's?" Sargent asked. "I wanted to come, but I've been so busy. I have a new commission to begin, so I must finish this picture soon."

"My show was a tremendous success. I have more work than I can handle. Of course, I'm refusing all the usual humdrum studio portraits. That type of thing pays well, but it's not art."

Sargent began tidying his paints and brushes.

"I have no one who depends on me for income—no wife, no child," the photographer went on. "It allows me the freedom to experiment, to continually test myself."

Observing the young man's clothing, Victoria wondered how he could afford to dress as he did if he made no money with his photography. Perhaps, like the Boits, he came from a rich family and lived on inherited wealth.

The maid returned with the older woman dressed all in black that Victoria had glimpsed in the hallway at the end of her last visit. The woman made a small bow to the gentlemen. "I beg your pardon, sirs," she said, "but Mrs. Boit is not well and asks that Mr. Sargent and Mr. Graham return another day when her health has improved."

Clifford Graham opened his mouth as though to argue the point, but Sargent spoke before the other man could utter a sound.

"Yes, yes, Madame Fouche," Sargent said, "I was just going. I'll walk back to the Rue du Bac with you, Clifford, if you're heading that way. Goodbye, everyone. We'll be back when Mrs. Boit sends word she's feeling better."

Jane and Florence began to protest, but the woman in black shushed them. They reluctantly dragged the camera equipment back across the room and handed it to its owner.

"I'll carry this, if you like," Sargent said to Graham, indicating the heavy box camera he still held.

"Yes, thank you, Sargent," Clifford Graham said. "I'll see you soon," he promised Jane and Florence. "We'll try again in a day or two." Then, hurrying to catch up with Sargent, he left the apartment.

"Come, girls," the older woman said sharply to Jane and Florence. "It's time for your lesson." She left the hall, not glancing back to see if the older Boit sisters were following.

Florence leaned in close to Mary Louisa and hissed loudly in her ear, "I suppose you'll be telling Papa how I insulted your darling Mr. Sargent."

"He's always been kind to you, Florie," Mary Louisa said. "I don't know why you're behaving this way."

Florence glowered at her little sister and retreated with Jane toward the back of the apartment.

At last, only Mary Louisa was left in the room. She darted around the screen and seized Victoria's hand.

"You're here, you're real," she breathed. "I didn't know if you were ever coming back."

"I did come back!" Victoria said. "But, you didn't see me— you were talking to Mr. Sargent. I was only here for a little while. Your sisters and that woman in the black dress nearly spotted me, so I couldn't stay."

"That's Madame Fouche, the housekeeper," Mary Louisa said. "She's always butting in where she's not wanted."

"Never mind," Victoria said. "I'm here now. Where's Julia?"

"Oh, Victoria," Mary Louisa said. "Julia's been asking for you, and I didn't know what to tell her. I'll take you to see her now. She's having a nap in our room, but she should wake up soon." Instead of moving, Mary Louisa stood, still clutching Victoria's hand, unable to take her eyes off the older girl. "I can't believe you're real," she said again.

Victoria felt equally amazed by the warmth and solidity of Mary Louisa's hand. Here stood a flesh-and-blood girl in the familiar red dress and white pinafore that Victoria knew so well from the painting. A speck of jam dotted the edge of her cuff and that, more than anything, made this moment feel so ordinary that Victoria forgot for a minute the bizarre circumstance of her arrival here. "What happened to the baby?" she asked.

"This one died before it was even born. Another boy. Mama won't stop weeping. She says she'll never have another child."

"Oh, Mary Louisa, how terrible." Victoria squeezed Mary Louisa's hand, and Mary Louisa squeezed back. "You must be heartbroken, all of you."

"Not Jane or Florence. They seem hardly to notice. They only want to talk about Mr. Graham, that photographer. I think he's cast a spell on them."

"You don't like him?"

"No, and neither does Julia. He talks baby talk to her, and she hates being treated like a baby."

"Is that why she doesn't like dolls?"

"Yes. But, not Popau. She *loves* Popau. She plays with him all the time. She's begun to think he's alive." Mary Louisa peeked out from behind the screen. "Wait here," she said. "I'll go see where they all are, then I'll take you to Julia."

She left and Victoria crouched down in the dark behind the screen. A few minutes later, Mary Louisa was back.

"The servants are in the kitchen, and Jane and Florence are with Madame Fouche in the study. Mama's still asleep. Follow me. No one will see us."

They left the big hall and went down the corridor opposite the one that Jane and Florence had taken, moving as quietly as they could. They passed a large dining room that contained a table and at least twelve chairs, then another large room with an imposing fireplace flanked by two rose-colored sofas. There wasn't time to notice everything, but Victoria liked the sky-blue wallpaper in the hallway and, high overhead, the elaborate plaster moldings that outlined the ceilings of each room.

Mary Louisa opened a door at the far end of the hall and led Victoria along a much narrower passage. "This is for the servants," she whispered, "but we use it when we want to sneak out of our bedroom and hide from Madame Fouche."

They emerged in another wide hallway, and then it was only a few steps to the bedroom Mary Louisa shared with Julia. Julia was asleep in a small bed pushed against one wall. A matching bed flanked the opposite wall. Victoria walked to a pair of floor-to-ceiling windows and looked out at a gloomy, overcast day, much like the one she had left behind in Boston. But in Boston, in spite of a late spring, green leaves were visible on the trees that lined the streets. Victoria could see that here in Paris, the trees were bare and the leaves lay decaying in the gutters. It looked like a typical late autumn day, the kind Victoria was used to experiencing in Boston.

Other differences were more startling. Victoria heard the unmistakable clatter of hooves on cobblestones and saw a carriage pulled by two shiny, black horses come into view and stop at the house across the street. It was followed by a heavily loaded cart drawn by an ancient, sway-backed nag. Except for the horses, she might have convinced herself she was having an amazingly realistic dream. But these living, breathing animals and the steaming piles of dung they were depositing on the pavement were too real to be disbelieved.

Mary Louisa sat on the bed beside Julia, gently shaking her awake. "Julia, dear, wake up. Victoria is here."

Julia sat up, rubbing her eyes sleepily. The minute she saw Victoria, she bolted from the bed and flung herself at the older girl, clinging to her arm as if to keep her from vanishing. Her voice rose in a desperate wail, and Victoria could do nothing but pat her shaking shoulders till she calmed down.

"Julia, stop crying. Someone will hear you," Mary Louisa said.

At last Julia was quiet. Victoria led her back to the bed and sat down beside her. Mary Louisa followed and sat on Julia's other side. "So tell me what's wrong," Victoria prompted. "Why are you so upset?"

Julia sniffed and wiped her nose on her sleeve. "The baby," she said. "If you came back, I wanted to show you the baby. But he died. We won't ever have a baby now, Mama says." Her voice trembled, and Victoria was afraid she'd start to wail once more.

"I know," she said softly. "Mary Louisa told me. It's very sad. I'm so sorry." The three of them sat without speaking. The idea of this house without a baby, without the possibility of a baby, felt to Victoria like the bleakest prospect in the world.

"Is your mother all right?" Victoria asked. "Is her health improving?"

"I don't know," Mary Louisa said. "She's not really sick—I mean she doesn't have an illness or anything. But she's so sad. She won't do anything. I can't wait for Papa to return. He'll make her get out of bed, at least."

"He'll be home soon?" Victoria asked.

"He's on his way," Mary Louisa said. "He had to go to Boston on family business. And he took some of his paintings to show to a collector."

"Papa's a painter, too, you know," Julia said with some pride. "A very good painter."

"And how have you been getting on while he's away, since your mother's been unwell?" Victoria asked, though she knew from eavesdropping during her last trip to Paris that life hadn't been easy for the little girls. "Who takes care of you?"

"Madame Fouche and the other servants are here. But mostly we take care of ourselves," Mary Louisa answered, looking slightly offended. "We're not babies."

"You take care of me," Julia corrected her.

"And you go to school?" Victoria asked.

"No," Mary Louisa said. "Madame Fouche teaches us French when she isn't having one of her headaches. We had a governess, but she left."

"We didn't like her, did we, Isa?" Julia said. "She made us eat prunes, and we hate prunes."

Victoria couldn't help thinking that the girls' education sounded very hit and miss, but they acted as though there was nothing unusual about it.

"And the painting's nearly finished?" Victoria asked.

Julia was the one who answered. "Mr. Sargent's been gone. He wanted the beautiful lady to pose for him, but she wouldn't agree. But now she has. He can't wait to finish with us, so he can paint her." She gave a theatrical sigh. "I wish he would stay. He promised to teach me how to be an artist."

"Oh, Julia, he'll be back!" Mary Louisa said. "He only stayed a little while today, but he said he'll be back. He promised to bring his sister Violet for a visit. And he told Mama he's going to paint her portrait soon."

Julia hung her head. "I like it when he comes," she said.

"So do I," Mary Louisa agreed. "He'll be back as soon as he can, and he'll give you more drawing lessons. But he says you've got to practice making pictures of the cat before he can show you how to draw people."

"He's going to take your portrait to the Paris Salon, isn't he?" said Victoria, casting around for something cheerful to talk about. "It's going to be a big success, don't you think?"

Mary Louisa looked at her curiously. "I don't know. I haven't seen it. No one has."

"Oh," said Victoria, realizing she was the only person here, besides Sargent, who had seen it. And even Sargent hadn't seen it in its finished state. "Well, I'm sure it will be wonderful. It's got to be. Look who painted it."

Mary Louisa smiled. "You sound like Julia. She says John Sargent is the greatest painter in all of Paris, maybe in all the world."

"You think so, too," Julia said to her sister, who nodded her assent.

"And so do I," Victoria said. "But that photographer who was just here thinks Sargent's paintings aren't as good as his photographs."

"Oh, him," Mary Louisa said, tossing her ringlets. "He won some big award and now he thinks he's an important artist."

"When photography gets really popular, I suppose it will put some portrait painters out of work," Victoria said, thinking about all the changes the invention of cameras brought about. With cameras came movies, then television—a whole new world that these Boit girls had no idea was coming.

"Maybe some, but not Mr. Sargent. He's not like the others."

"You're right," Victoria said. There were so many famous Sargent portraits. "He paints more than just a likeness. He paints what people are like inside."

Mary Louisa looked startled. "I never thought about that," she said slowly.

Julia's expression had turned peevish. "Was Mr. Graham here?"

"Yes, but Madame Fouche sent him away," Mary Louisa told her. "Jane and Florence were so angry. I heard him promise to take a special picture of them dressed as orphans and they've been making sad faces in the mirror all week to get ready."

"They're just silly," Julia said, shaking her head in disgust.

"They were very rude to Mr. Sargent just now," said Mary Louisa.

"Are you going to tell Papa?" Julia asked.

"I don't want to worry him," Mary Louisa said, staring back at her sister. "He has to take care of Mama when he gets home."

Victoria started to ask the girls to tell her more about Mr. Graham, when a sharp rap at the door startled them all.

"Julia! Mary Louisa!" a voice called. "It's time for your lesson."

"It's Madame Fouche," Mary Louisa whispered.

"You'd better go," Victoria whispered back.

"Wait here," Mary Louisa said. "We'll be back soon. I have so many questions."

Julia gave Victoria's hand a tight squeeze and rushed out of the room. Mary Louisa followed, smiling at Victoria as she closed the door carefully behind her.

Victoria moved back to her former spot at the window and looked out at the unfamiliar scene before her. All the buildings nearby looked the same as the one she was in, all five stories high and made of cool, gray granite with tall windows and ornate ironwork balconies. The sloping roofs were punctured by dormer windows placed at regular intervals along their length. Though not on the same epic scale, the architecture reminded her of the library and art museum back home in Boston.

A nursemaid, bundled up against the cold, hurried past on the sidewalk opposite, pushing an enormous black baby carriage. Two old women, dressed in elaborate fur coats and hats, walked by more slowly, followed closely by a young serving woman wearing a plain wool coat and carrying a large hamper. It looked incredibly peaceful to Victoria, accustomed as she was to the hubbub of Boston streets and the constant noise of cars and buses.

In spite of being nearly hypnotized by what she was seeing out the window, Victoria's mind continued to worry over Julia and Mary Louisa's situation. Jane and Florence's behavior was troubling. They seemed indifferent to their mother's miscarriage, to their little sisters' grief—in fact, the only person they seemed to care about was handsome Mr. Graham. Even though she knew Sargent was not their favorite, Victoria was surprised by their rudeness to him. He seemed like such a kind-hearted man. Was it just teenage moodiness, she wondered, or were these signs of the mental illness that she knew was coming, in Jane's case, very soon?

Victoria jumped in alarm as the same maid she had seen earlier in the entry hall came through the door of the bedroom carrying a pile of fresh linens. The maid moved purposefully toward Julia's unmade bed, but stopped short when she glanced toward the window.

At the same instant, Victoria experienced a sudden dimming of light. The last thing she heard was a gasp from the maid. Then she was gone.

Chapter Seven

Madame X

May, 1963, Boston

Returning from the Museum with her mother that Saturday afternoon, Victoria was too exhausted to talk. She slumped against the passenger side window, telling her mother she had yet another headache.

"Your aunt Margaret suffers from migraines," her mother said. "I think they started when she was about your age."

"I don't have a migraine, Mom," Victoria grumbled. As soon as they got home she went to her room. Her headache was nothing this time, but the disruption of time and space made her very tired. She crawled into bed and closed her eyes. When she awoke properly, it was already Sunday. She vaguely remembered eating an early supper in the kitchen with Rose, but for the most part, the past afternoon and evening had gone by in a fog.

She no longer felt tired, just helpless. She got up to dress, then sat on her bed to put on her socks, puzzling over what to do next. Her time with the Boit girls, though longer this time, had once again been interrupted. Each time she was with Mary

Louisa and Julia, someone else in their household had discovered her in a place she had no business being. Apparently, this was enough to flip her out of the past and back into the present. She could only guess how much time would pass in their world before she'd be able to get back.

She still believed the Boit girls needed her help. But how? What was the source of their trouble? She could think of several possible reasons, but none of them seemed exactly right. The family had lost another baby, but she was beginning to understand that miscarriages and infant death were not so rare in 1882 given that Sargent's family had suffered the same kind of loss. Mary Louisa and Julia didn't like the blonde photographer who kept coming around, but he looked pretty harmless to Victoria. She hadn't liked thinking about Jane and Florence going to his studio alone, but that didn't seem like enough of a reason for Mary Louisa to be so bothered by him. Jane was headed for a mental breakdown—did Mary Louisa have some premonition of that? Also, it was pretty clear the two younger girls were being neglected, but again, that wasn't a good enough reason for the vague but unshakeable fear she felt for their welfare. It was something much bigger than that.

Victoria pounded her still bare feet on the floor in vexation. Why couldn't she figure it out? Still, no matter how baffling and discouraging it was being in Paris, it was so much more interesting than being stuck at home. She couldn't imagine what her mother would say if she knew; her trip to Paris made James and Hillary's excursion to New York seem like a walk in the park.

Remembering that Hillary was at this very instant in New York at the Met made her mad all over again. Time traveling to Paris had given her an insatiable appetite for the freedom she craved. She was no longer willing to go along with her mother's strict rules about never leaving the house without adult supervision. It was time to make a stand. *Hillary goes where she pleases and her parents are fine with it,* she thought. *I deserve to do the same.*

Even if Victoria's mother wasn't ready to let her take a trip to New York with Hillary and James, she could at least let her go places on her own in Boston. Victoria put on her socks and shoes, finished tightening the straps on her brace and went down to breakfast prepared to do battle.

"Eggs?" said Rose in her usual abrupt way when Victoria entered the kitchen. "Bacon?" Rose was convinced that Victoria didn't eat enough and made it her solemn duty to fatten her up. She didn't smile or look at Victoria when she spoke, but Victoria knew she meant to be kind.

"Thanks, Rose!" Victoria said, raising her voice since Rose was getting quite deaf. "I'll just have cereal!"

Rose huffed and put the eggs back in the refrigerator. *It's going to be hard to replace her,* Victoria mused, *when she takes her well-earned retirement at the end of the year.* Though her personality was gruff, her cooking was marvelous and they were all used to her taciturn ways.

"Do you know where Mom is?!" Victoria shouted at Rose's back.

"She's down to see your aunties on the Cape," Rose told her. "She took the early train." Then the old housekeeper picked up her feather duster and walked out of the kitchen.

Victoria wasn't surprised to hear about her mother's plans, since this was a trip she made often on the weekend. Victoria's two middle-aged aunts lived alone in the family summer house on Cape Cod, and Victoria's mother, the oldest of the three siblings, treated them like they still needed a lot of looking after. Usually Victoria enjoyed the time her mother was away, but the fact that she chose today to disappear felt like bad luck. She could feel her determination to confront her mother already slipping away.

Victoria went to find her father in his study as soon as she finished breakfast. "When's Mom coming back?" she asked.

"Late," her father said, pulling her in for a one-armed hug, which she allowed. Her father was the one person whose hugs she didn't mind. He was always careful of her brace and never squeezed too tight. "She told us to eat dinner without her if she's not back in time."

Victoria sighed.

"Are you feeling better?" her dad asked. "I thought we'd go see *To Kill a Mockingbird* this afternoon if you're up to it."

Victoria perked up immediately. "I'd love to," she said. She'd been dying to see the film based on one of her favorite books.

"I need to finish some work," her father said. "How about we go to the four o'clock show?"

Victoria lingered behind her father's chair, watching as he sorted through a stack of files on his desk. His bristly, grayish hair had receded a lot in the last year and his narrow shoulders looked a bit more slumped. No wonder people sometimes mistook him for her grandfather. Everyone said she looked more like her mother, with her dark hair and eyes, but she clearly got her curls and long, skinny frame from her dad. Someday, Victoria hoped, she might turn out to be as pretty as her mom, but prayed, when it came to disposition, that she'd be easygoing like her dad.

"Dad?" she said. "Can I ask you something?"

"Hmmm?" said her father, not turning from the papers on his desk.

"Other girls my age get to go places on their own, but I never can." She hadn't meant to sound petulant, but a whining tone had crept into her voice.

Her father swiveled to face her. "What are you saying?"

Victoria tried for a more mature tone. "I'm asking why Mom never lets me go anywhere alone or with a friend. Do you know? Were her parents like that?"

Her father lifted his shoulders in a half shrug. When he answered, he spoke slowly, as if weighing his words. "Your grandparents could afford nannies to look after your mother and her sisters, and when they were old enough to go to boarding school, the headmistress was responsible for them. But your mother's parents never paid much attention to what their daughters were doing. After Randolph died, they seemed to lose interest in the children. They were busy with their own affairs."

This was news to Victoria. She'd heard about the death of Randolph, her mother's older brother, but only the fact of it, none of the details. She'd had no idea how that calamitous event had affected her mother or the rest of the family. Whenever Victoria tried asking her mother about it, her mother made it clear that the subject of Randolph was even more taboo than anything else about her mother's time growing up. "So, Mom got to go wherever she wanted?"

"During the summers, they stayed at their house on the Cape and the girls went to the beach and into town. Your mother probably went places with friends."

"Why won't she let me do that?"

Victoria's father fiddled with his pen, delaying his answer. "She thinks it isn't wise for young girls to go around without a chaperone."

"Chaperone!" Victoria rolled her eyes. "Dad, you sound so old-fashioned! Girls haven't had chaperones for decades."

Her father looked uncomfortable. "Perhaps that's the wrong choice of words. I mean to say unattended, unprotected—especially in a big city like Boston. When your mother was young, I'm sure the girls didn't go around Boston alone. It was only on the Cape, in that small-town setting, that they got to roam around on their own."

"Things are different now," Victoria insisted. "All the kids my age who live here are much more independent than I am."

She knew this was a weak argument. No parent liked a sentence that began, "All the kids my age . . ."

Her father didn't seem to be listening. He stared at the framed family photograph on his desk, as if recalling a long-ago conversation. "Your mother thinks her own parents were too uninvolved. When you were just a baby, she vowed to do a better job than they did."

"But, she never lets me go anywhere!" Victoria protested.

"Are you talking about this trip to New York with Hillary?" her father said, starting to sound a tiny bit annoyed. "You've only just met the girl. Don't you think it's a little soon to be planning a weekend trip with her?"

"You mean if I'd known her longer, you would have let me go?"

"Well, I can't speak for your mother, but if we knew the family better, including this brother of hers, and felt good about them, I would have considered letting you go."

"But not Mom?"

Her father took a moment before replying. "Your mother has different ideas about these things than I do."

"Can't you just tell her she's being unreasonable?" Victoria begged.

Her father met her eyes. "It doesn't pay to get your mother riled up, and, when it comes to your safety, that's much too easy to do."

"So, who's going to be on my side?"

Her father looked startled. "I am on your side, Victoria, but I have to try to see your mother's side of things, too." He sat up straighter in his chair. "How about this? Next time you want to go somewhere with Hillary on your own, somewhere closer to home, I'll do everything I can to get her to agree."

Victoria scowled.

"You're growing up to be a beautiful, resourceful young woman," her father went on, "and I want you to have the confidence to go out into the world without fear. I get it—it's important. I'll do my best."

Victoria smiled. "Thanks, Dad," she said, giving her father's shoulder an affectionate squeeze. "When should we leave for the movie?"

"Let's leave a little after three," her father said, smiling back, "so we can make sure to get good seats."

When she and her father returned from the movie that evening, Victoria's mother was still not home. The two of them talked about the movie while they heated the food Rose had left for them. They were both hungry and ate standing up at the kitchen counter. It was a nice change from their usual sit-down meals in the dining room.

"You know that line that Atticus says to Jem?" Victoria said. "Something like: 'There's a lot of ugly things in this world, son. I wish I could keep 'em all away from you. But, that's never possible.'"

"I remember," her father said.

"I think that's what Mom's trying to do—to protect me from *everything*."

"And she can't," her father sighed.

The phone rang, interrupting their conversation. "That could be your mother now." Victoria's father left the kitchen, but was back in a moment. "It's for you," he said. "It's Hillary."

"How was it?" Victoria asked, picking up the telephone receiver in the downstairs hall. She was eager to hear about Hillary's visit to the Met.

"Fantastic," Hillary said. "Everything was amazing, but seeing Sargent's painting of *Madame X*—that was the highlight for James and me."

Victoria had read about *Madame X* in her books on Sargent and seen reproductions. She knew the portrait had caused a terrible scandal when Sargent exhibited it at the Paris Salon in 1884, though she wasn't sure why. As far as she could tell, the only risqué thing about the original portrait was that the woman's gown was very low-cut and one of its straps had slipped off her shoulder. "Describe it to me," she said.

"It's huge," Hillary said, "at least as tall as the *Daughters of Edward Darley Boit*, so it towers over you. And the look on her face—so haughty! She was supposed to be a great beauty, but she has a really pointy nose and the whitest skin. She looks almost ill."

"Do you get the whole *Madame X* thing?" Victoria asked. "Why it caused such a fuss?" She picked up the phone and dragged the long phone cord behind her to the bottom step of the staircase.

"More than a fuss," Hillary said. "It ruined the woman's reputation, which wasn't so good to begin with. And almost ruined Sargent's as well."

"But why?" Victoria said, sitting, then leaning back against the stairs. "Other than the drooping strap, what was wrong with it?"

"Well, if you've ever seen a reproduction of the original, you have to admit, it was pretty racy." Hillary said. "The way it looks now, after Sargent repainted it with the strap back in place on her shoulder, is way less shocking. Remember, it was the Victorian era. They weren't used to seeing stuff like that back then."

Victoria found it hard to believe that, even in those days, the portrait could have been considered obscene. "Standards have certainly changed," she said, as she compulsively wrapped and unwrapped the coiled phone cord around her finger.

"What do you think the Victorians would make of miniskirts?" Hillary asked.

Victoria snorted. "Some of those skirts are so short they make it impossible to bend over. You have to squat to pick anything up from the floor."

"I know," said Hillary. "Nowadays it's not all about cleavage; it's also about too much thigh."

Victoria had a lot more questions, but she felt bad leaving her dad to finish his meal all alone. "I should go," she said.

"Hey," Hillary said before they hung up, "do you want to come over after art class next Saturday?"

Victoria was caught off guard. She did want to meet Hillary's family, but Saturday after class was her only chance to get back to Paris. "I can't," she blurted.

"How come?" Hillary asked, sounding disappointed.

"We're, um . . . busy that day, " Victoria said. "I'd love to come another time."

"What about Friday?" Hillary asked. "You can come after school and have dinner with us."

"Great!" Victoria said, relieved. "I'll ask my parents."

Victoria had just ended the call when her mother finally arrived home. Victoria asked if she could have dinner at Hillary's next Friday, and her mother said it sounded fine. "I can drop you off," she said. "And I'll give the parents a call to see if they want me to pick you up as well."

"Okay," Victoria said, "I can give you their number." Her mother's request was only to be expected. She seemed to like and trust Hillary, but she'd never met the parents and she wouldn't send her daughter off to visit complete strangers without at least talking to them on the phone.

Her mother turned to hang her coat in the hall closet, and Victoria couldn't resist saying, "Hillary and James had a great time at the Met, by the way."

"Oh?" said her mother. She straightened her coat on the hanger, refusing to rise to the bait. "Did Hillary tell you what they saw?"

"She mentioned Sargent's *Madame X*."

"Yes, I've seen it," her mother replied. "I don't like it. It's the only one of Sargent's portraits I truly dislike."

"Why?" Victoria asked.

Victoria's mother turned to face her daughter. Her expression was somber and Victoria thought she saw a slight shudder run through her body. "I can't really say," she said, with uncharacteristic vagueness. She shut the closet door and walked away down the hall.

As she got ready for bed, Victoria thought about her mother's odd reaction to her mention of *Madame X*. Her mother was strange, there was no doubt about that. Still, it had been a good day overall—the movie and spending time with her dad. She was glad to be going to Hillary's on Friday and even more thankful to be returning to the Boit girls the next day. She wasn't going to worry about anything else for now.

Intrigued by Hillary's description of her favorite painting at the Met, she took one of her library books to bed with her and read more about Sargent's painting of *Madame X*. It had occurred to her that the "beautiful lady" Julia Boit had mentioned might be Amelie Gautreau, the woman depicted in the famous *Madame X* portrait. After checking the dates—Madame Gautreau's portrait was begun early in 1883, just after Sargent finished his painting of the Boit girls—Victoria was convinced of it.

When school ended on Friday, Victoria's mother picked her up and drove her to Hillary's house. Hillary answered the door and led Victoria inside. Looking around, Victoria saw signs of children everywhere: an overloaded coat rack in the front hall, crayon drawings tacked to the wall, and roller skates in the dining room. In the smallish living room, an old tabby cat had draped itself over the back of a lumpy sofa, and in the bathroom, which Victoria asked to visit first thing since she was feeling a bit nervous, towels hung in damp bunches on the bars.

The smell of some exotic spice wafted in from the kitchen, where Hillary's mother was busy at the stove. "Hello, love," she said over her shoulder, when Hillary introduced Victoria. "Nice to meet you." She smiled warmly, then turned back to her steaming pots and pans. She was wearing a pair of roomy, wide-legged cotton pants under a big, patchwork apron, and her hair was pulled back in a messy ponytail. A few escaped tendrils stuck to her sweaty face. To Victoria, she looked busy, but cheerful.

Hillary's house was such a contrast to her own spacious, well-ordered home that Victoria couldn't help feeling a little claustrophobic. Hillary seemed unaware of the clutter and made no apologies for the state of her room, which she shared with her younger sister, Peg. She pushed aside a pile of books and clothes and spread out some of James's drawings and watercolors on the bed.

"James said it was okay to show you these," she said. "Some of his stuff isn't finished yet, but these are more or less done."

Victoria was instantly drawn to James's work, many of them portraits of the family. Victoria could see that he had exceptional talent, a whole level above Hillary's. He'd made many sketches of Erin, who, at five, was the baby of the family. He'd drawn her in all moods: sleeping and laughing and looking inexpressibly sad.

A pen-and-ink drawing of his mother, sitting at the kitchen table with a cup of coffee, was Victoria's favorite. James had caught his mother during what must have been a rare moment of quiet contemplation.

"He's really good," Victoria said. "This one of your mother reminds me of Sargent's portrait of his sister Violet at breakfast."

"James is crazy about Sargent," Hillary said. "He thinks *Madame X* is the best painting at the Met."

"So, Sargent repainted the strap as soon as he got the portrait back from the Salon?" Victoria asked, eager to continue the conversation about *Madame X*.

"And, according to James, ruined the lines of the picture in the process," Hillary said.

"What's 'according to James'?" said a voice. A boy with thick, brown hair and wire-rimmed glasses stuck his head in the door and grinned at them. He had a small frame, like his sister, and the same dark, penetrating eyes. "What are you saying about me, Hil?"

"James—you're back," Hillary said. "Come in and meet Victoria."

"Hello," James said, coming into the room and leaning against the dresser.

"Hello back," Victoria said, trying to look James in the eye in spite of feeling shy. He looked younger than Victoria had imagined, more like a sixteen-year-old than a senior in high school. Victoria guessed he was about her height, maybe a little shorter, with a smile that made her want to smile back.

"We're talking about *Madame X*," Hillary said.

"Did you know she took arsenic to make her skin white?" James asked.

"What?" Victoria said, startled.

"Amelie Gautreau, the notorious *Madame X*. Sargent used a lot of blue in the skin tones, but that's apparently how she really looked. It was fashionable to have really pale skin, so she took small doses of arsenic every day to turn her skin that deathly shade of white."

"She could have killed herself!" Victoria said.

"Yeah, but think of all the ridiculous things women have done throughout history to make themselves beautiful," Hillary said, "like binding their feet or trussing themselves up in corsets or having ribs removed so they could have tiny waists."

Victoria thought of her own mother's insistence on "proper" attire. Stockings and garter belts or girdles weren't exactly torture, but they were horribly uncomfortable—almost as bad as wearing a back brace for scoliosis. "I know, but taking poison!" she said. "Did people know that—about the arsenic? Is that why they were so bothered by the portrait?"

"I think it was more than that," James said laughing. "I read that one reviewer called it a 'flagrant insufficiency' of clothing. I love that description!"

"Everybody said Amelie Gautreau was promiscuous," Hillary said. "Have you seen Sargent's portrait of Dr. Pozzi, the famous gynecologist? According to the rumors, he and Amelie were lovers. She called him 'Dr. Love.'"

Victoria did remember a portrait of a devilishly handsome doctor that she'd seen in a book of Sargent prints. "You mean that amazing painting of the guy in the long, red bathrobe?"

"That's the one," James said. "The fellow with the wonderful bedroom eyes."

"But, wasn't Madame Gautreaux married?" Victoria protested.

"Yes, and so was he." James laughed again. "That didn't stop them."

"So, Sargent knew all this when he painted her?" Victoria asked.

"Of course," James said. "I'm sure it was all just business as usual in Paris in those days. He was as surprised as anyone by all the uproar her portrait caused."

Victoria knew that most of the earliest reviews of *Madame X* were negative, many of them mocking, though a few applauded Sargent's courage. "I read he changed the title of the picture to *Madame X* to protect her identity," Victoria said, eager to show off her recently acquired knowledge.

"That's true. It was—" Whatever James had been going to say was cut short by shrill voices from the hall. Hillary's younger sister, Peg, burst into the room, followed a moment later, by Erin, the only one of the O'Brien girls with bright red curls. Erin reminded Victoria of Julia. The little girls were more or less the same age and had the same round cheeks.

"James! James!" Erin cried. "Mum let me use the finger paints and I made you a picture."

"And got paint all over the kitchen and the cat," Peg said, with nine-year-old disdain.

"You said you'd read me a story," Erin cried, holding up a copy of *Where the Wild Things Are*.

"Oh," James said to Erin. "That's a good one." And then to Victoria, "I'm a sucker for Sendak's art."

James read the story to Erin while Victoria listened, and then they all went out to the back yard. Victoria had brought along her camera and took some candid shots of James and Hillary as they played a game of hide and seek with Erin and Peg. It was her first attempt at photographing people, and she decided she liked it better than taking pictures of clouds or spiderwebs covered in dew. If these shots came out well, maybe she'd focus on portraits from now on.

When Hillary's two other brothers, Ralph and Patrick, returned from a tennis match, Victoria was introduced to them as well. By now, Victoria was feeling thoroughly overwhelmed; O'Briens were coming out of the woodwork. The two boys, who looked only a little older than Hillary, appeared nearly identical. Both were taller and thinner than James, wore tennis clothes, and had longish hair that constantly flopped into their eyes.

"We borrowed the Dylan album from Josh," Patrick said to James.

"Just don't play it around Dad," James said. "He thinks Dylan sounds like a sick donkey."

"Are they twins?" Victoria whispered to Hillary.

"Irish twins," Hillary whispered back. "Eleven months apart."

"Do you like Dylan, Victoria?" James asked.

"He's okay," Victoria said. Victoria had heard the Bob Dylan album once and, though she wouldn't admit it here, agreed with Mr. O'Brien about his voice.

Mr. O'Brien was last to make an appearance. "Home at last," he announced, striding into the dining room just as dinner was about to be served. He sat at the head of the table and, after intoning a brief prayer, said, "Let's eat."

Victoria decided Hillary's father looked a lot like James, only taller. He had the same dark hair and a grin that cracked open his face in much the same way. He told them he'd been over at a neighbor's house watching President Kennedy's most recent televised news conference, which began with a statement by the president condemning the outrageous treatment of Dr. Martin Luther King Jr. and the people who had joined him in a peaceful protest in Birmingham, Alabama.

Victoria felt herself withdrawing as Mr. O'Brien guided the conversation, addressing all of his children as he rehashed what the president had to say. Victoria could imagine her own mother's disapproving reaction to this conversation. "Politics is not a polite topic for the dinner table," she'd heard her mother say.

"What about you, Victoria?" Mr. O'Brien asked. "Are you in love with our president like all the women in this family?"

Victoria blushed. She did, in fact, have a secret crush on the handsome JFK. She looked around at the ring of friendly faces and was able to smile and say, "I guess."

Everyone laughed and Victoria, feeling suddenly brave, said. "He makes me feel safe."

Mr. O'Brien, who wasn't laughing, asked, "Why is that?"

Victoria's cheeks grew hot, but she didn't retreat. "Last fall," she began, keeping her eye fixed on Mr. O'Brien, who nodded encouragingly, "when we all were afraid the Russians were going to start World War III, I thought President Kennedy handled things really well."

"Ah, the Cuban Missile Crisis," said Mr. O'Brien. "Yes, I think he deserves a lot of credit for standing up to Khrushchev the way he did." Then he smiled wickedly and added, "But, you have to admit, it doesn't hurt that he's so *very* good-looking."

"He's not just a pretty face, Michael," Mrs. O'Brien said. "I'm convinced he's going to do more to help the civil rights struggle in this country than any president we've ever had."

"Hey Ma," Patrick said. "Josh's brother—the one who goes to Brandeis—heard that Martin Luther King is planning a big march in Washington next summer. His brother is going, and Josh wants to go, too. He said I should come."

"Maybe we'll all go," said his mother, "our own little contingent of freedom fighters."

There were cries of agreement from everyone, including Victoria. She had a vision of herself marching side by side with James and Hillary and the rest of the O'Briens singing the movement's anthem, "We Shall Overcome."

The conversation went on, ranging over a variety of topics. The O'Briens got a kick out of arguing, in a good-natured way, about everything. No subject was forbidden and the children were encouraged to voice their own opinions.

As Victoria listened to the animated chatter, her thoughts returned to the Boits. She tried, and failed, to picture Mr. and Mrs. Boit and their four daughters having a dinner conversation like this one. It seemed no more likely than it would be at her own dining table.

It was around ten o'clock when Mrs. O'Brien dropped Victoria at home. Victoria's mother and father were waiting for her in the living room and wanted to hear all about her visit to Hillary's. "It was exhausting," she said. "They're such a big family; it's like watching a play with all three acts happening at once."

What she didn't say was what she found herself thinking about James. He was kind of short, but very attractive and *so* friendly, besides being enormously talented. If she had a boyfriend like James, she thought as she climbed the stairs to her room, they'd never lack for things to talk about. It was impossible, of course: she was much younger than he was. And then there was the problem of her brace—she'd pretty much given up on the idea of having a boyfriend while she was required to wear it. Nevertheless, she fell asleep imagining what it would be like to amble through Central Park with James, on their way to a day at the Met.

Victoria was happy to see Hillary, dowdy clothes and all, in art class the next day, but as the last hour drew to a close, she began to feel anxious about her trip to Paris. She had to leave quickly after class or she'd miss her chance to enter the painting and time travel back to the Boits' apartment. As she and Hillary walked out of the classroom together, Hillary was talking about James's college plans and, as much as Victoria was eager to hear anything that had to do with James, she was burning to get away. She made several attempts to end the conversation, but Hillary wasn't taking the hint.

"Hil," she said finally, cutting her off mid-sentence, "I've got to go."

A hurt look clouded Hillary's bright face as Victoria turned to leave, but she didn't say anything more. Victoria would have to make it up to her, but she couldn't worry about it now. She walked off purposefully and as soon as Hillary was out of sight, raced to the Sargent gallery and, without hesitating, walked straight into the painting.

Chapter Eight

The Waif

November, 1882, Paris

Mary Louisa's attention was riveted on the feathered shuttlecock she was bouncing off her badminton racquet, so she didn't turn when Victoria appeared in the entry hall just behind her. Glancing around to make sure the girl was alone, Victoria saw that the painting was still there, but it no longer faced the wall. It was turned outward and partially hidden behind the red screen. A shiver ran through her. So, it must be finished! She couldn't wait to examine it.

"Mary Louisa," she called softly, not wanting to startle her.

Mary Louisa jerked in surprise, inadvertently sending the birdie flying upward with a sudden whack. It lofted into the air, traced a wobbly arc and fell, of all places, into the mouth of the nearest vase.

"Victoria," she gasped, looking over her shoulder. "Look what you made me do!"

"Sorry," said Victoria. "I didn't mean to sneak up on you like that."

Mary Louisa gave her a rueful look. "It's all right," she said, breaking into a big smile. "I'm just glad you're here."

"That was quite a shot," Victoria said, grinning back.

"Papa would be furious if he knew I batted a shuttlecock into his precious vase," Mary Louisa said, her smile turning wicked. "It's not the first one either. I popped two in last week!"

"Well," said Victoria. "I doubt he'll find out. I don't imagine those vases get emptied very often."

"Never, as far as I know," said Mary Louisa.

"Then you're safe," said Victoria, still grinning. She was happy to see that Mary Louisa looked no worse than she had the last time they'd met. Hopefully no further disasters had occurred in the Boit household during Victoria's absence. "I won't tell if you don't."

"Let's go find Julia," said Mary Louisa, leaning her racquet against the wall and reaching for the older girl's hand. "She was heartbroken to find you gone last time."

Victoria waved toward the painting behind the screen. "I want to look at it before we go." She stepped around the screen and had her first good look at the newly completed masterpiece. The paint was still fresh enough to smell and the colors glowed. It felt like a tremendous honor to be among only a handful of people who had seen it so far. "It's incredible," she said, taking in a wondering breath.

"I know." Mary Louisa stood beside her nodding, then pulled again on Victoria's hand. "We need to go before anyone comes," she said. The two girls crept cautiously down the hall to the sisters' bedroom. Julia was sitting on the floor playing with Popau, but jumped up when she saw them and rushed over to greet Victoria.

"You're here!" Julia cried. "Why did you have to leave?"

"I'm sorry, " Victoria said. "I couldn't help it." She gave Julia a sideways squeeze. "How long have I been gone? Tell me what's happened."

"Wait," said Mary Louisa. She dragged a rocking chair in front of the door and positioned it under the handle. "We don't want anyone to barge in and find you."

"Good thinking," said Victoria. The three girls sat side by side on Mary Louisa's bed with Popau on Julia's lap. It was early afternoon and, though sunlight streamed through the windows and lit up the gold streaks in Mary Louisa's curls, the room was cold. Julia was dressed in a nubby woolen dress that emphasized her round tummy and Mary Louisa wore a thick, hand-knitted sweater. Victoria shivered in her oversized cotton shirt. For once she was grateful for the second layer of warmth provided by the leather back brace.

"Mama's better," Mary Louisa said, "and Papa's come home. He makes her get out of bed for supper."

"But Mr. Sargent's gone," Julia said sadly. "He's busy with his new portrait. Ours is finished."

"I know," Victoria said. "I saw it." She was eager to ask about the new portrait—it had to be Sargent's painting of *Madame X*—but she wanted to talk about the girls' portrait first. "Do you like it? What do you think?"

"We love it, Mary Louisa and me, and Popau," Julia said, bending to look the doll in the eye for confirmation, "but, Florence and Jane hate it."

"We think it's grand and mysterious," Mary Louisa said. "But, they say it's dark and ugly." She sighed. "They're mad because Mr. Sargent painted them in the background and Julia and me in front. Florence is especially unhappy."

Victoria nodded. "And your parents, do they like it?"

"Oh, they think it's a great work of art," Mary Louisa said. "And Papa is pleased that his vases are so handsomely displayed."

"Yes, the vases are lovely," Victoria said, though, in truth, Mr. Boit's preoccupation with the vases irritated her. She had yet to lay eyes on the man, but was starting to believe he cared more about the vases than his own daughters. "But, what does he think of your portrait and Julia's?"

"He thinks it's nice of Julia and me," Mary Louisa said in her most earnest voice, "but he says he can understand why Jane and Florence are disappointed. He offered to have their portraits painted by someone else, but they say they'd rather sit for photographs. Painting is too old-fashioned for them."

"That's because they like Mr. Graham so much," Julia said, wrinkling her nose.

"The photographer?" Victoria asked.

"He's been coming every day," Mary Louisa said. "We think he's annoying but Papa likes him. Mama says they went to the same school in Boston, but not at the same time."

"Mama still likes Mr. Sargent best!" Julia said, smoothing Popau's dress.

Mary Louisa nodded her agreement. "Jane and Florence can't stop talking about Mr. Graham, how handsome he is, how clever. Not around us, though. If Julia or I come into the room, they stop talking and leave. They're always busy getting their costumes ready for the next photograph." Mary Louisa sat with her hands in her lap, her fingers pinching the folds in her skirt as she talked. "Mr. Graham tries to get Julia and me to pose. We've said no, but he pesters us so much—I'm afraid we'll have to do it."

Julia sighed extravagantly.

"I miss Mr. Sargent," Mary Louisa continued, her own sigh echoing Julia's. "Papa's busy taking care of Mama. And when he's not doing that, he's painting or seeing his friends. He doesn't spend time with us the way Mr. Sargent does."

Just as I suspected, Victoria thought. "So, Mr. Sargent isn't coming back?" she asked.

"He's getting ready to paint a lady who's a great beauty," Mary Louisa said. "I heard Mr. Sargent tell Papa her skin is the color of blotting paper!"

"He thinks blotting paper is pretty?" Victoria asked.

Julia giggled.

"I guess," Mary Louisa said. "He said if he gets it right, it will be his best portrait yet." Mary Louisa looked doubtful, but Victoria knew she would never seriously question Sargent's judgment when it came to his own art.

"Well, he's not exaggerating," Victoria told her, excited that her guess about the new portrait was correct. "That lady he was talking about has a very unusual sort of beauty. Her portrait will be one of his greatest achievements, but it's going to cause him a lot of trouble at first."

Both Mary Louisa and Julia stared at her.

"Trouble? What kind of trouble?" Mary Louisa asked.

"Well—" Victoria hesitated, looking at Julia.

"She knows," Mary Louisa said.

"Mary Louisa told me you know what's going to happen, even before it happens," Julia said, patting Popau's head complacently. Her matter-of-fact attitude to time travel made Victoria bold.

"Okay," Victoria said. "So it's going to be a hard picture to paint. It will take him a whole year, and he'll have to start over many times. And the lady, Madame Gautreau, will be very difficult—always late to her sittings, always busy with other things. But the worst part will be when he shows the finished portrait at the Paris Salon."

She paused in her narrative to build the suspense. Both girls were leaning forward, their breathing audible in the quiet room.

"Tell us," Julia begged.

"Everyone will hate the painting. They'll say her dress is too revealing. Mr. Sargent is going to paint her with one strap slipping off her shoulder and people will be very shocked when they see it. I guess they think the whole dress might fall off and there she'd be, naked for the world to see." Victoria laughed at the idea of a painted dress falling off a painted lady.

Julia laughed, too, but Mary Louisa looked dismayed.

"He's painting a naked lady?" Julia asked, still giggling.

Victoria made her face serious again and tried to explain. "No, she actually won't be naked. It's just the idea of nakedness that upsets everyone. It will ruin Mr. Sargent's reputation in Paris. He'll be so devastated, he'll leave Paris and travel to England to recover."

"Poor Mr. Sargent!" Mary Louisa said. "We have to warn him. He mustn't paint that picture! He mustn't leave Paris!"

Victoria realized she'd said too much. She'd started to see herself as the younger Boit sisters' protector, and here she was worrying them with her knowledge of Sargent's future difficulties. She felt ashamed.

"You don't understand," she said, scrambling to figure out a way to take back what she'd just said. "Mr. Sargent has to paint this picture, and he has to paint it exactly the way I described. It's a wonderful painting. Very dramatic, very unusual, and—" she said reassuringly, "—it will make Mr. Sargent famous for all time. People from all over the world will come to New York to see it. So, you mustn't do anything to stop him." She looked at the girls imploringly, hoping they would realize how serious she was. "That would be the worst thing you could do."

"Even though everyone hates it?" Mary Louisa asked, looking skeptical.

"Remember, they only hate it at first," Victoria insisted. "Later, people love it."

"But you said Mr. Sargent's reputation will be ruined!" Mary Louisa said.

"Not forever! Listen—" Victoria took a deep breath and spoke as solemnly as she could. "Mary Louisa, Julia—we can't interfere. It might mean Mr. Sargent never gets recognized as a great painter. And painting is what matters most to him. We can't interfere with his future." She paused and looked at each girl in turn. "You have to promise to say nothing about what I've told you—not to Mr. Sargent, not to anyone."

Mary Louisa nodded slowly. Julia followed her sister's lead and nodded, too.

"We promise," Mary Louisa said.

Victoria relaxed. Knowing about the future was a nerve-wracking business. She warned herself to be more careful from now on and never try to influence the choices made by the Boits or Sargent, no matter how great the temptation.

Her thoughts were interrupted by a light tapping on the door to the bedroom and a thin, high voice calling to them in French.

"*Un moment*," Mary Louisa responded, then whispered to Victoria, "It's Bella, our maid. She says Papa wants to see us in his study right away!" She stood and pulled Julia to her feet, yanking her rumpled dress down and straightening her hair ribbon. "We'll be quick. Put the chair back in front of the door as soon as we leave."

"Wait for us, Victoria!" Julia said, a worried look on her face.

The two sisters hurried out, and Victoria replaced the chair as directed. This time she wanted to stay as long as possible and was taking no chances on being discovered. After pacing the perimeter of the room several times, Victoria heard a faint knock on the door.

"Open up," Mary Louisa called in a soft voice. The sisters came into the room breathing hard, as though they'd run up several flights of stairs.

"Just as I told you," Mary Louisa moaned, throwing herself face down on her bed. "We have to pose for Mr. Graham—today, right now. Papa ordered us to come as soon as we change. He says we're being unkind to his friend and he won't stand for it."

"It's only a photograph," Victoria said. "It won't take long. You'll be back in a little while and we can go on with our talk."

Mary Louisa shook her head. "You're wrong. Mr. Graham's

photographs take forever. First, he'll have to make us stand just so, moving our arms up, then down, pulling us this way and that. I peeked in when he was working with Jane and Florence. He won't be satisfied until he's taken the same photograph a hundred times."

"We have to dress in costumes," Julia complained, "like children in a story."

"And make faces and pretend to be something we're not," Mary Louisa added. "At least Mr. Sargent's painting is real, it's about *us*, even if Jane and Florence don't like it. But these photographs—they're just playacting."

"What do you have to wear?" Victoria asked.

"Some old nightgown. He's got shawls to drape over our heads," Mary Louisa told her. "Jane and Florence are already dressed in their costumes. We're supposed to look like child Madonnas, all saintly and sad. Mr. Graham wants a photograph of the four of us, all dressed the same." She flounced onto her back on the bed and stared up at the ceiling, her expression bleak.

"I guess if he's trying to win that bet with Mr. Sargent he needs a photo of all of you," Victoria said.

"I know, but we don't like Mr. Graham," Mary Louisa protested. She got up off the bed, stomped over to the bureau and started pulling nightgowns from the drawers and dumping them on Julia's bed. Mary Louisa handed a nightgown to Julia and took another for herself from an adjacent drawer. After helping her little sister unbutton her wooly dress, she dressed her in a plain, long-sleeved nightie. "I don't know why Papa's making us do this," she said as she pulled her own sweater up over her head, her words muffled by the thickness of the knit. The girls' objections made sense to Victoria, but she could see how their father might not understand.

"I'm cold," Julia said, hugging her chubby arms to her chest.

"Let's wear our winter leggings underneath," Mary Louisa

The Waif

suggested. She slid open another drawer and began to dig. "Did you ever find your white ones, Julia?"

"No," Julia said, her face a mask of dejection. "They're gone."

On impulse, Victoria stood. "I'm going with you," she announced. She'd be lending the girls her moral support, but she was also dying to get another look at Clifford Graham. "I'll find a hiding place and watch."

"But you can't!" Mary Louisa said. "The servants will see you. Papa's giving a dinner party tonight, and they're rushing around getting ready."

"She can wear a nightie, too," Julia said. "And a nightcap. They'll think she's Florence."

"But what if Florence comes out? Then we'll have two Florences," Mary Louisa said. She thought for a minute. "We could dress you like a boy—a serving boy."

"Like the boys who bring the coal!" Julia cried.

Victoria considered this. "My pants and boots will look all right. Can you find me a jacket and cap?"

"The boys leave their muddy gardening clothes in the basement and put them on when they come to work in the morning," Mary Louisa said. "I guess we could borrow something of theirs." She looked dubious, but Julia was eager to give it a try.

"I'll go look," Julia said. She ran out of the room and returned a few minutes later, carrying what looked like a bundle of rags.

"Did anyone see you?" Mary Louisa asked.

"No, I ran fast," Julia said.

Victoria put on the jacket and tucked her hair out of sight under a filthy cap.

"Will I do?" she asked, turning around.

"Pull the cap down over your eyes a little more, so we can't see your face," Mary Louisa instructed.

Victoria did as she was told, and Julia clapped her hands. "You look just like a boy!"

"Wait! What happens if we meet Mama or Madame Fouche in the hall? You'll have to take off your cap to them. None of the gardener's boys would leave his cap on in the presence of a lady," Mary Louisa said.

"It's okay," said Victoria. She pulled off the cap and ducked her head in a show of deference. "My hair is short enough that, even without the cap, I probably look like a boy to most people. What do you think?"

"It might work. But what if Jane and Florence see you?" Mary Louisa asked, still not convinced.

"Or Mr. Graham?" Julia said.

"We'll just have to take our chances," Victoria answered. "I'll follow a little behind you and then hide somewhere while you get your picture taken. If Mr. Graham acts too obnoxious, I'll jump out and scream. It will scare him to death."

"Oh, do!" Julia said. "He'll run away and never come back!"

They trooped down the hall, and though the tiny maid Victoria had seen before hurried past, she didn't stop to question them as they went by. When they reached the large drawing room, Victoria saw that both doors stood open to reveal an elaborate backdrop the photographer had erected using tables and chairs covered in tablecloths. Florence and Jane were posed on one side of this construction, arms thrown carelessly over one another's shoulders, eyes fixed on the ceiling.

Clifford Graham was busy adjusting his camera, peering through the lens at the two older sisters. He didn't notice the younger Boit girls as they entered the room or see Victoria hide behind the heavy brocade drapes that covered a hallway window opposite the room's wide double doors.

Peeping between the curtains, the first thing Victoria noticed was the camera on its tall tripod, a complicated contraption made of gleaming wood and brass with a lens at the front and a strange bellows-like section attaching it to the photographic plate at the rear. Then she focused on the photographer himself, as he finished fussing with his equipment and exposed one of his photographic plates. Finally, he signaled to the older Boits that it was time to break the pose.

"You took long enough," Florence said, when she lowered her gaze and noticed her two younger sisters standing there quietly. "Papa said you were coming right away."

The photographer saw them and hurried over. "Girls!" he gushed. "Mary Louisa, Julia—at last."

Mary Louisa and Julia stared at him stony-eyed.

Victoria watched as the photographer brushed strands of hair away from his eyes and beamed a welcome at the younger girls. He inspected Mary Louisa's gown, then turned to Julia and touched the blue satin ribbon in her hair. "Take that off, will you, Julia? Your hair must be loose for this photograph." His eyes lingered on her face and his smile intensified. "Such perfect skin—like the first ripe peach of summer." He reached out to stroke her cheek, but Julia ducked out of reach.

"I don't want to take it off," Julia said, her mouth turned down in a fierce pout. "Mr. Sargent gave it to me."

"It won't do," Graham said. Julia tried to elude him, but he succeeded in grasping the blue ribbon and it slid from her hair.

Mary Louisa let out an exasperated breath and moved between them. "What do you want us to do?" she said to Graham in her most peremptory tone.

"Come, both of you," the photographer said, turning instantly brusque. "I need you here, Mary Louisa. Kneel down in front of Florence, and Julia must lean against you. Cover your heads with these." He handed each of them a shawl, then pushed Mary Louisa into position on the floor. He placed Julia next to her, draping one of her pudgy arms over her sister's neck. He stood back to survey the composition, then darted in to readjust Julia's limbs and tilt Mary Louisa's chin to one side. He frowned in concentration and the girls did likewise.

"No scowling!" he cried, when he stepped back to look at them. "You must look angelic, otherworldly. Think of blue skies and towering white clouds. Think of a cathedral."

Julia looked like she was about to break into giggles; in contrast, Mary Louisa looked furious. Only Jane was able to adopt the requisite beatific expression, while Florence stifled a yawn.

The photographer clapped his hands and changed his tone from scolding to coaxing. "Come, come girls. The quicker you do as I ask, the quicker you'll be able to run off to your tea."

Victoria saw Mary Louisa give Julia's arm a squeeze. They both cast their eyes down and looked solemn. The two older sisters gazed heavenward, expressions of rapture on their faces.

Graham took several photographs, adjusted the girls' positions slightly, then took several more, changing the plate at the back of the camera each time. It was a lengthy process, but at last he was satisfied. "All right girls," he said to Mary Louisa and Julia. "You may go."

Mary Louisa and Julia flung their shawls to the floor and headed for the hall. They paused in front of the curtain where Victoria was hiding, but the photographer was close on their heels, accompanying them to the door. Victoria saw them look back once, but Clifford Graham remained in the wide doorway watching them walk away, his back to Jane and Florence.

Graham pulled Julia's blue hair ribbon, from his pocket. Victoria expected him to call to Julia to come back, to tell her she'd forgotten it, but he did no such thing. Instead, he brushed it against his lips, breathed in its scent, then hastily stuffed it back into his pocket and turned to reenter the drawing room.

"Let's try a few more poses, girls," he said to Florence and Jane, as he strode back to his camera.

While Graham was busy positioning the two older girls, Victoria slipped from her hiding place. Julia and Mary Louisa were waiting for her in the entry hall, and the three of them hurried together to the safety of the little girls' room.

"I'm glad that's over!" Mary Louisa said.

"You were so quiet, Victoria," Julia said, bouncing up and down on the bed in her excitement. "I forgot about you—then I remembered!"

Victoria nodded. "The good thing is, I'm sure no one else knew I was there."

"So what did you think of him?" Mary Louisa asked, her face serious. She didn't appear to be sharing the elation both Victoria and Julia felt over the success of their ruse.

Victoria wasn't sure how to reply. Mild mannered though he seemed, Clifford Graham's behavior with the ribbon was definitely weird. She didn't think she should say anything about it to the girls, but it worried her. "He's very sure of himself," she said. "And very silly. 'Think of a cathedral,'" she intoned.

"Why does he call me a peach?" Julia grumbled. "I'm not a fruit. And he always tries to pinch my cheek."

A line from Hillary's sister Erin's picture book, *Where the Wild Things Are*, popped into Victoria's mind. She could almost hear the Wild Things chanting, ". . . we'll eat you up—we love you so!"

"Don't worry, Julia. Victoria won't let him bother you," Mary Louisa said reassuringly. "She's almost as tall as he is, and she knows things."

Mary Louisa exaggerated Victoria's physical strength, but she was right about one thing, Victoria thought: she did know things. *I know what will happen to Sargent and even a few things about the Boit girls' future. But*, she realized, *I know nothing whatever about Clifford Graham.* Why did he keep Julia's ribbon instead of returning it? It felt wrong.

"How long will Mr. Graham stay?" she asked.

"Till tea time," Mary Louisa said. "Madame Fouche will have to shoo him out."

"May we skip our tea today?" Julia asked. "Since Victoria's here?"

"We need to eat," Mary Louisa said shaking her head. "Will you promise to wait, Victoria?"

"I can wait," Victoria said, "I want to stay as long as possible this time."

The girls left to see if their meal was ready, and Victoria settled in to wait for their return. A moment later, to her surprise, she heard Clifford Graham's voice out in the hall. What was he doing in the bedroom wing of the apartment? She quietly opened the door a crack, straining to hear what was being said.

"Show me the chemises you want to wear for our next portrait," Graham said. "I'll tell you if they're appropriate."

"They're just in here," Jane said. "I'll get them." Victoria heard her open the door of a bedroom down the hall.

Florence must have stayed in the hall with Graham, because he continued speaking. "Tell your mother you're invited to my studio tomorrow," Graham said. "There are props there we'll need to set the scene."

"What time is convenient?" Florence inquired, sounding very grown up.

"Here they are," Jane said, as she came back into the hallway.

"Yes, those will be fine," Graham said. "I'll call for you at ten o'clock tomorrow. My valet can arrange a small picnic luncheon for us, if that's all right with your mama."

"Yes, Mr. Graham," both girls answered in the same breath. Jane giggled, but Florence silenced her with an irritated, "Hush!"

Victoria risked a peek out the door. She noticed the high color in Jane's cheeks and Mr. Graham's ingratiating smile.

"Will Madame Fouche accompany you this time?" Graham asked.

"She'll want to come," cried Jane. "She loves a picnic."

"We meet tomorrow then," Graham said. He started to leave, then turned back. "I think I left my extra plate holder on the sideboard. I need to go back for it."

"I'll go," said Jane.

"No, no, girls. I don't want to make you late for tea," the photographer said. "Julia and Mary Louisa are there already. Madame Fouche will be angry with me if you don't go immediately. I'll see myself out."

The girls walked away leaving Graham standing alone in the hall. Instead of heading for the drawing room, Graham turned toward the bedroom where Victoria was hiding. She ducked behind the door, flattening herself against the wall in horror as it was pushed noiselessly open and Graham slipped inside.

Victoria held her breath. If he closes the door now, he'll spot me, she thought. She knew this meant getting flipped back to her own time and that was the thing she most wanted to avoid. But Graham, as if on a mission, went straight to Julia's bed and began rummaging through the heap of nightgowns Mary Louisa had dumped out of the drawer. He snatched one up, stuffed the garment into his jacket and strode quickly out of the room, pulling the door closed behind him.

In a surge of protective fury, Victoria forgot her fear. *First the hair ribbon, now this? What does he think he's doing,* she fumed, *stealing Julia's things?* It was outrageous, and creepy besides. No longer caring if Graham or anyone else saw her, she charged down the hall after the thief. He was moving fast. He had grabbed up his heavy box camera and was out the front door by the time she reached the entry hall. Without a second thought, Victoria followed him through the outer door and down to the pavement below.

This was the first time she'd stepped outside the Boits' apartment. In other circumstances, she would have stopped to look around, to take in all the sights and sounds and smells of this Paris street. Instead, she focused all her attention on Clifford Graham's retreating back. He was halfway down the block, moving quickly through the fading afternoon light. Fueled by adrenaline, Victoria broke into a run to catch up. It'd been quite some time since she'd tried to run and her brace rubbed and pinched as she moved, but she didn't slow down. She had no idea what she'd say to Graham when she caught him, but she wasn't going to let him get away with stealing from a child.

The sun, which was hanging low in the sky, sank beneath a layer of gray cloud and suddenly it was night. Graham turned several corners, and Victoria almost lost him. When she spotted him again, he was mounting the stairs of a tall apartment building similar to the Boits' building. Victoria hurried as fast as she could, but she was too late. A woman dressed all in black opened the door, greeting Graham with a curt nod as he disappeared inside.

Victoria stood at the bottom of the stairs, panting. She didn't dare enter the building, afraid the lady guarding the door would stop her. As she caught her breath, she finally took a moment to assess her situation. It was fully dark now and so cold Victoria was grateful to be wearing the heavy woolen gardening jacket Julia had borrowed for her. What was she thinking, following the photographer out into the night? She had no idea where she was or how to find her way back to the relative safety of the Boits' apartment. She was alone on a Paris street, in an unknown neighborhood, in an unfamiliar time.

Badly frightened now, she decided her only hope was to wait and see if Graham came out again. If he did reappear, instead of accosting him, she would think of a plausible excuse to approach him and ask for directions to the Boits' apartment. *He might be the only person in this neighborhood*, she thought, *who speaks English and knows where the Boit family lives.*

Victoria loitered near the steps, hopping up and down to keep warm. The street was deserted. There was no traffic, and no one walked by. Across the road was a little park with a marble fountain in its center. It was so quiet she could hear the splash of the water as it fell into the pool below. How she wished she was walking down this pretty street on a warm summer day, instead of cowering here in the dark and cold, alone and afraid.

Victoria was beginning to think she should leave and try to find her way back to the Boits' apartment on her own, when Graham came out of the front door with a camera—a smaller one this time. He had changed his clothes. Instead of his soft hat and long coat, he was wearing a short, dark jacket and cap, not unlike the clothes Victoria wore, only cleaner and less threadbare. She stepped forward to speak to him, then lost her nerve. He turned and walked quickly away. She waited a minute, then followed, not sure what else to do. She was too scared to approach him and too scared to let him out of her sight.

After several minutes of fast walking, they left the wide boulevards and majestic apartment buildings behind and reached an open area with trees and flowerbeds lining the path. The air felt colder, and Victoria realized why when Clifford turned left and led her across a bridge. When she glanced over the stone balustrade, she saw light reflected on the surface of moving water. *This must be the Seine*, she thought, the fabled river that wound its way through the heart of Paris, crossed by countless ancient bridges.

On the other side of the bridge they entered another world. This was a crowded neighborhood of twisting lanes and narrow alleys, with men, women, and children packing the sidewalks and spilling out into the street. As she wound her way further into this warren close on Graham's heels, Victoria's heartbeat accelerated and her breath came in tight gasps. She had no hope now of ever finding her own way back to the Boits' neighborhood. She was truly lost.

This was obviously a commercial district, populated by working people who were busy ducking in and out of small restaurants and shops. Sharp odors assaulted Victoria's nose, a disagreeable mix of unwashed bodies and the smoke from hundreds of chimneys. At intervals, gas street lamps supplied a wash of weak, yellow light that briefly lit the tired faces eddying around her. As she pushed forward, a door opened and a man stumbled out, followed by a burst of loud music and the reek of tobacco and alcohol. Victoria stepped quickly aside to avoid being pushed into the gutter. In all her life, she'd never been in a neighborhood quite this dirty and disreputable. She wondered if the poorer sections of Boston looked anything like this.

Victoria's disguise allowed her to mix easily with the crowd and no one gave her a second glance. Most of the men wore rough jackets and caps like hers, and the women held tightly to the collars of their drab woolen coats. They hurried along with their heads bent against the cold, packets of food or jugs of wine clutched to their chests. Here and there children wearing ragged clothing crowded into the doorways of shops, seeking the warmth of the heated rooms within. Gangs of young boys huddled together near the people waiting in line for their turn at the butcher's shop or bakery. One especially hungry-looking child was handed a roll by a kind-hearted shopper. The boy immediately sat down on the curb and tore greedy bites out of the coarse bread.

Voices rose and fell around Victoria in a chorus of unintelligible French. At one point, a woman collided with her, and swore fiercely, but Victoria paid no attention, focusing only on Clifford Graham as he made his steady progress through the crowds.

Victoria began to notice women and girls loitering on the street corners and near alleys. Some of them were very young—teenagers dressed in gaudy costumes clearly not intended to keep out the cold. She watched as a short, thick man wearing a dented top hat left his horse and cart by the curb and approached one of these girls. They spoke briefly, then walked off together into a dark side street, passing close enough that Victoria could smell liquor on the man's breath.

Though she couldn't quite believe it—*they're so young!*—Victoria realized that these girls must be prostitutes. She had read about prostitutes, had understood the references to "fallen women" in novels by Charles Dickens and Jane Austen, but she had never actually seen one and had no idea someone so young might be forced into this way of life. Many of these girls weren't much older than she was and some seemed even younger. One girl, she was sure, had to be the same age as Mary Louisa.

Clifford Graham slowed his pace, and Victoria slowed hers to match. He stopped and spoke to a tiny, frail girl, no older than six or seven, Victoria guessed. The child wore a faded gray cotton dress and had wound a bright red scarf many times around her long neck. She reminded Victoria of an exotic crane, standing with one thin leg wrapped around the other, shivering in the cold.

Graham bent down and spoke to the girl in a low, urgent tone. He held out his camera and showed it to her. Victoria moved closer, trying to hear what he said, but he was speaking French and she understood nothing. The girl did not react to Graham's words, and Victoria was astonished to see Graham bring out Julia's hair ribbon and nightgown and hold these out to her. She shook her head. Graham then reached into his pocket and pulled out a fat leather purse. He removed several coins. The girl shook her head more vehemently, and Victoria gasped as Graham seized the child by the arm as if to drag her away.

The girl looked up, fear in her eyes, and stared straight at Victoria. In the next instant, Victoria was shoved roughly from behind. A group of boys, the same sort of street urchins she'd observed milling around the shop entrances, rushed past her and plowed into the crouching Graham, sending him sprawling.

His camera flew in one direction and his purse in another. Quickly the boys snatched up the purse and camera and set off at a dead run down the street. The girl ran after them.

Graham pulled himself to his knees and shouted at the young thieves as they sped away. He clambered to his feet and turning, lunged at Victoria, still shouting in French. She had no idea what the words meant, but guessed that, dressed in her costume, Graham thought she was part of the gang that had robbed him. He came at her with fists raised, ready to strike. Victoria stepped backwards off the curb in a mad scramble to get away.

She felt herself falling. As she hit the ground, her skull cracked against the pavement and a sharp pain rippled down her spine. She struggled to her feet as a blessed darkness settled over the scene. The light from the street lamp faded and the angry sounds issuing from Graham's mouth died away with a hiss. The Paris street disappeared in a gray haze. When Victoria could see again, she was back in Boston, back in her own time once more, far away from the eerie nighttime world of the back streets of Paris in 1882.

Chapter Nine

The Search Begins

May, 1963, Boston

Victoria emerged from her latest journey to Paris still wearing the muddy wool jacket and cap belonging to one of the Boits' servant boys. She pulled off the shabby garments and, balling them up, thrust them into the trash bin outside the Sargent gallery.

Her eyes welled with tears at the sight of the museum's familiar hallways. She couldn't remember ever feeling this relieved. The back of her head ached, and when she touched it, her fingers came away sticky and red; she'd cut herself falling into the gutter. Her brace was twisted, and her back hurt more than her head. She headed toward the restrooms, one hand on her side to ease the pain, sure she must look even more disheveled than she felt.

As she reached the door to the ladies' room, she saw the familiar Black guard walking toward her. Seeing her obvious distress, he stopped. "Are you all right?"

Victoria took a deep, unsteady breath before she replied. "I have scoliosis," she said, surprising herself; she never mentioned her back problems to anyone. "I stumbled on the stairs just now and hurt my back."

"Do you need help?" he asked, his fuzzy salt and pepper brows drawing together in concern. "Are you here alone?"

"My mother's meeting me in a little while," she said, and gave him a weak smile. "I'll be fine." Inside the restroom, she swabbed the back of her head with wet paper towel, washed her face and tried to straighten her hair.

When she came out, the guard was waiting for her. And standing next to him, talking excitedly, was her mother. *Good grief,* Victoria thought, *this is all I need!*

"What happened?" her mother cried. "This gentleman said you got hurt!"

"It's nothing," Victoria said standing as straight as possible. "I stumbled on the stairs and twisted my back."

"I waited to make sure you were okay," the guard said. "Then your mother came along looking for you. I recognized her from the other day." He lowered his gaze, looking awkward as they all recalled the circumstances of their first meeting. "I told her you were hurt."

Victoria's mother was searching her daughter's face, looking for signs of serious discomfort. Victoria turned away from her and, smiling widely, thanked the guard for his concern.

"I wanted to make sure you were okay," he said again.

"Yes, thank you," said Victoria's mother absently, opening her handbag. For one dreadful second, Victoria was afraid she was going to hand the man a tip. Instead she pulled out a tissue and wiped away a last bit of grime from her daughter's forehead. Then, after a final inspection of Victoria's face, she turned her full attention to the guard. "You've been very kind," she said, sounding sincerely grateful.

"Not at all," said the guard, giving a polite nod as he continued on his way. Victoria watched him walk away, thinking, *Maybe my mother isn't prejudiced after all.* What a relief that would be, if it were true.

At home that afternoon, Victoria managed to convince her mother that she hadn't done anything to her back that rest and an ice bag wouldn't fix. She went up to her room, closed her door and was finally alone with her thoughts.

What exactly had happened in Paris? As frightened as she'd felt following Clifford Graham through the nighttime streets, in retrospect she didn't think she'd been in any real danger. By now, she'd made enough trips back and forth from Boston to Paris to realize, at least in her experience so far, time travel had rules. If things stayed calm and her presence remained a secret from everyone but the younger Boit girls, she was able to stay in the past. But if trouble threatened—if she panicked or was in danger of being discovered somewhere she had no business being—she popped instantly back to her own time.

What concerned her more than her own safety was the safety of the Boit girls. Now that she knew that Clifford Graham was a liar, a sneak, a thief and—recalling his rough treatment of the child prostitute—a violent bully, her worry about her young friends intensified.

Initially, the man had seemed harmless. She'd thought Mary Louisa and Julia's dislike of him was due to the rivalry between the painter and the photographer, between the younger and older siblings. But clearly it was something more serious. She was sure Clifford Graham was up to no good.

What could she do? She had no control over getting back to Paris in a timely fashion. But then, her entire understanding of time as a fixed entity was eroding fast. She needed to get back to the Boits' apartment, but her Saturday art class was her only chance to visit the painting. Apart from cutting school or sneaking out of the house and taking a taxi on her own to the museum—and giving her mother a real reason to call the police—there was nothing she could do but wait.

Victoria sat on her bed staring at the wall. She couldn't get the girl with the red scarf out of her head. Whatever Graham had proposed, it had frightened her, maybe more than the usual requests she got from men. It had something to do with the camera and also something to do with Julia's ribbon and gown. Graham was willing to pay her a lot of money—even get rough with her—to get her to cooperate. Did he want her to pose for him wearing Julia's things? To pretend to be Julia, since he'd had so little success getting the real Julia to agree to be photographed? She wondered why the girl with the red scarf, who agreed to have sex with strangers for money, would refuse to take money for being photographed?

Victoria's mind whirled. The more she thought about it, the more sinister it seemed. If the gang of boys hadn't put an abrupt end to things, what would have happened? She liked to think she would have intervened, pushed Graham aside herself and seized the little girl by the hand to run for safety—but she wasn't at all sure what she would have done. In all her previous trips to Paris, she'd only watched, too afraid of being discovered to intrude on anything that was happening, until now, when she'd acted impulsively and chased after Graham when he stole Julia's nightgown. Next time, she might need to do more. *It's my job to protect the Boit girls*, she thought. More and more she was sure this was her true purpose for traveling back in time, her only reason for being in the Boit girls' lives at all.

She made a vow: If she ever again saw anyone threaten to hurt a child, in the Boits' world or her own, she would do everything in her power to stop it.

On Monday, in history class, Victoria was assigned to write a ten-page term paper on a topic of her own choosing. It only took a moment to decide she wanted to write about the history of photography, focusing on the early years. It meant she could do her school work and have a legitimate reason to investigate Clifford Graham at the same time.

With her mother's express permission this time, she went back to the library after school to look for books on the history of photography, but also for information about Paris in the 1880s. She'd been shocked by the plight of the children she'd seen—the girl prostitutes and hungry young beggars who'd taken Clifford Graham's camera and coin purse. What she'd been taught about sex was that it was something you got to choose, when you were ready, with someone your own age. But, what if, instead of being a girl from a privileged family, she was like the little girl in the red scarf, hungry and alone? Things would be very different then. She needed to know more about the conditions that existed back then.

The reference books she looked at confirmed her worst fears. In those days, street children survived mainly by stealing or prostitution. Of the thousands of Paris prostitutes, half of them were children. The more she read, the more horrified she became. Wealthy men were willing to pay huge sums for little girls, especially virgins under the age of twelve. In 1863 the legal "Age of Consent" was bumped from eleven to thirteen. *Some victory!* Victoria thought. *Why would any thirteen-year-old "consent" to having sex with a dirty old man, unless they were starving and it was their only way to pay for food?*

Victoria sat back in her chair in the reference room, shaking her head. In her sex ed class she'd learned that there were laws today that protected girls: a man could be arrested if he had sex with a girl who was younger than eighteen, even if the girl said yes. And sex between a child or young teen and an adult was considered a serious crime.

She'd had no idea things were so bleak for young girls in

the prior century. She was pretty sure kids in her time were still being abused, but at least there were laws that tried to stop what she had seen happening right out in the open on the streets of Paris. It was one thing to know about it and another to see it happening. It made her feel outraged in a whole new way. How could she just sit at home and be safe, when stuff like that was happening?

Above all, she needed to make sure the Boit girls were okay. They weren't poor, like the girl prostitute, and they had parents to look out for them, so she was sure they would never wind up on the streets. But Clifford Graham was a creep. Mr. and Mrs. Boit had welcomed him into their home, and worse, allowed the older girls to visit him in his studio. *What went on there?* she wondered.

She did a new search, this time for information about Clifford Graham. If he was famous enough to have made it into the history books, she wanted to know. The more she could learn about him, the better prepared she'd be to stop him from doing any harm to the Boits. She did find lots of books on the history of photography, but nothing about anyone named Clifford Graham. His name didn't appear.

"Victoria, I'm in here," her mother called when Victoria walked through the front door with her stack of books. Victoria followed her mother's voice to the study, where she found her bent over a desk strewn with papers and books. "You've been gone for hours," her mother said, half-turning to peer at her daughter over her reading glasses.

"I found lots of material for my history project," Victoria said, dropping her stack of books on a chair.

"Hmm," said her mother. She glanced at the books, then resumed scribbling on a yellow pad. "I'm preparing my first docent tour. You can ask Rose for a snack."

"Mom," said Victoria. "Do you know anything about a photographer friend of John Singer Sargent's?"

"I know nothing about photographers," her mother said, not looking up from her pad.

"Do you know anyone who does?" Victoria persisted.

"My friend Martha might," her mother said distractedly. "Martha Grimke? I know her from college. She's an archivist at the Gardner, and I think they have her cataloging the photographs."

"Would you introduce me?" Victoria asked, feeling a thrill of excitement. The Gardner was the perfect place to search for clues about Clifford Graham. It was even possible Isabella Gardner had known him and collected his work. After all, he was from Boston and a friend to both Sargent and the Boits, who were also friends of Mrs. Gardner. "Maybe Martha could show me some of the photographs in the Gardner's archives—ones that aren't on public display. It would be great for my report."

"I can give Martha a call," her mother said, turning finally to look at her daughter more closely. "This report is turning into quite a project. Does your teacher really expect you to do this much work?"

"He's giving me extra credit," Victoria said, hoping it might be true.

"I see." Her mother's eyes strayed back to her work. Victoria wanted to ask when she might be talking to Martha, but refrained. Her mother was preoccupied, and it would only make things worse to pester her. She might refuse to speak to Martha at all.

Victoria managed to contain her excitement during dinner, but couldn't settle down in her room afterwards. She tried reading the library books she'd found on the history of photography, but wasn't able to focus. *I'll call Hillary*, she decided, and went downstairs to use the hall phone. She couldn't tell Hillary about her scary experience in Paris, but it would be good to hear a friendly voice—at least she hoped Hillary would be friendly.

The two girls hadn't spoken since the last art class, and Victoria wondered if Hillary was still upset with her for leaving so abruptly.

"How are you?" she asked, when Hillary came to the phone.

"All right," Hillary said. Victoria's fears were confirmed. There was a distinct coolness in the other girl's voice.

"What have you been up to?" Victoria said.

"I've been busy," Hillary said.

"What with?"

"Oh, homework mostly."

"I got my snapshots back from the print shop—the ones I took of you and James and Erin in the backyard. Some of them are pretty good, I think."

"That's nice," Hillary said, sounding uninterested.

"How's James?" Victoria asked, desperate to find a topic that would keep Hillary engaged.

"He's working on his scholarship application for Columbia," Hillary said. "I said I'd type it for him."

"I hope he gets it," Victoria said. Hillary didn't reply. She wasn't making this easy. Victoria raised her eyes to the ceiling and wished she could think of a good excuse for her rudeness the previous Saturday, but nothing occurred to her.

"It must be great to know exactly what you want to do with your life—for James, I mean," Victoria said, making one last try. "Sargent was like that, too."

"Lucky for Sargent he was successful at such a young age," Hillary said, still sounding stiff.

Desperate, Victoria plowed on. "I've read he had to take care of his mother and his sisters after his father died. Maybe that explains why he never married."

"I don't know," Hillary said. She paused, as if debating whether to continue. "James thinks he wasn't attracted to women," she said eventually. "He told me Sargent drew a lot of male nudes. His family donated them to the Fogg Museum at Harvard after his death. James says they're pretty explicit."

Victoria felt a rush of understanding. "So, you think he might have been homosexual?"

"Nobody knows for sure, but it hardly matters—he was married to his art," Hillary replied. "That's what he really loved."

Victoria took a moment to take this in. The fact that Sargent might have been homosexual was something she'd never considered. She'd read that Oscar Wilde and Sargent's friend, Henry James, were homosexuals, but they were part of the past and she knew very little about them. In a bizarre way, she felt she knew Sargent, having seen him a few times and read about him a great deal. She'd never known anyone who was homosexual, at least, not to her knowledge, since no one talked about it. Hillary was right. It didn't matter, in the sense that it didn't detract in any way from the brilliance of his art and it didn't change who he was. He was a kind man, who loved children and his sisters, and who painted like an angel. It didn't matter whether he loved women or men. The knowledge helped Victoria understand Sargent better. Maybe having a secret of his own made him more sensitive to the secrets of others and explained why his portraits always seemed to hint at hidden truths about the people he painted.

"You're awfully quiet all of a sudden," Hillary said.

"Sorry," Victoria said. "I was thinking."

"Well, I'm tired," Hillary said, sounding cool again. "I need to go to bed."

Victoria said good night, then sat glumly by the phone, aware that Hillary was still mad at her. She felt more anxious now than she had before she called. Up until now she hadn't given a lot of thought to her relationship with Hillary; it had just happened without much effort on her part. But she'd clearly hurt Hillary's feelings by rushing off last Saturday, and now she needed to make amends. Victoria wished she could tell Hillary about the Boits and her trips into the past. It was hard keeping it a secret, and not being able to confide in Hillary was standing in the way of their becoming real friends. *But if I share this,* she thought, *and Hillary decides I've lost my mind, I risk losing her friendship altogether.*

It was a strange friendship—they came from such different worlds. Victoria's family was rich; Hillary's was, if not exactly poor, then most likely scraping by. And when it came to politics and religion, the families were miles apart. But, unlike the snooty girls at Winslow, Hillary never seemed to judge and never acted like their differences were reasons they couldn't be friends. Victoria appreciated that quality more than she could say.

On her way up to bed, Victoria paused on the landing to admire the small painting that had hung there for as long as she could remember. It was the portrait of two bonneted old women sitting close together, their heads tilting toward one another, their gnarled hands wrapped around glasses of what looked like red wine. It was a quiet picture, painted in somber browns, but Victoria had always liked it. Her father said his mother, Victoria's dead grandmother, who was its original owner, used to joke that it was a portrait of herself, sitting in contented, slightly drunken silence with her best friend, Marie.

Looking at it now, Victoria wondered, *Will I ever have a friendship as close and comfortable as that?* Like the one she'd had with Pam, but better, more lasting. Like the one she'd like to have with Hillary.

While she was studying the painting, Victoria heard her parents talking below. Her mother stood in the doorway to her father's study, apparently about to head up to bed herself. They must have assumed Victoria was already shut away in her room since they sounded like they were arguing. They never argued in front of her.

"What are you saying?" her mother said, clearly angry. "You think I'm too strict with her?"

"A little independence might do her good," her father said. His voice was less audible, but loud enough for Victoria to hear. "I told her I would speak to you."

"You don't know what you're talking about," her mother fumed. "Girls her age are much too vulnerable. I won't have her flitting around the city alone."

"Not alone," her father countered. "With her friend, with Hillary. They can watch out for each other."

"Hillary's no bigger than a minute! What could she do to protect your daughter in a bad situation?"

"She's bright and resourceful and probably has more street smarts than Victoria!" her father shot back. "Aren't you glad Victoria's made a friend? She spends far too much time in her room by herself."

Victoria didn't hear her mother's reply because she chose that moment to step into the study and close the door. Victoria waited, but hearing nothing more, crept up the remaining stairs to her room. She was glad her father was trying, but she knew he'd never change her mother's attitude overnight.

The next day, her mother got through to Martha at the Gardner. They set up a visit for Friday after school.

"I'll deliver you to Martha and pick you up at five o'clock," her mother said. "Do you want to ask Hillary to come with us and have dinner here afterwards?"

Victoria rushed to phone Hillary. This invitation—a behind-the-scenes tour of Hillary's favorite museum—would be a perfect peace offering.

"Will you come?" Victoria asked, after she'd explained the reason for her call.

"I wouldn't miss it," Hillary said. Victoria could hear the pleasure in her voice.

On impulse, Victoria asked, "Do you want to sleep over?" Her parents wouldn't mind. Then she remembered the problem of her brace. She guessed she could always change into her nightclothes in the bathroom—being modest was certainly no crime.

"I'd love to," Hillary said.

When she got off the phone, Victoria felt less depressed than she had all week. Hillary was acting friendly once more and though she knew she wouldn't stop worrying about the Boit girls, having Hillary over would be a good distraction. And Saturday was not far off. She'd be back at the Museum and, with luck, be able to make a trip to Paris. The long week of waiting would be over.

Victoria's mother dropped the two girls at the curb by the Gardner's front entrance on Friday, and Martha—looking every inch the serious archivist with her sensible shoes and messy bun—met them at the elevator and took them up to the Gardner's fourth floor.

"I've always wanted to see the grand apartment where Isabella Gardner spent her final years," Hillary said to Martha. Hillary, who was acting like her former cheerful self, looked disappointed when they were ushered into the cramped office where Martha cataloged photographs.

"This is my work area," Martha said, indicating a drafting table and chair. She switched on the lamp over the table and pushed her glasses up higher on her nose. "I examine the photographs and look for identifying information. Many of them are labeled, but some of the older ones aren't. We're trying to establish the provenance of each one."

"Do you work only on photographs?" Victoria asked.

"That's what I was hired to do," Martha said, "but I sometimes help out with letters and manuscripts. Eventually, everything's going to be cataloged so students and researchers can find what they need when they come looking for a piece of information or a particular artifact. The collection's so extensive it draws people from all over the world." She pulled out drawers as she spoke. Inside were carefully preserved documents and photographs.

"Did Mrs. Gardner intend all of this to be exhibited some day?" Hillary asked.

"I don't think so, or she would have built two palaces, instead of one," Martha said. "I think she just liked collecting and could never resist buying or saving things she thought were significant."

While Hillary looked at letters in one of the drawers Martha had opened, Victoria asked to see more photographs. Martha led her into an even smaller room next door.

"I understand you're doing a report on the history of photography," Martha said.

"Yes, but I'm focusing on the earliest period," Victoria said. "Do you know much about the Victorian photographers?"

"Well, yes, quite a lot actually. They loved using costumes and props—creating scenes from the Bible or from fairy tales. In my opinion, they were more inspired by theater than the visual arts."

"I read that some of them tried to make their photographs look like paintings," Victoria said.

"That's true," Martha said. "Sometimes they colored their prints with oil paint after they were developed. It was a fad for a while. Then people decided it looked too artificial and tried for a more natural look." Martha moved to a cabinet on the other side of the room. "There are a few Victorian portraits in here."

The photos in this drawer were encased in sleeves made of clear, heavy plastic to protect them from fingerprints. Martha cautioned her not to remove them since the photographic paper they used back then was not nearly as durable as the paper used today.

Martha pulled one out and showed it to Victoria. "Look at this," she said. It was a photograph of a pale child lying on a bed with her eyes closed and hands folded. "In the early days there was a demand for photographs of babies or children who had died—something for the parents to remember them by. Then photographers started taking pictures of children who were posed to appear dead, like this one."

"How strange," Victoria said, feeling a little sickened by the staged death scene. Martha showed Victoria several other old pictures, but none were from the years Victoria was most interested in.

"Have you ever heard of a photographer named Clifford Graham?" Victoria asked, trying to sound offhand.

"What period?" Martha asked.

"1882 or thereabouts."

Martha considered. "The name sounds familiar, but I don't know if any of his photographs are here."

"He was a friend of John Singer Sargent's, so I thought maybe Mrs. Gardner might have known him too. He came from Boston."

"Was he important?"

"I don't know for sure, but I know he won a big photographic prize in Paris in 1882."

"What else do you know about him?"

"Nothing really," Victoria said, glancing away. "Never mind. Do you have any photographs from the early 1880s? I'd love to see them."

"The photographs are categorized by date for the most part. Anything from that period would be here." Martha indicated a drawer further down in the file. "Tell you what—if you want to look through them, I'll take Hillary out and give her a little tour of the fourth floor."

As soon as Martha and Hillary left, Victoria pulled out the

drawer and started going through the photographs one by one. Most were of individuals or family groups, with a few landscapes mixed in. Not all of them were art pieces; some were obviously taken to commemorate events. Victoria recognized none of the names of the subjects or the photographers.

Before long, Martha and Hillary returned and Martha announced it was time for her to head home. Victoria's disappointment must have shown in her face.

"You're welcome to come back another day," Martha said.

"I'd love to," Victoria said.

"Great!" Martha said. "When you come back, please bring that fancy new camera your mother told me about and maybe some of your photographs as well. I'd like to take a look."

They still had a few minutes before Victoria's mother was due to pick them up, so the two girls ducked into the tiny gift shop on the ground floor. Hillary inspected everything in the shop and Victoria trailed along behind her. She was disappointed with her lack of results—she'd hoped to find a photo by Clifford Graham in the Gardner's collection—but she wouldn't give up. She fully intended to return.

When Victoria spotted a small Sargent calendar that had the portrait of the Boit girls on the cover, she decided to buy it. As she approached the cash register, her eye was caught by a postcard of Zurburan's Madonna and Child, the one Hillary had shown her on her birthday. Beside it was a card showing a locket with a portrait of baby Jackie, Isabella's poor dead son. She compared the two faces and decided they really did look alike. She purchased both cards and the calendar and turned to go.

"These are for you," she said, handing the cards to Hillary when they got to the sidewalk outside. "To remember our first visit here." Hillary smiled her thanks. All seemed to be forgiven.

Dinner was one of Rose's specialties: pot roast and Irish potatoes, a potato casserole made with onions and cream that

Rose had made in Hillary's honor. The recipe came from Rose's Irish grandmother who had come over during the potato famine, according to Rose. Since this was one of the few bits of personal history Rose had ever shared, the family never failed to mention it when she cooked this dish. The food was delicious. Victoria's father kept up the conversation, asking Hillary questions about her brothers and sisters. Her mother, Victoria noticed, wouldn't look at her father. Was she still angry at him for criticizing her parenting the other night?

After dinner the girls went up to Victoria's room.

"I'm stuffed," Hillary complained, stretching out on Victoria's big bed.

Victoria had hoped having Hillary over would divert her, but her thoughts kept returning to the Boits. She found it hard to concentrate. She paced back and forth, picking up objects and putting them down, her nerves too jangled to allow her to settle. Tomorrow, she hoped to be back in Paris. But what would she tell Mary Louisa when she got there? She wished she'd found out something about Clifford Graham today!

"What's up?" Hillary asked. "You seem restless."

The impulse to confide in Hillary was strong. Victoria almost blurted it out, but she knew she couldn't. Her friend would surely think she was nuts.

Trying to steer her thoughts in another direction, Victoria asked, "What do you want to do when you finish college? James knows what he wants—I've been wondering what you want to do."

"Maybe work in an art museum," Hillary said. "I could study to be a curator, but I'll have to keep my grades up. With so many of us, I need to get some kind of financial aid if I want to go to college." Hillary looked embarrassed. She gestured to Victoria's mahogany bedstead with its elegantly carved bedposts and matching side tables. "I guess that's not something you have to worry about."

The bedroom set, as well as many of the other antiques in the house, had come from Victoria's mother's childhood home, the family mansion on Beacon Hill. Hillary was obviously more sensitive about the differences in their economic circumstances than Victoria had imagined.

"I don't," Victoria replied, making a wry face. "Apparently my college fund was fully endowed before I was even born!"

"What about you?" Hillary asked, changing the subject. "What do you want to be?"

"Oh, I don't know," Victoria said, pacing again. "I like taking pictures. Maybe I could travel the world taking photographs for *National Geographic.*" She gave a little laugh. "If they'll have me, that is."

"You'd have to have boatloads of talent," Hillary agreed.

Victoria took off an imaginary top hat and bowed. "Well, it turns out my great-great-grandfather, whose name was Gardiner Greene Hubbard, was the first President of the National Geographic Society. So . . ." Victoria smiled so Hillary would realize she was not being serious. "If I can't get a job on my own merits, I'll use my family connections."

"You're joking—" Hillary said, "—right?"

Victoria felt awkward again. Did Hillary think she was bragging? "Yes, joking about getting a job with *National Geographic.* Not joking about my great-great-grandfather. He really was their first president."

"That's so cool," Hillary said, laughing. "I'm pretty sure my great-great-grandfather was a potato farmer."

"Not much help there," Victoria said, relieved that Hillary was laughing. She hadn't taken offense at Victoria's attempt at humor. "But really," she said, no longer joking, "I think I'd like to be a psychologist."

"Oh?" Hillary said, looking surprised. "Why?"

"I don't know," Victoria said, feeling unsure of herself. It was a new idea and she hadn't thought it through. "It's just something I think about sometimes. I like trying to figure people out—to discover their secrets."

"Everybody has some sort of secret," Hillary said. She was studying her feet when she said this, but Victoria had the feeling Hillary might be talking about her. Was she aware that Victoria was keeping something from her?

"I don't mean secrets, like private thoughts," Victoria said, keeping her voice level. "People need to keep some things private. I mean secrets that hold people back. Things they're afraid to talk about because they're big and important and scary."

"I get that," Hillary said. "Things that people need to get off their chests, so they can move on."

"I think I'd like to work with kids," Victoria continued. "Not that I've had much experience with kids, being an only child . . ."

"What about having kids of your own?" Hillary asked.

"I'd like to have kids," Victoria said, "though not as many as your parents."

"Yeah," Hillary said, "my folks kind of overdid it." They laughed again.

Victoria sat down at last, dropping her shoes to the floor as she pulled her legs up under her on the bed. Hillary scooted over to make room.

"I'm not quite sure how women manage marriage and kids *and* a career," Hillary said. "My mom was a teacher, but she quit when she married my dad—that seems to be what's expected."

"My English teacher just read a book called *The Feminine Mystique*," Victoria said, "and gave us a big lecture about not settling for being only a wife and mother. Apparently, we girls need to have 'meaningful work' or we'll never be happy." Victoria shifted back onto the bed to get more comfortable. "It makes me wonder if my mother's happy."

"Does she seem unhappy?" Hillary asked, then reddened. "I hope that didn't sound nosy."

"No, it's okay," Victoria said. "She's not unhappy exactly, but, she seems like she needs more to do. I mean, she's studying to be a docent, but that's not really enough. I think maybe she'd be happier if she had her old job back. It would give her something to worry about besides me."

"What was her job?" Hillary asked.

"She worked as an art appraiser. That's how she met my dad. Her firm sent her to evaluate the art in his parents' estate after they died."

"Did she like the job?"

"I guess," Victoria said. "She doesn't talk about it much."

"My mom seems happy, most of the time," Hillary said, "but she misses teaching." She paused, her hand idly plucking at the tufts on the heavy chenille spread. "I don't think I'd be happy being only a wife and mother."

"But you want kids?"

"I do." Hillary's eyes wandered to the bookshelf.

"What about James?" Victoria said, glad Hillary wasn't looking at her when she asked the question. Her voice went a little funny when she talked about James.

Hillary didn't seem to notice her discomfort. "He insists he's never getting married."

This was not what Victoria expected to hear. "Did he say why?"

"I'm not sure," Hillary said. "He's pretty reserved around girls—not us, of course, but girls his own age. He never goes on dates."

Victoria felt a little tremor of excitement when she heard this. If James was a late bloomer, there might be hope for her after all. "Maybe he's waiting till he gets to college," she said.

"I guess." Hillary sighed. "I worry about him. He doesn't have a lot of friends."

Hillary fell silent, and Victoria studied her face. *Maybe,* Victoria thought, *if I become James's girlfriend, Hillary won't have to worry about him so much. Then, when Hillary finds a boyfriend, the four of us can go on double dates, and, after we marry, our children can play together. . .* She stopped herself—it was easy to let her imagination run wild.

"So what will you name your first child?" Victoria asked, hoping to get Hillary talking again.

"Barnaby Ulysses," Hillary said without hesitation.

"You can't!" Victoria gasped. "Poor child! What if it's a girl?"

"Veronica Maude."

"Even worse!"

"Well, I'm not naming her Suzy or Patty. Too boring."

"My names are not much better than yours," Victoria said. "I like the literary ones, like Ramona or Heloise."

"And Abelard for a boy?" Hillary suggested.

"Good one!" Victoria said.

"Dickens has some great names. I like 'Charity Pecksniff.'"

The names got sillier and sillier, and when Victoria's mother came to say goodnight, the girls were hanging off the sides of the bed, laughing.

"What's so funny?" Victoria's mother asked, hands on her hips.

"Nothing," they said and started laughing again.

It was time to put on their pajamas, so Victoria went into the bathroom and shut the door for privacy. On impulse, she decided to skip the brace for one night and, removing it, hid it under the bathroom sink. The doctor would be furious, but she didn't care.

When she emerged after brushing her teeth, she found Hillary, already changed into a flannel nightgown, standing in the middle of the bedroom studying the pages of a slim volume called *Charles Dodgson, Photographer of Children*. It was one of the many library books Victoria had found on Victorian photographers, but hadn't had time to read.

"This is really odd," Hillary said, looking up. "You know Lewis Carroll, the guy who wrote *Alice in Wonderland*? I knew his real name was Charles Dodgson, but I didn't know he was a photographer. He liked taking pictures of little girls." She turned the page. "Yikes! Look at this one!"

A quiver of apprehension made the hairs on Victoria's arms stand up. She looked at the page Hillary was indicating. The photograph showed a very young girl, identified as Evelyn Hatch, lying on her back on a couch, completely naked. She was posed with her elbows cocked back, her hands on either side of her head. Her eyes looked straight at the camera, but seemed to see nothing. The expression on her face was unnerving: bland and unsmiling, somehow resigned.

Victoria sat down on the bed, her knees suddenly weak. All her worst fears came flooding back. Perhaps this was what Clifford Graham had had in mind for the girl in the red scarf—or, god forbid, Julia!

"Look at her eyes," Hillary said. "It's like she's not a child at all, but a little fox or something. Her eyes are so empty."

Victoria nodded numbly.

"Why would her parents let him photograph her like that?" Hillary said.

"Maybe she didn't have parents," Victoria said, thinking of the girl prostitute. Then, thinking of Mr. and Mrs. Boit, "Or, if she did, maybe they didn't know what was going on."

"This girl looks about the same age as my little sister Erin," Hillary said, still staring at the photograph. "I can't imagine anyone taking a picture like this of Erin—she wouldn't allow it! I mean, she's okay being naked at bathtime, but she'd never pose like this for a photographer."

Victoria's throat constricted. She looked at Hillary's shocked face and wished with all her might that she could tell her what was careening through her mind.

"I always thought Lewis Carroll was this great children's author," Hillary said. "Not some pervert taking nude pictures of little girls." She looked up, aware that Victoria was not saying anything.

Victoria found her voice again. "Did you ever read *Alice in Wonderland*? I hated it. It used to give me nightmares."

Both of them grew quiet as they paged through the rest of the photographs in the book. They found no other nude studies, but one, showing a partially dressed child, was almost as disturbing as the picture of Evelyn Hatch.

In this photograph, a girl of about six was posed lying on her side on a tiger pelt, her bare shoulder loosely draped in white linen, a dreamy look on her face. A richly brocaded cloth covered the rest of her body. From beneath the cloth, the child's legs stuck out, her feet shod in short, white socks and black strap shoes. Beneath the photograph, in careful, childish script was the name "Irene MacDonald," written with two backward n's, the letters scrunched together to fit.

"You think this was the Victorian's answer to *Playboy*?" said Hillary, shaking her head in dismay. "Using kids instead of women?"

Victoria had never seen a copy of *Playboy*, but Hillary had three older brothers—maybe she had. She took the book out of Hillary's hands, closed it and put it on the bottom of the stack of library books.

They said nothing more about the book, but got into bed and turned off the light.

Hillary fell asleep almost at once, but Victoria lay awake, wondering what would possess a person to take pictures like the ones she'd just seen. Children, especially naked children, were beautiful, but in Lewis Carroll's photographs they looked too self-conscious, or not conscious at all, and anything but childish.

In paintings, children were sometimes naked. Victoria thought of the painting of the Madonna and the naked Christ child she'd seen at the Gardner, and the mother and child paintings by Mary Cassatt. But painters almost always included a tender, protective figure in the frame. She couldn't think of a single painting that featured a naked child all alone and posed to look deliberately seductive.

When she finally slept, she had troubling dreams that woke her in the night.

The next morning, breakfast seemed to take forever. At last, Victoria's mother drove the two girls to the museum. They arrived at their art class just as their teacher was starting the lesson.

An hour later, Victoria excused herself to go to the restroom. Instead of heading to the toilets, she went straight to the Sargent gallery. A trip to Paris and back took no time at all; she'd be able to return to class before anyone noticed she was gone.

Tucked into the inside pocket of her rain jacket was the book containing those dreadful photographs by Charles Dodgson, which she planned to show to Mary Louisa.

There was almost nobody in the gallery when she entered. As Victoria walked up to the painting of the Boit daughters, the walls of the museum fell away. She entered the painting with no transition at all. One instant she was in Boston and the next in Paris, eighty-one years before her time.

Chapter Ten

Who Is Neddie?

December, 1882, Paris

When Victoria arrived at the rear of the enormous entry hall, the Boit family was in an uproar. Not only were they all there—Mrs. Boit and the four Boit daughters and a man Victoria assumed must be Mr. Boit, as well as John Singer Sargent and the house-keeper, Madame Fouche—they were all talking at once. *What has happened?* Victoria wondered. *Am I too late?*

Everyone was focused on Sargent's huge portrait, which was facing outward on full display. The red screen had been moved to the opposite side of the room, and Victoria was able to slip behind it without making a sound. The others were so busy arguing, they didn't notice her sudden arrival in the room.

Peering through the crack, Victoria got her first good look at Mr. Boit. He bore a striking resemblance to the portrait Sargent had painted of him, which Victoria had seen in a book of Sargent reproductions: a man with strong, handsome features, a balding head, and huge brushy mustache. He looked totally in command of himself and his surroundings, like a person who was used to being obeyed. Sargent was speaking, but Mr. Boit cut him off.

"For heaven's sake, John, you scruple too much!" Mr. Boit said. "Of course you'll exhibit the picture at the Salon. It's a masterpiece, one of your best. These girls will get over their silly objections when they hear the thing being praised all over Paris."

Julia's small voice quavered shrilly above the rest. "Papa's right. Mary Louisa and I think it's wonderful, and we have a say, even if we are the littlest."

The two older Boit daughters had stopped speaking, but their dark expressions told it all. Their mother appealed to them. "Please, girls, tell Mr. Sargent that he has your consent to display the picture. He wants to hear that you approve."

Jane stepped forward and faced her mother. "If he's going to show that painting, Florence and I want to go home to Boston as soon as we can book passage. We can't stand to be in Paris while that picture hangs in a public gallery for everyone to see."

Jane turned to Florence for support, but Florence wouldn't look at anyone. Mary Louisa was likewise silent. She looked from one face to the other, as though trying to fathom the true feelings of each person.

For several seconds, no one else spoke. Madame Fouche took a small bottle out of her pocket, removed the stopper, and held it delicately to her nose. When she sniffed loudly, it seemed to break the spell.

"Well—" said Sargent, regarding the two older girls solemnly. Victoria was struck by his obvious concern for them. "I very much desire your approbation, both of you, but I have to agree with your father and Julia. I think it's a fine picture, and I'd like to see if the critics agree. Granted, it's not your usual sort of portrait—I was trying for something different. But I hope viewers will be fascinated by it."

"Fascinated by how extremely strange you find us," retorted Jane.

"Jane! Stop this impertinence!" said her father. "No one will think any such thing. The worst you can expect is that they won't think of you at all. You and Florence are in the background. Julia and Mary Louisa are really the featured subjects." He paused and smoothed his fine mustache with two large fingers. "While this may make you feel less important, you must overcome your objections."

"Please, listen to your father," pleaded Mrs. Boit. Victoria observed the dismissive expression on Florence's face. She seemed hardly aware that her parents were speaking.

"I'm sure it wasn't Mr. Sargent's intention to injure your feelings," her father went on. "He was trying for something new, as he just told you, and I believe he's accomplished it. The painting is unique, and I'm sure the composition will be studied and discussed for some time to come."

"We must consider it from the point of view of art," Mrs. Boit said, speaking earnestly to the older girls, "and not simply as a portrait. I know you two will come to see it that way eventually."

Florence turned abruptly and walked out of the room without a backward glance. Madame Fouche threw a despairing look at her mistress and hurried after the retreating girl.

Jane watched them leave, then fixed her glare on Sargent. "See what you've done," she hissed. "She'll be silent for a week, and it's all your fault!" Then she, too, ran after Florence.

"Jane!" Mr. Boit shouted, "Florence! Come back here this minute and apologize. This is madness—both of you come back at once!" He strode after his oldest daughters, then stopped and turned back to speak to his friend with obvious embarrassment. "I apologize, John. That was uncalled for. They grow more troublesome the older they get."

Mrs. Boit laid a hand on Sargent's sleeve. "Don't pay any attention to them. You must go ahead with your plans to exhibit the painting at the Salon. We're quite clear about that."

Sargent shook his head. "I've upset them. Their unease, their withdrawal—they don't like to see it in the painting." Mr. and Mrs. Boit both turned to him. "I didn't mean to make things worse for them."

"Good heavens, man," cried Mr. Boit. "They'll be fine. They're just young girls, high-strung and strong-willed." He paused, staring at his friend's worried expression. "There's nothing wrong with them, if that's what you think. Why, we had the doctor here just the other day for Mary Louisa's sore throat, and he checked on all four girls. 'The picture of health,' he said. Those were his very words."

Mrs. Boit exchanged a glance with Sargent. "You're not to blame, no matter what Jane says to the contrary," she told him quietly.

When Sargent spoke, it was with an obvious effort to sound less concerned. "It's a difficult age, I know. My sister Violet is about to turn thirteen, and I've noticed a great change in her these last few weeks. She's much more stubborn and seems to find fault with everything our parents do. And she was always such a good-humored child."

"Well, I can't say Jane and Florence have ever been extraordinarily good-humored," remarked their mother, "but lately they seem intent on turning the smallest setback into a tragedy of Shakespearian proportions."

Mary Louisa spoke at last. "Will you take the picture today?" she asked Sargent.

"Yes, my dear," he said. "The Salon is not till May, but I plan to exhibit it at a small gallery here in Paris as soon as possible, with luck before the Christmas holidays."

"Jane and Florence will be better when the painting is out

of the house," observed Mary Louisa. The three adults turned to look at her.

"I daresay you're right," her mother murmured, but she sounded less than convinced. She excused herself to go check on the older girls.

Mr. Boit suggested that he and John retire to the study and ring for the servants to give instructions on how to package the painting for removal.

"Come, Julia," said Madame Fouche, coming back into the room. "It's time for your nap." Julia followed her out with uncharacteristic meekness.

When everyone but Mary Louisa had left the entry hall, Victoria stepped out from behind the screen and called to her.

"Oh, Victoria!" Mary Louisa cried. "You've come! Did you hear? What a fuss this portrait has caused!"

"Jane and Florence don't like it," Victoria said. "Just as you told me."

"Yes, but now they're beside themselves," Mary Louisa said. "They can't stand it that Sargent wants to enter it in the Paris Salon. They say they're ashamed to have it exhibited in a public gallery."

"Well, they'll just have to get used to the idea," Victoria said. "It's going to be exhibited, and people are going to love it."

"Yes, but meanwhile, Florence won't talk to anyone," Mary Louisa said, "and Jane is being so unpleasant. She tells me to go away whenever I try to talk to her."

Victoria had other things on her mind. "Is there some place we can talk?" she asked, fingering the book through the fabric of her jacket. "Where no one will interrupt us?"

"Let me check to see if anyone's in the hallway," Mary Louisa said. "I'll be back in a minute. Hide yourself in the cloakroom, just in case."

Victoria ducked into the cloakroom and waited. She heard

footsteps and rose to look out the door, but stepped back quickly when she saw it was Florence and Jane, not Mary Louisa, coming toward her. Victoria concealed herself behind a man's bulky, full-length dress coat. Peeping out, she glimpsed the older Boit girls as they entered.

Florence started fumbling her way into a raincoat and boots and Victoria was struck by how boyish she looked. Her long, thin body was all angles and knobs, and her movements were fast and jerky. Jane's body, though slight, was a softer version of her sister's and her attitude was less defiant than it had been a few moments before.

"You can't just leave," Jane said, wringing her hands in agitation. "It's raining and you'll—"

"Leave me alone," Florence barked. "I'm only going for a walk around the block. I have to get out of here. You heard what Papa said—he called us mad. He thinks we'll go insane like Neddie."

Jane gasped. "He didn't mean it, Florence. It was only an expression."

"But, it could be true, you know," Florence insisted. "It's in our blood. Sargent thinks so, too. That's why he painted us hidden away in the dark like demented ghosts."

Jane moaned and rocked from side to side. "Don't say that, Florie. I can't bear it."

"You don't remember what it was like—what Neddie was like. You were only a baby. I was three and I remember. It was awful. He wouldn't stop screaming."

"Please don't talk about him," Jane said, rocking faster now, her voice rising in pitch. She looked like someone on the verge of a hysterical fit, and it took all of Victoria's will power to keep from rushing from her hiding place to try to calm her. Florence opened her mouth to say something, but closed it when Mary Louisa appeared in the doorway.

"What are you doing in here, Florence?" Mary Louisa asked in a high, breathless voice. "Why do you have your coat on?"

Florence stormed out of the cloakroom and through the front door, slamming it behind her. Jane grabbed a coat and ran after her. When they were gone, Victoria stepped out from among the hanging coats.

"Follow me," Mary Louisa commanded, grabbing Victoria's hand and shushing her when she tried to speak. "We have to get you out of here before they come back." Silently she led the way to a music room at the far end of the hall, taking care to shut the door of the study, in case her father or Sargent looked up as Victoria went by.

The music room was small, most of the space occupied by a beautiful Steinway piano piled high with stacks of sheet music. Mary Louisa pulled Victoria inside and shut the door, then struggled to push a heavy side chair against it. Victoria moved to help her.

"Did my sisters see you?" Mary Louisa asked, looking worried.

"No, but they were acting so strange!" Victoria exclaimed, glad to be finally able to talk. "Jane was so upset she was shaking."

"She's just angry about the painting," Mary Louisa said, dismissively. "My mother says she makes mountains out of molehills. She makes things up, just to get people to feel sorry for her. I never believe anything she says when she gets like that."

"She didn't look like she was faking," Victoria said. She walked to the piano and stared at the sheet music that stood on the piano's music rack, not really seeing it. She felt as though she'd just witnessed evidence of Jane's impending breakdown. She knew from her reading that the girl was about to experience a psychotic episode that was bad enough that she'd have to be sent away from home and put under a doctor's care. Should she tell Mary Louisa? No one in this house seemed to be taking

Jane's moods as anything more serious than adolescent bad temper and Victoria knew it was something much worse than that.

"Do you play?" Mary Louisa asked.

"No," Victoria replied, still distracted.

"Most of the music belongs to Jane," Mary Louisa said. "She plays constantly. Too much, father thinks." As she spoke, she pushed back the drapes to let some sunlight into the room, then sat down on a pale green love seat. Victoria left the piano and came to sit beside her. *Concentrate*, she told herself. She was here to talk to Mary Louisa about Clifford Graham.

"What happened to you last time?" Mary Louisa asked, showing no interest in talking further about Jane. "You said you'd wait, but when we came back from our tea, you were gone."

Victoria wasn't sure how much to tell Mary Louisa about what had happened last time. She didn't want to frighten her unnecessarily, but she did need to warn her about Clifford Graham. How to begin?

"I did something a little scary," she said. "I followed Clifford Graham when he left your house that day."

Mary Louisa gasped. "You went out by yourself?"

"I was fine. I still had on my disguise. It was risky, but I didn't get hurt." Victoria told her the story, leaving out the part about the young prostitute, but including the part about the gang of boys knocking Graham down and taking his money and camera.

When she described how Graham had attacked her, Mary Louisa asked anxiously. "But you got away?"

"I got away, back to my own time. So, I'm fine, really," Victoria said. She took a breath to try to calm her nerves. "But, tell me— how are things here? Is Clifford Graham still coming around?" She felt her jaw clench as she waited for Mary Louisa's answer.

Mary Louisa nodded. "He's here all the time. But I think he's finally given up on trying to photograph me or Julia. We had our picture taken one more time, but we wouldn't do anything he asked us to do. We looked away or moved just when he was about to take the picture. He was so angry!" She giggled as she remembered. "But we decided that's what we had to do to make him stop pestering us. And he has. At least for now."

"Was that your idea, Mary Louisa?" Victoria said. "How clever of you!"

"It's good he's not bothering us anymore," Mary Louisa said. "But he's taking so many pictures of Jane and Florence. They've been to his studio, just the two of them. Madame Fouche is supposed to go with them, but if she has a headache, they go without her."

"And your mother lets them go alone?"

"I'm not sure she knows."

"Doesn't Madame Fouche object?"

"Oh, Madame Fouche thinks Clifford Graham can do no wrong. He always brings her big bunches of flowers. I don't doubt she's half in love with him."

"And Jane and Florence, too, I suppose," said Victoria.

"Yes, head over heels. Well, Jane at least, more than Florence. He's always telling them how pretty they are, how smart. He pays attention to everything they say, except when Mama and Papa are around. Then he talks just to the adults. But I think he really likes children more. He likes to play silly games and tell jokes. Jane and Florence think he's so much fun, but Julia and I don't." Mary Louisa pinched her mouth into a hard line. *She's not a person who puts up with idiots*, Victoria thought, imagining how formidable Mary Louisa would be as an adult.

"Have you seen any of the photographs he takes?" Victoria asked.

"One or two," said Mary Louisa. "But he says he's still not satisfied with the photographs he's taken of the four of us. He wants to take a picture to rival Mr. Sargent's painting."

"What are they like, his photographs?" Victoria asked cautiously. "Are they any good?"

"I suppose, if you like that kind of thing. I don't really like photographs."

Victoria hesitated. The thin book in her pocket felt as heavy as a brick. The question she needed to ask was dreadfully embarrassing and she didn't know how to ask it in a way that wouldn't mortify her young companion. But she plunged ahead. "Does he ever take pictures of your sisters with their clothes off?"

Mary Louisa looked shocked. "What do you mean?" she said.

Victoria pulled the book from her pocket. "I found this in the library," she said. "It was taken by the man who wrote *Alice's Adventures in Wonderland.* I saw that book in your room, so you must know who I'm talking about. He was—I should say he is—a photographer, as well as a writer. And—" she turned to the page with Lewis Carroll's nude photo of Evelyn Hatch, "—he likes to take pictures of little girls."

"Is this Alice?" Mary Louisa whispered, staring at the photo of the naked child. "Is this what happened to her when she fell down the rabbit hole?"

"No, it's not Alice. Alice is a real girl, not just a character in a story. Her name is Alice Liddell, and she's all grown up by now. Lewis Carroll took lots of pictures of her when she was young, but this is another little girl, Evelyn Hatch. This picture was taken," Victoria paused to look at the caption, "about four years ago. In your time."

She looked at Mary Louisa to see if this mention of the time difference confused her, but Mary Louisa was too busy studying the photograph to notice. "Why would he take a photograph like this?" she asked Victoria.

"That's what I wondered, too," Victoria said. "Most people who see this think it's disgusting. Lewis Carroll must know that, because he's keeping it secret. This photograph won't be discovered till after his death, so not for many years from now."

Mary Louisa looked at her. "Why did you show me?"

Victoria looked straight into Mary Louisa's eyes. "Because I wonder if other photographers take pictures like this one."

"Mr. Graham," Mary Louisa said at once, her eyes growing round with alarm. "You think he wants to take a photograph like this of Julia."

"I don't know for sure," Victoria said. "But, he's always pestering you to let him take pictures of Julia. You don't trust him. I don't trust him."

Mary Louisa looked once more at the photograph and then said, with a catch in her voice, "Please put it away."

Victoria put the book back into her jacket pocket. "Mary Louisa," she said tentatively. "There's something else. Something I didn't tell you last time." Then she told Mary Louisa about Clifford Graham taking Julia's hair ribbon, and later, her nightgown.

"He's stealing Julia's things?" Mary Louisa said, spots of color appearing high on her cheeks.

"Is Julia missing anything else besides her ribbon and nightgown?"

"We can't find her white leggings. And this morning she told me her wool scarf is missing. I thought she'd misplaced it."

"Maybe she did. But maybe Mr. Graham took it. Was he here yesterday?"

"Yes. And he was in the drawing room where Julia left her scarf, so he could have stolen it." Mary Louisa put her hand over her mouth. "Oh, Victoria, what should we do?"

"Maybe you should talk to your parents," Victoria said.

"But they won't believe me!" Mary Louisa said. "Mr. Graham will say it's not true."

"Can you at least warn Florence and Jane to stay away from him?" Victoria asked.

"You don't know them," Mary Louisa said. "If I tell them about this and it turns out we're wrong, they'll never let me forget it. I wish we knew for sure."

Victoria felt desperate. "I've tried to find out more about him. I've checked the Gardner museum and the library, but there's nothing. I don't even know if any of his photographs survived into my time. I'll keep looking, but I think we need to do something right now."

"We should go to his studio!" Mary Louisa said, jumping up in excitement. "If he's taken any pictures like that one—" she pointed to Victoria's pocket, "we can find them and prove he's a villain!" She seized Victoria's hands. "You can come with me—you can wear that boy's jacket and cap again!" She stopped to study what Victoria was wearing. "You still have them, don't you?"

Victoria shook her head. "I threw them away," she admitted. "I wasn't thinking. I'm sorry. The poor boy will have no warm coat to wear when he has to work in the garden."

"Don't worry," Mary Louisa said. "There are lots of old jackets in the basement." She frowned in consternation. "But now we have to get you a new disguise."

"I'm not sure that plan would work anyway," Victoria said. "How would we find his studio? I followed him to his apartment, but his studio is most likely somewhere else."

"You're right," Mary Louisa said glumly, sitting down again. "I've never been there. I have no idea where it is."

"And how would we get in?" Victoria went on.

Mary Louisa shook her head and looked miserable. Victoria thought of several more reasons why breaking and entering would never work, but decided not to mention them.

"So, what can we do?" Mary Louisa asked.

As the two girls sat side by side, thinking, Victoria's mind drifted back to the conversation between Jane and Florence she'd overheard in the cloakroom. She turned to Mary Louisa. "Who is Neddie?" she asked.

"Who told you about Neddie?" Mary Louisa whispered.

"I heard Florence and Jane talking about him in the cloak-room. Florence said they might go mad like Neddie. That's when Jane got so frantic. Do you know who he is?"

Mary Louisa's chin dropped and her hair fell forward over her face. "He's our brother," she muttered. "Our secret brother. Mama and Papa don't like to mention him, but I know about him. My uncle told me."

Victoria put a hand on Mary Louisa's shoulder. "Where is he? Why isn't he here?"

"He's in a special school in Massachusetts," Mary Louisa said, "pretty far from Boston. He's very ill. He doesn't speak—he just sits in his room and plays with sticks." She stopped and cleared her throat, trying to control the tremor in her voice. "He was fine until he was two and then he stopped talking and started having tantrums. My parents thought the doctors at the school could help him, but my uncle says he's not getting better." Mary Louisa avoided Victoria's gaze. "I wanted to visit him, but my uncle said no."

"How old is he?" Victoria asked.

"Sixteen or seventeen, a few years older than Florence. I've never met him, but I've seen a photograph of him when he was a little boy. He was so beautiful, but he would cry if anyone touched him." Mary Louisa's voice had lost all of its usual confidence; she sounded like a much younger child.

Victoria felt an urge to take this suddenly fragile girl into her arms, but suspected Mary Louisa would resist. "When did you find out about him?"

Just then Mr. Boit's stern voice called through the door. "Mary Louisa, come out please. I need to talk to you."

Mary Louisa clutched Victoria's arm and put a finger to

her mouth. Her father spoke again, more loudly. "Mary Louisa, come out here, please." He knocked on the door and, when Mary Louisa still didn't answer, said, "I'm coming in."

Both girls stared at the door. It didn't open right away, but as the girls watched, the chair they'd used to block it began to slide slowly forward. "What the devil are you up to?" Mr. Boit said, and they knew he was about to put his head around the door.

Mary Louisa looked at Victoria in horror. As their eyes met, Victoria's vision began to blur.

This time, Victoria fought hard against the forces that were flashing her forward into her own time. But, no matter how hard she resisted, she was powerless to reverse the process once it had begun. As had happened each time before, Victoria found herself back in the museum—leaving Mary Louisa alone again to fend for herself.

Chapter Eleven

Bernadette's Story

May, 1963, Boston

Victoria stumbled out of the Sargent gallery, reeling from her abrupt return to the present. She hurried back to art class and sat like a zombie through the last hour.

"Are you okay?" whispered Hillary.

"I feel sick," Victoria answered. "I think I might throw up."

She was only half pretending, and it gave her the excuse to make a quick exit after class without worrying about hurting Hillary's feelings. She was quiet on the ride home with her mother. As soon as they got back she used her school report as a reason to stay in her room until dinnertime.

Dinner was an ordeal. Victoria was too upset to eat much, but she managed to rearrange the food on her plate in a convincing enough manner to fool her parents, then returned to her room to brood. *If only I could have stayed long enough with Mary Louisa to figure out a plan*, she thought. Now the girl was alone again, doing her best to protect Julia on her own. And there was Jane's mental state to worry about, too. It was all too much.

Charles Dodgson's picture of the naked child filled Victoria's mind, only it wasn't Evelyn Hatch, it was Julia she saw lying there, alone and exposed. She knew Clifford Graham was stealing Julia's things; beyond that, and what she'd seen of his rough behavior with the young prostitute, she had nothing to prove he was dangerous. It was all just a hunch and maybe she was wrong about all of it.

Mary Louisa was doing a good job of keeping Julia away from the photographer, but how long could an eight-year-old fend off the unwanted attention of a determined adult? *So far*, Victoria thought bleakly, *I haven't been much help.*

With no evidence and no idea how to produce any, Victoria felt at a loss. Finding the photograph of Evelyn Hatch had put her on the right track, she hoped, but she didn't know what to do next. And, unless she was willing to tell someone about her predicament, there was no one to turn to for help. With a growing sense of panic, she concluded, once again, that she, like Mary Louisa, was on her own.

Even though she knew she couldn't ask for help, when it was nearly bedtime, she called Hillary just to talk. Ralph answered and went to find his sister. After what seemed like a very long time, Hillary came to the phone.

"I didn't throw up after all," Victoria said. "I'm feeling better. Just bored. What are you doing?"

"Nothing," Hillary said. "I can't talk." She didn't sound like herself. She sounded distracted, her thoughts far away. "I can't talk," she said again.

"What's up?" Victoria asked. "Is something wrong?"

"It's not a good time," Hillary said. "I'll call you tomorrow." She hung up.

Victoria waited all day Sunday, but Hillary didn't call back. Not wanting to bug her, Victoria decided she'd have to wait until Hillary was ready to talk on the phone or else find out in class next Saturday what was troubling her friend.

The following Wednesday, the teachers at Victoria's school had a meeting, so the students were given a day off. As it happened, Victoria's mother was planning to visit the Gardner that day to ask for Martha's help in finding material on Velazquez for one of her upcoming docent tours.

"May I come along?" Victoria asked at breakfast. "I want to take another look at the photographs. And Martha asked to see my new camera and some of my snapshots." She was excited about showing her photos to Martha, especially the ones she'd taken at Hillary's house.

"It's fine with me," her mother said. "But, don't take up too much of Martha's time."

"It was Martha's idea," Victoria grumbled, feeling stung. "I wouldn't dream of *wasting* her time." She flounced out of the dining room before her mother could respond.

They rode to the Gardner in silence, but on their way in Victoria's mother suggested they stop in one of the small rooms on the first floor. "There's a Sargent portrait of Mrs. Gardner you should see," she said, "a watercolor." Victoria didn't protest. As anxious as she was to get upstairs, she wouldn't turn down the chance to see a Sargent painting she'd never heard about.

"I used to come here when I was in college," Victoria's mother said, as the two of them stood looking at the painting. "I always made a point of visiting this picture. It was painted shortly before Isabella's death, after she'd suffered a stroke and was partially paralyzed." Her mother was holding forth as usual, but for once Victoria didn't mind. This time she was actually interested.

The painting showed Isabella seated in a chair and wrapped mummy fashion in swaths of white fabric. Only her face was visible. "It has a hidden element you might not have noticed,"

Victoria's mother was saying. "The face just above the folds of cloth on her shoulder—do you see it?"

Victoria stepped closer to the painting. It was true: over one of Mrs. Gardner's white shoulders were swirls of darker paint that looked very much like a merry little face.

"I like to think Sargent was giving the viewer a hint of the way Isabella used to look, when he first got to know her," her mother went on. "She had a very playful personality, even when she was in her forties. There's a famous story about them chasing one another around the gymnasium at the Groton School here in Boston."

Victoria looked at Isabella's sunken eyes as they peered out from her white turban, noticing the way she stared straight ahead. It was possible she was seeing her own death, since she was eighty-five years old and had just had a stroke. But she didn't look afraid. She looked as though she was ready to face whatever was coming, the same way she'd faced all the obstacles in her life, with stubborn resolve.

I'm not alone in this search, Victoria realized. *All this time I've had these others—Sargent for sure, and Isabella, too—there to encourage me, ready to guide me when I feel lost.* It made her more determined than ever to find what she'd come to find.

When they arrived on the fourth floor, Martha greeted them warmly. "I see you remembered to bring your camera," Martha said, as she opened the room with the photographic files for Victoria. "I'll be back in a bit to take a look. I need to show your mother the things I've found for her on Velazquez."

"Great. I also brought some of my snapshots to show you," Victoria said, giving her mother a pointed glance, "like you asked." Her mother paid no attention, busy looking for something in her purse.

As soon as Martha and her mother left, Victoria immediately started flipping through the photographs from the late

1800s. She hoped Martha wouldn't come back too soon; she wanted time to do a more thorough search this time. After going quickly but methodically through everything in the first drawer, she returned to the drawer she'd examined on her previous visit. She studied each photograph in turn, determined not to miss anything.

As she laid a plastic archival sleeve face down in the pile, she noticed the corner of a second photograph poking out from behind the one on top. Martha had cautioned her not to touch the photos themselves, but she was desperate. *To hell with the rules*, she thought. As she opened the plastic sleeve and pulled the concealed photograph out into the light, a sharp cry of surprise escaped her and her hand flew to her mouth.

The face that looked out at her was Jane Boit's.

This was Jane at twelve, looking the same as she had when Sargent painted her, the same as she had each time Victoria had seen her in Paris. There was no mistaking the curly, brown hair framing the narrow face; the startled eyes and tentative smile. In the photograph, Jane was dressed in a thin slip that hung loosely on her slender frame. One strap of the chemise had slipped off her shoulder and small budding breasts, about the size of Victoria's own, were visible through the light fabric covering Jane's chest.

"Just like *Madame X*," Victoria whispered, seeing the drooping strap—only it wasn't really. This was the picture of a child and *Madame X* was a mature woman, able to make adult decisions about how she wanted to be portrayed.

The picture didn't shock Victoria as much as the photograph of Evelyn Hatch, but it flooded her with an unspeakable sadness. She was used to seeing photographs of girls in skimpy halter tops—they appeared in every teen fashion magazine sold these days—but this was a picture from a very different time.

How, she wondered, remembering the uproar caused by

Amelie Gautreau's fallen strap, *could a girl of Jane's era consider posing in such a flimsy garment?* It was so reckless! Jane must have known how shocked her parents would be if they ever saw this photograph. Did she think Graham would keep it a secret?

Mary Louisa claimed her big sister was in love with Clifford Graham and would do anything he asked. But a more dismal explanation occurred to Victoria. Had Graham found it easy to take advantage of a girl whose mind was already slipping into confusion? Did Jane even understand what she'd done?

Slowly, Victoria turned the picture over. Just as she'd expected, the words *"From the Studio of Clifford Graham Esquire, Portrait Photographer"* were embossed on the back, along with the date: January, 1883. Victoria's mind worked furiously. When she'd last visited the Paris apartment, she was sure the month was still December—Sargent had mentioned exhibiting the Boit girls' portrait before the Christmas holidays. Perhaps, if the photograph hadn't yet been taken, it might be possible to prevent it!

She hadn't expected to find anything this damning in the archives. She'd hoped for a Clifford Graham photograph of some other child—an echo of the Lewis Carroll photographs, perhaps—something she could use to prove that Clifford Graham had a sick interest in young girls. But she'd never imagined finding a photograph of Jane in her slip!

I have to get this to Mary Louisa right away, Victoria thought. She can show it to her parents and get Clifford Graham kicked out of the Boit's home for good.

But how? For a moment, Victoria considered stealing the photograph from the Gardner, but she hesitated. She didn't want to violate Martha's trust or risk getting her into trouble. Then, she remembered her camera. Without wasting a second, she pulled it from its case, laid the photograph on Martha's drafting table, and turned on the powerful lamp.

She took several quick shots of Jane's portrait, praying the light settings were correct. Hearing Martha's footsteps coming back along the hall, she slipped the original photograph into its protective sleeve and was stuffing her camera into its case when Martha came through the door.

"Oh, don't put it away," Martha said. "Let me take a look."

Victoria's hands were trembling as she handed the camera to Martha. If Martha noticed, she didn't say anything. She started talking about aperture openings and shutter speeds, and as she talked, Victoria picked up the plastic sleeve that contained the photograph of Jane and carefully slipped it back into its proper place in the drawer, using the time to get her nerves under control.

"What about your snapshots?" Martha asked. Victoria handed her the packet. "This is good," Martha said, choosing one of the pictures of Erin. She was holding the photograph under the lamp and looking at it with real appreciation, when Victoria's mother appeared in the doorway. "I like the way you've caught her looking away from the camera," Martha said, "with the sunlight falling on one cheek."

Victoria's mother stepped into the room to take a look. "That's very nice, Victoria," she said. "The picture of innocence."

Victoria was surprised. This was high praise, given her mother's complete lack of interest in photography. But she was also struck by her mother's having hit upon the stark difference between her own picture of Erin and the photograph of Jane Boit. For a second, she was tempted to show Jane's photo to her mother and Martha—just to see what they would say. But she resisted. It was time to go. Victoria picked up her camera, and, thinking of the important images it contained, clasped it to her chest. She and her mother thanked Martha and left.

That same afternoon, Victoria got her mother's permission to take her film to the one-hour photo shop two blocks from her house. She came home and counted the minutes anxiously until it was time to return to the shop to collect her small package of prints. A few minutes later, she sat on her bed and stared at the evidence spread out before her on the coverlet.

The pictures were quite clear. She'd done a good job with the camera settings and there was no mistaking the identity of the girl in the pictures: it was Jane Boit and she had almost nothing on. A feeling of accomplishment took hold of Victoria. This was it. This photograph was all she would need to put an end to Clifford Graham's influence over the Boit sisters once and for all.

She felt pleased with herself, but worried, at the same time. *What will happen when I take this picture to the Boits?* she wondered. *Will I make the situation better or somehow worse?* It was a terrible responsibility, and it went against the warning she'd given to Mary Louisa and Julia about the dangers of tampering with the future.

She was sitting on her bed, mulling it over, when her mother came into the room holding a dry-cleaning bag in one hand.

"That was quick," her mother said. "Did you get your pictures already?" Before Victoria could react, her mother had crossed the room and picked up one of the prints lying on her bed. "What on earth?" she said, letting the dry cleaning drop to the floor.

It had been a new roll of film, and, though Victoria had used only part of it, all the pictures were of Jane. As Victoria's mother stared at the photograph, a look of revulsion and disbelief spread across her face.

"It's a photograph I found in the Gardner," Victoria said quickly. "I mean, it's a photograph I took of a photograph." She gave up. There was no good way to explain.

Her mother was still staring at the picture. "My God," she said. "When was this taken?"

"1882. No, 1883, in January."

Her mother turned a sharp eye on her daughter. "Who was the photographer? Did you know he took pictures like this?"

"His name is Clifford Graham," Victoria said. "He was that friend of Sargent's I was trying to track down."

"Clifford Graham!" Her mother gasped and released the photograph as if it had burned her fingers.

"Mom, what is it?" Victoria asked. "What's wrong?"

Her mother put both hands over her mouth. "No, it can't be," she moaned. "That long ago?"

Victoria froze. Could her mother actually know something about Clifford Graham? She'd never mentioned his name to her mother, as far as she could recall, but it clearly meant something to her.

Her mother sat heavily on the bed, unaware she was crushing some of the duplicate pictures of Jane. Finally, she spoke. "I need to know how you got that photograph," she said. "And why you have it."

"I found it in the archives, at the Gardner. It's by that friend of Sargent's." Victoria tried to speak slowly and carefully, but her mind was racing and her hands were ice cold. "I was interested in his work. I found just that one portrait, and I photographed it. I wondered about the girl in the picture—it didn't say who she was." Victoria was sure the holes in her explanation were obvious, but her mother didn't seem to notice.

"Graham," her mother said, hesitating, as though it was difficult for her to say his name. "Clifford Graham? You're sure?"

Victoria nodded.

"Well, the coincidence is too extraordinary." Her mother's voice was thick with emotion. "I knew Clifford Graham—when I was a girl."

Victoria had never seen her mother like this. "How?" she asked. "Where?" Then, seeing that her mother was struggling, "Mom, please tell me."

"I don't like to talk about it," her mother said, giving Victoria a look that held equal parts panic and resolve.

"I need to know," Victoria said, thinking this was true in ways her mother couldn't even guess.

Her mother paused so long that Victoria wasn't sure she'd heard. "It's a long story," she finally began, her voice not much louder than a whisper. "I have to go back to when I was eleven. My brother, Randolph, died that year. He was sixteen—a beautiful young man. I loved him, idolized him really. He died in the influenza pandemic of 1919. I've told you about that."

She stopped and appeared to be gathering her thoughts. "My parents never recovered. We girls—me, Constance and Margaret—were never enough for them. They wanted a son to carry on the name and take over the family business. But Randolph died and they seemed to lose interest in their other offspring. We had nannies and school mistresses and so forth, but no real anchor. We felt lost. I mean—my parents made sure we had the best of everything, but we felt no sense of belonging. We were like decorations, little girls in pretty dresses—but nothing more." She went on, her voice a little stronger now. "When I was fourteen and Constance eight and Margaret six, they hired a famous Boston photographer to make a portrait of the three of us to hang on the wall."

Victoria knew now where the story was going. "Clifford Graham," she said.

"Yes. He was old, in his sixties, but still quite the favorite with society ladies. He came to our house in Boston to take photographs and then turned up again later in Falmouth—just by chance, I thought. He said he had a summerhouse near ours and a studio in town. He was lying, of course, but I didn't know that. I was just a kid." Sighing deeply, Victoria's mother rolled her shoulders, then continued speaking.

"My sisters and I would run into him on the beach. He talked to me mostly, told me I was beautiful, that my face reminded him of the movie star Clara Bow. I was an awkward teenager, very slow to mature, and no man had ever called me beautiful. It went to my head. He called me Bernadette, not Birdie like everyone else, and it made me feel very grown up. He wanted to take more photographs of us, art photographs, just for himself—no charge to our parents. I agreed to come to his studio. Sometimes my sisters would come along and sometimes I went alone. I should have known better, but he was so polite—so grandfatherly. Later he changed, but in the beginning he acted like a perfect gentleman."

Her mother took a deep breath, obviously steeling herself for what was coming next. "He took hundreds of pictures, just ordinary shots at first, and then he started insisting I take off my clothes." She sat up straighter at this point, and pushed her hair behind her ears. Her face was stony. "It was art, he said. And he considered the nude the 'highest form of art.' I did what he asked. He took lots of photographs of me in the nude, but then he grew bored, and began asking me to bring Margaret and Constance to the studio. And I did." She shook her head. "I don't know why I did it—I've never forgiven myself." She stopped and a sob escaped her throat. "He molested Margaret. I wasn't there when it happened—but I know he molested her!"

Victoria was appalled. "Aunt Margaret?" she said. "How did you find out?"

"Constance told me," her mother said. She rubbed at one eye with the heel of her hand and took a moment to get her voice under control. "She was there and she said he tried to molest her, too, to touch her in places she knew he shouldn't, but she wouldn't let him. She took Margaret away as soon as she realized what was happening. Margaret never talked about it—I'm not sure she's even aware of what really happened. But she was never carefree after that. She'd always been such an airy child—so light, always dancing around. It was my fault. I should have known what kind of a man he was. I wanted to believe he was really interested in art—perhaps to excuse my own behavior. I finally understood he was only interested in having his way with little girls."

Victoria was pretty sure she knew the answer to her next question, but she asked it anyway. "Did you tell your parents?"

Her mother shook her head. "When I confronted him, he threatened to show my parents the nude pictures he'd taken of me. He made me promise not to tell and to make sure Constance and Margaret never talked about what happened. He left the Cape the next day and I never saw him again, though I would read about him in the newspapers from time to time. When I came across his obituary a few years later, I was glad he was dead."

Her mother picked up one of the photographs and studied it. "This is how he'd begin—just the strap falling off the shoulder. Then, eventually, all the clothes would come off. For art." She laughed, but there was no humor in her voice. She sat stiff and unmoving on the bed. Victoria tried patting her shoulder, but she didn't seem to feel it.

Victoria's heart broke for her mother. It was easy to imagine the shame she must feel for having been so gullible and the guilt she still suffered over her little sister's fate. *Why*, Victoria wondered, *did I never guess that something terrible had happened to her long ago?* Instead she had hated her mother for being controlling, which was something she would regret for a long, long time. As desperately as she wanted to think of something comforting to say, words seemed completely inadequate. "I'm so sorry," she said, then lapsed into a painful silence.

"I've been so determined that nothing like that would ever happen to you," her mother said, smiling bitterly, "but your father thinks that's another mistake I've made."

"Does he know—about Clifford Graham?" Victoria asked.

"No. I never told him. He knows I had a difficult time as a teenager, but he doesn't know the details." Her mother reached over and squeezed Victoria's arm. "I'll have to tell him, now that you know." She stood, then picked up the dry cleaning she had dropped, shook it out and hung it carefully in Victoria's closet, smoothing the crumpled plastic before she closed the closet door.

"Wait," Victoria said, seeing that her mother was about to leave. "I need to show you something." She went to her desk and removed the photograph of her mother posing as a coy glamour girl and handed it to her. "This photograph makes sense to me now, but it didn't before."

Her mother drew in a sharp breath. "Where did you get this?" she asked. "I thought I'd destroyed them all."

"I found it in the attic," Victoria said, "in the pocket of your old beach robe."

"You never mentioned it," her mother said.

"I was—I don't know." Victoria struggled to find the right words. "I thought it might embarrass you."

Her mother nodded.

"But I did wonder," Victoria said, "what kind of girl you were back then—" She regretted her words the minute they were out of her mouth.

"Well, now you know," her mother said, with an angry shake of her head. "Not an especially nice girl."

"I don't agree!" Victoria said. "He tricked you, Mom. He made you pose like that, like some movie star."

"That may be true, but just the same, I should have refused. I knew it was wrong from the start, but I was so starved for attention, I just ignored my misgivings." She looked at her daughter and sighed. "We'll talk about this again," she said, "another time." She walked out the door, closing it quietly behind her.

Victoria stared at the door, trying to digest what her mother had told her. Clifford Graham certainly wasn't the only one preying on little girls. Victoria thought of Charles Dodgson's pictures of Evelyn Hatch, of how hard it must have been for Evelyn, when she got older, to forgive herself for letting him take those photographs of her.

All of these children grow up, she realized, *and they're not the same. Their trust is broken and they live with guilt and shame for the rest of their lives.* Victoria was grateful that her mother had confided in her, but she knew she wouldn't be able to share her own secret in return. Her mother had been deeply hurt by what had happened to her; it had made her afraid. If Victoria told her about traveling through time and meeting Clifford Graham as a young man—and if her mother believed her, even a little bit—her response might be to forbid her daughter to go anywhere near the museum and the painting of the Boit girls for as long as she lived.

But Victoria had to get back to Paris right away; she just wasn't sure what she would do once she got there. Her strong words to Mary Louisa and Julia about never meddling with the future were coming back to haunt her.

She realized she'd struggled with this problem on her own long enough; she had to get help. Without second-guessing her decision, she went downstairs to call Hillary.

"It's Victoria," she said in a rush, when Hillary answered, pitching her voice low so no one could overhear her. "I know I've been acting weird, and I haven't been completely honest with you. There's a reason, though, and I need to tell you about it— but not on the phone."

"Okay," Hillary said cautiously. "When?"

"Can you meet me tomorrow, after school—at the library?"

"Yes," Hillary said. "But, Victoria?"

"What?"

Victoria heard Hillary take a calming breath. "I've been weird, too. I'll tell you everything when I see you."

Hillary and Victoria met in the Public Library courtyard and sat down on a stone bench under the roof of the arcade. The day was overcast and a light, warm rain had begun to fall, making the shrubbery shine. The girls could hear rain drops plinking into the small reflecting pool at the center of the outdoor space. No one else was in the garden, so they had the place to themselves.

"What is it?" Hillary asked. "You look scared."

"I *am* scared," Victoria said. "Scared you won't believe me when I tell you what's been happening to me."

Hillary studied her. "Just tell me," she said.

Victoria started at the only place she could: at the beginning. She told Hillary about her first experience of seeing Sargent's painting of the Boit girls, the day her mother had yelled at the museum guard, about the mesmerizing effect the painting had had on her.

"That day, the day I saw you for the first time, you were sketching Mary Louisa. Do you remember? I stayed in the gallery after you left, and I could swear I heard voices coming from the painting. It's hard to explain, but I was being pulled forward and I couldn't help it, I walked up close and I—I walked into the painting."

Hillary stared at her. "You what?"

"I mean I was there, in the room with the painting. I went to Paris. I was in the Boits' apartment."

Hillary's laugh—a disbelieving bark—rang out in the stone corridor. She turned to look out at the dripping garden.

I shouldn't have told her, Victoria thought, panicking. *I can never tell anyone.*

Hillary turned back to her. She wasn't laughing now. Her

brown eyes looked darker than usual, and she was regarding Victoria with concern.

"I'm not crazy!" Victoria insisted.

"I know you're not," Hillary said. "Tell me again."

"I walked into the painting and then somehow I was there, inside the Boits' house. I was there, in the painting, in 1882." She took a breath and then plunged on. "And so was he."

"Who?"

"John Singer Sargent."

"What do you mean? Why was he there?"

"That's the weird thing. He was there painting the portrait. It wasn't finished yet. The girls were there, posed just like they were for the finished portrait, but he was still painting it."

"Wait—how old was he?"

"Young, only twenty-six, but he looks older. He's very tall and has a dark beard and is beginning to get a little fat. He looks kind of middle-aged." Victoria was staring into Hillary's eyes and saw her friend's expression visibly soften. Without realizing it, Victoria had slipped into the present tense and this, more than anything, Hillary told her later, convinced Hillary she was telling the truth.

"So you're telling me that you not only walked into a painting, but you also went back in time?" Hillary said. "And you expect me to believe you?"

Victoria kept her gaze steady. "Yes. You've got to believe me. If you don't, no one will."

The two girls sat there, momentarily speechless. At last, Hillary spoke. "I don't believe things like that happen, but I believe *you*."

Victoria exhaled. It was a first step.

"Tell me everything," Hillary said. "I'm just going to assume you're not crazy. We'll see where we get."

Victoria gave her a brief smile of thanks and started talking.

Hillary listened with rapt attention. She asked questions, but kept her expression neutral, never once showing the skepticism Victoria knew she had to be feeling.

Victoria talked and talked. She told Hillary about the Boit girls' interactions with Clifford Graham, about her nighttime journey through the back alleys of Paris. She told about seeing the photographer with Julia's hair ribbon and about the other missing items, about making the connection to the photograph of Evelyn Hatch that Hillary had seen the night she slept over.

The rain stopped and the shadows on the grass lengthened, but no one came out to interrupt them. When she'd finished describing most of the events that had occurred so far, Victoria pulled the photograph of Jane out of her pocket and handed it to Hillary. This was her trump card. It was the only tangible thing she could show Hillary to support her story. Hillary took it and studied it.

"This reminds me of someone," she said at last.

"It's Jane Boit, the second oldest sister in the painting. She's in the background, but you can see her face clearly enough."

Hillary nodded. "And you say that Clifford Graham took this picture of her?"

Victoria told Hillary the rest of it, of finding the photograph at the Gardner, of her fears for Julia and Jane, and her determination to prevent Clifford Graham from taking any more pictures of the Boits. "If he has some horrible plan in mind—and I'm convinced he does—I have to stop him."

"What other choice do you have?" Hillary asked.

Victoria looked at her friend with relief. It was true. She had no choice. Once she'd found the photograph of Jane, her course was determined. She'd been sent to the Boits for a reason, and she believed it was to protect them from Clifford Graham. This photograph was the proof she needed to get him banished from the Boit's house forever.

"So, you think I should interrupt the future?"

"You have to—*you* specifically—because you're the one who traveled back in time. I don't know why you got picked, but you did."

Victoria nodded, chewing her lower lip. The other piece, of course, was the part she hadn't told Hillary, about her own mother's involvement in this whole mess. Even though it proved conclusively that Clifford Graham was a child molester, at least in his later years, it seemed too private to talk about. That part was her mother's secret, and she needed to keep it to herself.

"Just think," Hillary said, grabbing Victoria's arm. "You've seen John Singer Sargent! Do you realize how many people would give anything to be in your place? To be in the presence of a great artist, to watch while he painted one of his most famous works? It's incredible. I wish I could tell James."

Victoria gasped. "But you can't! You can't tell anyone!"

"I know, I know," Hillary said. "I won't. I promise. But that doesn't mean I don't want to. It's *such* an amazing story. It must have been so hard to keep it to yourself."

"I suppose," Victoria said. "But, I was afraid to tell you, to tell anyone. I was so sure no one would believe me." She shut her eyes, afraid she might cry. "It's been hard, having no one to talk to."

"I'm sorry," Hillary said, with a catch in her voice, "that was a stupid thing to say."

Victoria opened her eyes, surprised by the emotion in Hillary's voice.

"Thank you for trusting me," Hillary said. She paused, looking uncertain. "I've been feeling shut out. I mean, I knew you had something you weren't telling me—now that I know what it is, I understand why you couldn't say anything—but it's been hard for me, too." She stopped again. "I thought it was just me, that you didn't consider me a good enough friend to let me in on your big secret."

"I wanted to tell you!" Victoria said. "I just didn't know how. But you're the one I wanted to tell, of anyone. Only you." As soon as the words left her mouth, Victoria knew they were true.

Hillary gave her a wobbly smile. "I'm glad." Then her look turned serious again. "I have something I've been wanting to tell you, too—or tell somebody." She hesitated. "But, I wasn't sure you wanted to hear about my problems."

"But I do!" Victoria protested.

"You were so—well, distracted." Hillary gave a little laugh.

"Just tell me," Victoria said echoing Hillary's own words.

"Okay," Hillary said. "It's about James." She ducked her head as she spoke, letting her braid fall forward. She tugged on it, looking miserable.

"Is he in trouble?" Victoria said.

"I guess you could say that," Hillary said, keeping her head down. "I just found out he's a homosexual."

"He likes boys!" Victoria exclaimed and wondered if having a crush on a boy who was a homosexual was something she ought to feel dumb about or not. Now that she knew, it seemed obvious. James had always reminded her of Sargent, and that alone should have been a clue.

"But, he doesn't know I know," Hillary said.

Victoria frowned. "So, how did you find out?"

"I overheard him talking to his best friend, Alec, in his room." Hillary stood up, and rocked nervously onto the balls of her feet. "There's a heating vent that goes between his room and mine and it's usually closed, but it was open last Saturday and I heard them, even though they were whispering." She paused and looked ashamed. "Maybe, because they were whispering, I listened extra hard."

"What did they say?"

"I heard James say, 'I can't—I'm scared' and then Alec said something I couldn't hear. James said, 'I love you, too!' kind of loud. I couldn't hear anything more until he said, 'It'll be easier when we're both in New York next year. We can be together all the time.'"

"Wow," Victoria said, a little stunned. "What are you going to do?"

"I don't know," Hillary said, tugging on her braid again. "I'm worried. My parents will be beside themselves when they find out."

"You're not going to tell them!" Victoria didn't know what it would mean to his family that James was homosexual, but she felt certain he shouldn't be punished for it.

"No! I can't be the one to tell them. James has to do it. When he's ready."

"What will they say?"

"I don't think they're going to disown him or anything, but they won't be happy."

Hillary plopped down on the bench again and fell silent. Victoria studied her out of the corner of her eye. She was feeling protective of James, more than disappointed for herself. She'd actually known all along he wasn't interested in her romantically—it was just a daydream she'd enjoyed for a time. But, if he wasn't interested in *any* girls, somehow it made her feel a little better about his not liking her.

"What are you thinking?" Victoria asked.

"I don't know what to think," Hillary said, chewing her thumbnail. "I mean, I always thought we'd both get married, James and I, and have kids, eventually. The kids would be cousins and play together; now all that seems impossible. I feel like I've lost something even before I had it."

"I get that," Victoria said. She hesitated before saying what she wanted to say next, not wanting Hillary to feel criticized. "But what about James? He's suffering, too. You need to talk to him. He needs to know you're on his side, and that you won't give him away."

"But don't you see?" Hillary burst out. "That's what's so hard. He's going to be furious at me. I invaded his privacy."

Victoria shrugged. "James will understand. He knows you love him. You have to talk to him."

Hillary seemed to be thinking it over, then gave Victoria a weak, grateful smile. "You're right. I have to talk to him. Soon."

They sat a few minutes longer. Victoria was exhausted and could tell that Hillary was too. Sharing their secrets had completely worn them out. When they parted on the front steps of the library, Hillary gave Victoria a fierce hug. It happened so fast, Victoria had no chance to fend her off. Victoria was sure Hillary could feel her brace through her clothing, but Hillary said nothing.

"I wish I could go with you," Hillary whispered into her ear, "just to see what it's like—just to be there!" She let go and looked Victoria straight in the eye with an expression that conveyed such strength and caring that Victoria felt more heartened than she had in weeks.

"There's one more thing," Victoria said, knowing it was time to get everything out on the table. "Something else I haven't told you." She pulled up her blouse and showed Hillary the brace.

"I know," Hillary said. "Your brace. I've known for a while. What's it for?"

"How did you know?" Victoria said, surprised.

"I saw it—that night I slept over. I was looking for a roll of toilet paper under the sink."

"Oh," Victoria said, feeling foolish. "I should have told you earlier."

"It's okay," Hillary said. "I thought you'd get around to it eventually."

"It's for my scoliosis," Victoria said. "I won't have to wear it forever."

"Scoliosis," Hillary said knowingly. "A girl at my school has that. Her back hurts sometimes and she can't play sports."

Wouldn't you know, Victoria thought, *Hillary needs no explanation. She knows everything already!* "Yeah," she said, breathing with relief now that her last secret was out, "my back hurts sometimes, too, less since I've been wearing this thing. But it's a drag. It makes me feel like a freak."

Hillary gave her arm a squeeze. "You're very good at not complaining," she said, and there was real admiration in her voice.

Chapter Twelve

Exposed

December, 1882, Paris

I may not know what's going to happen, Victoria thought as she stepped into the painting and entered the Boits' apartment, *but at least Hillary believes I'm doing the right thing.*

Mary Louisa greeted her in the entry hall, which looked emptier than usual now that the huge painting was gone. As unperturbed as ever by Victoria's sudden appearance, Mary Louisa led the older girl quietly down the hall to her bedroom, where Julia waited. Instead of noisy lamentations, Julia buried her head against Victoria's stomach and put her arms around the older girl's waist, sighing with contentment at having Victoria back. Victoria was sure Julia could feel her brace, but, if so, she gave no sign.

"I told Isa you'd come," Julia said. "When we need you, you come."

Victoria hugged her back. "Yes, I've come." She smoothed the child's bangs away from her high, round forehead, then sat down in the rocking chair and turned Julia around so she could pull the chunky four-year-old up into her lap, hoping the buckles on her brace wouldn't poke the girl's soft flesh. "Tell me what day it is. It's very important."

"It's almost Christmas, silly," Julia said, snuggling back. "Don't you know that?"

Victoria felt some of the tension go out of her body. "That's good. Then we still have time."

Mary Louisa sat down on the hassock. "Time for what?"

"Time to stop Clifford Graham from taking this picture." She pulled the photograph of Jane from her jacket pocket and, removing it from its protective wrapping, held it over Julia's head to show to Mary Louisa. In an attempt to make it look like the original, she'd glued the snapshot to a thin, pasteboard mat she'd taken from the back of one of her father's childhood photographs.

Mary Louisa stared in astonishment at the photograph. "Mama and Papa would be so angry if they saw this." She took the picture from Victoria and studied it closely.

Refusing to be left out, Julia leaned forward to get a look at the picture. "That's Jane," she said disapprovingly, "and she's wearing her petticoat."

"When did he take it?" Mary Louisa asked Victoria.

"That's just it," Victoria said. "He hasn't taken it yet. At least, I don't think he has. The date on the back of this photograph said January, 1883."

Mary Louisa looked confused for a moment and then her face cleared. "So he's going to take it after the New Year," she said. "Do you think we can stop him?"

Julia shook her head. "He takes pictures of Jane and Florence whenever he wants."

"We have to get Papa to do it," said Mary Louisa. "We'll show him this picture and he'll throw Mr. Graham out on his ear." She looked quite pleased as she said this, but slowly her expression changed. "Victoria," she said, "didn't you tell us we can't do anything to change the future, even the bad things? Because that might change something else that's really good?"

Victoria sat up straighter, pulling Julia up with her. "You're right, Mary Louisa, I did say that. I've thought about this a lot for the last few days, and I think we have to do it, even so. If we don't, Clifford Graham is going to go on taking pictures of your sisters. What if he takes a picture like that one I showed you of Evelyn Hatch?"

"Who?" Julia asked, craning her neck to peer at Victoria. The older girls ignored her. She sank back against Victoria and put her thumb in her mouth.

Mary Louisa fixed her bright hazel eyes on Victoria. "We have to do it. For Florence and Jane and—" she said, then stopped. Sounding horrified, she asked, "Do you think there might be other girls?"

"I know there are," Victoria said.

Mary Louisa's brows came together in a bewildered scowl. "What should we do?" she asked.

"We need a plan," Victoria said. "You need to take this photograph to your parents right away. But I'm worried about what they'll do when they see it." There was a risk the adults would notice how different the modern photographic paper looked from the prints they were used to seeing. "It's only a copy of the original photograph. I did my best to make it look authentic, but what if they think there's something strange about it?"

Mary Louisa studied it again. "It looks fine to me," she said.

"What if they ask Jane?" Victoria asked. "Won't she tell them she never posed for this photograph?"

Mary Louisa shook her head. "It doesn't matter—they won't believe her. Jane always says it wasn't her. Whatever it is, she says someone else did it."

"And we need to figure out what you should tell them," Victoria said, "about where you got it."

"I'll say I found it in Jane and Florence's room—in Jane's drawer," Mary Louisa said. "I'll say I was looking for Julia's leggings."

"But will it work?" Victoria asked, unable to hide her fear.

"Don't worry. I'll convince them." Mary Louisa brandished the photograph aloft and moved toward the door. "I'm taking this to Father. Julia, you stay with Victoria."

Julia started to whimper. "What's going to happen, Isa?"

"Wait!" Victoria said. "Don't you want me to come with you? I could keep out of sight."

"No, you need to stay here with Julia," Mary Louisa said. She left the room, closing the door firmly behind her.

Julia began crying in earnest. Even if she didn't understand what was going on, she knew it was urgent.

Victoria patted the little girl's shoulder. "Everything will be all right," she said. "We hope your papa will send Mr. Graham away. You'd like that, wouldn't you? Maybe Jane and Florence will have more time to play with you, if he's not around."

Julia shook her head and sniffled. "They won't. They never do. Even before." She took a shuddering breath, then settled her head once more against Victoria's shoulder. "But, it's all right," she said dreamily, "because Violet's coming again. Violet will play with us."

"Violet?" Victoria asked, forgetting for a moment how she knew that name.

"Mr. Sargent's sister," said Julia happily, her tears forgotten. "She's twelve, like Jane, but she's *much* nicer than Jane."

"Mr. Sargent brought his sister to meet you, just like he promised!"

"Yes, and he's been coming, too. He gave me a drawing lesson today."

"That's wonderful, Julia." The little girl was growing heavy in her arms. Victoria started rocking back and forth and singing softly. "If I had a hammer, I'd hammer in the mo-o-rning . . ." By the time she got to the third verse, Julia's eyes had closed. Victoria carried her to her bed and pulled the quilt up over the sleeping child.

The fire in the bedroom grate was burning low, so, after some fumbling with the tongs, Victoria added more lumps of coal. December in Paris felt as cold as winter in Boston. The sky beyond the window was ominously dark, and Victoria guessed a storm was on the way.

Minutes passed. Victoria grew sick of staring at the china clock next to Mary Louisa's bed. She had just opened the door to peek out, when Mary Louisa came running down the hall.

"Shh," Victoria said. "Julia's sleeping."

Mary Louisa motioned for Victoria to follow her. The two of them scampered to the entry hall and into the cloakroom, leaving the door open a crack so they could see out. They sat side by side on the bench beneath the hanging scarves and jackets.

"I took the photograph to Father," Mary Louisa whispered. "He was in his study with Mr. Sargent. They asked me ever so many questions. Then he sent for Mother and told me to go back to my room. They're in the study now."

"What are they going to do?"

"I don't know," Mary Louisa whispered excitedly. "But Mr. Graham is expected any minute."

"What did they ask you?" Victoria said.

"They wanted to know where I got the photograph."

"What did you say?"

"I said Mr. Graham took it, just as we agreed—that I found it in Jane's drawer. I was sure they'd know I was telling a lie, but they were so busy staring at Jane's petticoat, they didn't look at me." Mary Louisa stopped to take a breath, then hurried on with her account. "Mr. Sargent recognized the vase of peacock feathers in the background as a prop from Mr. Graham's studio, so they believed me—at least the part about Mr. Graham taking it."

"They were convinced it was his photograph?" Victoria asked.

"Yes."

A knock sounded on the front door and the girls leaned forward to get a better view into the entry hall. The little maid came from the back of the apartment to answer the door, but Edward Boit strode from his study with Sargent and waved her away. The maid retreated toward the kitchen.

Victoria was struck by how alike Mary Louisa's father and Sargent appeared. Even though Mr. Boit was many years older, both men were tall and dignified, with the same steely look in their eye. They glanced at each other, then Mr. Boit pulled open the heavy outer door.

Clifford Graham stood there, weighed down by his usual assortment of camera equipment.

"Come in, damn you," Mr. Boit ordered. "I want to talk to you."

"Hello Ned, Sargent," Graham said, half-smiling, obviously taking his friend's odd greeting as a jest. He rubbed his hands together. "It's freezing out there. It might—"

Mr. Boit cut him off. "I'm surprised you have the temerity to show your face in this house after what you've done."

"I—done? What do you mean?" Graham lowered his heavy camera to the floor and, straightening up, peered at his host.

Mr. Boit held out the photograph of Jane. "This. This is what you've done. What do you have to say about it?"

The photographer took the picture and gazed at it. His face turned deathly pale above the dark collar of his coat. "What—what is this?" he stammered. "Who took this?"

"You did!" Mr. Boit roared. "Do you deny it?"

Sargent spoke quietly. "There's no point denying it, Clifford.

That's your studio. I recognized the props right away—that tall urn of yours with the peacock feathers is clearly visible."

"That is my studio," Graham said, shaking his head. "But you're wrong. I never took this picture."

"No one else has been photographing my girls," Mr. Boit said through clenched jaws. "It's your work all right—and damnable work, in my opinion." He looked at Graham with loathing, then continued, his voice low and full of threat. "You won't be taking any more pictures of children, not if I can help it. John and I know a lot of people and, God help us, we won't be silent on this matter."

"But you can't!" Graham's rigid shoulders suddenly sagged. "That kind of talk would ruin me!"

"You should have thought of that before you decided to take advantage of innocent young girls," Mr. Boit said, and began pacing furiously around the spacious entry hall.

"I never—" Graham began, but Mr. Boit wouldn't let him speak.

"You've betrayed my trust. I invited you to my house, allowed you to befriend my children, and now this. I won't have it." Mr. Boit grabbed the photographer roughly by the arm and shoved him toward the front door. The photograph fell from Graham's hand and, without noticing, Mr. Boit kicked it aside. It skidded across the smooth parquet floor and lodged under a corner of the carpet. "I want you to leave this instant and never come back."

"There must be some mistake!" Graham cried.

"The only mistake was letting you through that door in the first place," Mr. Boit shouted.

Graham held his ground.

"You'd better leave," Sargent told the photographer. "You're no longer welcome here."

Without further protest, Graham turned and walked out. Mr. Boit banged the door shut behind him, then muttered to

Sargent, "Mrs. Boit and I must speak to Jane immediately." He strode toward the study, calling to his wife.

Mrs. Boit emerged, her face white with strain. She murmured something to Sargent that the two girls in the cloakroom couldn't hear, then hurried after her husband. Sargent rubbed his forehead as if feeling the start of a headache, then retreated to the study, shutting the door behind him.

Mary Louisa and Victoria looked at one another and then out into the empty hall. Graham's camera, the one he had set down when he came in, was still sitting on the floor where he'd left it. The incriminating photograph lay nearby.

"We shouldn't leave it there," Victoria said, meaning the photograph. "They'll be sure to come back for it and if anyone examines it too closely, they might get suspicious."

"I'll get it," Mary Louisa said. She darted out of the cloakroom and was just picking up the photograph, when there was another knock on the door. When she opened it, Clifford Graham was standing on the threshold.

"I left my camera," he said, avoiding Mary Louisa's eyes. "I need to get my camera." His voice trailed off. He waited, his body drooping, his handsome face rubbery with disbelief.

"It's here," Mary Louisa said. She stood aside to let Graham step into the room to retrieve it, holding the photograph tightly to her chest with both hands.

As Clifford Graham stepped forward into the room, Mary Louisa glanced toward the cloakroom, where Victoria crouched in the doorway. Graham followed the younger girl's gaze straight to her hiding place. Feeling a chill of horror, Victoria stepped back, but she wasn't quick enough. She was sure Graham had seen her and waited for the familiar darkness to whip her away, back to her own time.

But nothing happened. If Graham saw her, it was as though he saw right through her.

"Please get your camera and go," Mary Louisa said sternly. Victoria could hear some of Mr. Boit's forcefulness in her tone.

The photographer didn't move to pick up his camera, but stood transfixed, his eyes now searching Mary Louisa's face. "I never took that photograph," he said. "You can ask Jane."

"She'll deny it," Mary Louisa said, "but I'm sure my parents won't believe her. They've seen the photograph."

"Who did take it?" Graham asked. "It wasn't me."

"But," Mary Louisa whispered, "you would have if we let you." She glanced again toward Victoria's hiding place, unable to suppress a look of triumph.

Graham dropped his gaze from Mary Louisa's face and, turning, strode across the entry hall to the cloakroom, where he flung open the door.

"Come out!" he demanded. "Who's hiding in there?" He reached around the door and grabbed Victoria's arm, dragging her into the room. As he stared at her, a look of recognition came over his features. "I've seen you before," he said. "I never forget a face."

"No," Victoria gasped. "I never—"

Graham didn't let her finish. "I don't know where, but I know I've seen you." His eyes narrowed and his already red face darkened. "What are you two up to? Have you been spying on me?" He shook Victoria's arm roughly and she cried out in pain.

"Stop it," Mary Louisa yelled, launching herself like a small bulldog at Clifford Graham's leg. "Let her go or I'll start screaming and my father will come and thrash you with his cane."

At the mention of Mr. Boit, Graham seemed to come to his senses. He released Victoria's arm, but he wasn't ready to leave.

"Why are you doing this?" he demanded. "This will destroy me!"

"Yes," said Victoria, finding her voice. "We know. We know

what you've been doing. You've been stealing Julia's things and—and trying to get her to pose for you." She could tell by the photographer's suddenly widened eyes that her words had hit home. "And poor Jane—you made her fall in love with you so you could do whatever you want with her. But it's going to stop. All of it. We're going to stop you!"

Clifford Graham's expression was stubbornly evasive. "You don't know what you're talking about," he said, but his voice lacked conviction. He stared about him, as though he didn't know where he was.

Victoria stood with her arms folded across her chest, not giving an inch.

Suddenly, with a furtive duck of the head, Clifford Graham grabbed his camera from the floor and rushed out the door without saying another word.

Mary Louisa, looking dazed, sat on the floor where she had landed after her furious attempt to tackle Clifford Graham. She spied the incriminating photograph lying nearby and crawled across the carpet to pick it up. Victoria held out her hand.

Mary Louisa stood up and handed her the photograph. "What are you going to do with it?" she asked.

"I'm going to throw it away," Victoria said. "No one wants to look at this anymore." She folded the photograph and, on impulse, strode to the nearest vase and, with one flick of her wrist, tossed it in.

Mary Louisa gasped. "Not in the vase!"

"Why not?" asked Victoria.

"Papa will be furious."

"He'll never know."

"But, he'll come looking for the photograph when he realizes he doesn't have it. He'll want to show it to Jane."

Victoria thought about this. "Tell him Graham took it away with him when he came back to get his camera." Mary Louisa looked unsure, but Victoria took her by the hand and said, "Let's leave before anyone sees us."

The two of them raced back down the hall to the girls' bedroom. Once inside, they stood with their backs to the door to catch their breath. Julia was still asleep.

"Do you feel sorry for Mr. Graham?" Mary Louisa whispered.

"No!" Victoria said, a rush of anger making her face grow hot.

"But this will end his career," Mary Louisa said.

"I'm glad!" Victoria answered. "I don't feel sorry for him for a minute. What he did was unforgivable." She thought of her mother's anguish, of Aunt Margaret and of the girl in the red scarf. She hoped Graham would never become the famous art photographer he dreamed of being, but she knew he would never stop taking pictures of little girls.

Julia moaned and turned over, rubbing her eyes. "Is he gone?" she asked before she was fully awake.

"Yes!" said Mary Louisa and Victoria in unison.

"Good," she said and smiled.

Victoria pulled back the covers and, scooting Julia down, climbed into her bed, pulling Mary Louisa in under the quilt beside them.

"We did it," Mary Louisa exulted. "We got rid of him!"

"Yes," Victoria agreed. "I think my job here is done."

"But, you'll come again, won't you?" Mary Louisa asked. "After today, I mean?"

Victoria had been wondering about this herself. "I don't know," she said. "If my reason for being here was to stop Clifford Graham, then I may not be *able* to come back." What she meant was the painting might not let her back in.

"But why?" Julia cried, clinging to her. "Why won't you come again? You're our friend! You need to come back."

Victoria felt her throat tighten with emotion, but kept her

voice calm. "I need to live in my own time," she said, gently stroking Julia's hair. "Besides you have a new friend—Violet, Mr. Sargent's sister. You told me she's coming to see you again soon."

"That's right, Julia," Mary Louisa chimed in, ready to help forestall another fit of tears. "She said she'll come back tomorrow and bring her little dog. You told her you wanted to meet her dog."

Victoria couldn't help feeling jealous. She wished she was the one coming tomorrow, not Violet.

Julia looked up, her face sad, but resigned. She moved closer to Victoria and put one chubby arm over her chest. No one said anything for a time and Victoria tried to capture the moment in her mind—it was the closest thing to having sisters she'd ever known.

Julia lifted her head and looked curiously at Victoria. "What's that?" she asked, pointing to the top edge of the brace that was poking out of the neckline of Victoria's blouse. "Is it your corset?"

Victoria couldn't help laughing. "No, it's not a corset."

Julia looked unconvinced. "Mama wears a corset when she goes to dinner parties."

"It's not a corset," Victoria repeated, still laughing.

"What is it?" Julia persisted.

"It's a brace for my back," Victoria told her. "I have a curve in my spine, and the brace is helping to make it straight."

"Can I see it?" Julia asked.

"You mean the brace?" Victoria said. "Or the curve in my spine?"

"The brace," Julia said.

Victoria pulled aside her jacket and lifted her blouse to expose the brace with all its straps and fastenings.

"Does it hurt?" Mary Louisa asked. "It looks like it's squeezing your skin."

"The brace keeps my back from hurting," Victoria said, "but it does squeeze. And it makes me hot and itchy sometimes."

"When I was a baby, I had to wear hard shoes to keep my feet from turning out," Mary Louisa said. "Is it like that?"

"Just like that," Victoria said, smiling.

As she shifted her body to get more comfortable, Victoria felt a lump in her jacket pocket, the same light jacket she'd been wearing on her last visit to the Gardner Museum with Hillary. She pulled it out and saw that it was the small Sargent calendar she'd bought at the gift shop that day and forgotten all about. On the front was Sargent's painting of the Boit girls.

"Look, Julia," she said, "I brought you a present." She handed it to the little girl.

"It's us," Julia said. "We're on the cover!"

"See, you're famous." Victoria opened the calendar and read aloud. *"The Daughters of Edward Darley Boit.* Everyone knows this painting. It's one of Sargent's most famous pictures, and whenever people visit the Museum of Fine Arts in Boston, they want to see it." She tapped Julia's forehead with a finger. "Can you guess what everyone likes best about it?"

"What?" Julia asked, her eyes round with wonder.

"You—with your bangs and your cheeks and your big blue eyes."

"But, what about Mary Louisa?" Julia asked. "Do they like her curls?"

"Of course they like Mary Louisa's curls. Everybody likes Mary Louisa's curls." Victoria tickled Julia's tummy and she laughed.

"May I look?" Mary Louisa asked, taking the little calendar from Julia's hand. She turned the pages until she came to the portrait of Madame X. "Who's this?" she asked.

"It's the portrait of Amelie Gautreau," Victoria said, "the woman that Sargent is about to begin painting. It's the portrait

I told you about—the one that causes Sargent so much trouble." The three girls studied the picture together. "In this version the strap is painted up on her shoulder, but the one he'll take to the Paris Salon in a year has the strap falling down."

Mary Louisa looked at Victoria, her eyes full of alarm. "But, that's just like the photograph of Jane."

Victoria took the calendar from her and stared at the page. She remembered that in those first stunned moments after finding Jane's photograph at the Gardner it made her think of *Madame X*. But she hadn't thought of it since. After discovering the photograph of Jane, all she'd thought about was finding a way to warn the Boits. *Madame X* had gone completely out of her head.

"It must have been Clifford Graham's photograph that made him think of it," she said slowly.

"Why? Why would he do that?" Mary Louisa cried.

"I don't know," Victoria said, her faith in Sargent suddenly shaken. "Maybe he didn't realize what he was doing, maybe he was in a hurry."

Her mind searched for possible reasons. She'd read about how much Sargent had struggled with the portrait of Amelie Gautreau. As she stared at the picture in the calendar, she could see it in her mind's eye—could see Sargent painting Amelie over and over in different poses and costumes. Nothing satisfied him until he dressed her in a long, black skirt and a low-cut bodice held up by thin jeweled straps, her red hair piled high on her head.

Victoria studied Amelie's pose. She'd pulled her shoulders back and turned her head sharply to the left so that her profile was on display. She clutched her skirt in her left hand, while her right arm, oddly twisted, gripped the edge of a side table. With the right shoulder slightly lower than the left, it looked as though the strap could have slipped out of place on its own.

Whether it happened by accident or by Sargent's direction, the painter must have seen in an instant how perfect it was. Victoria could imagine him painting faster and faster, this detail just what he needed. Had he hesitated when he thought about the reaction of Jane's parents when they saw what he'd done? Or did he not think about Jane at all? Maybe the regret came later—in the moment, he only knew he'd created a masterpiece.

Victoria tried to think of what she could say to comfort Mary Louisa, who had turned her face to the wall and was clutching the bedcovers tightly to her chest. Oblivious to her sister's change of mood, Julia took the calendar back from Victoria, flipping to the cover to study her own likeness.

"Don't worry, Isa," Victoria said, using Mary Louisa's nickname for the first time. "Sargent repaints it as soon as he can. There's no drooping strap in the portrait that hangs in the museum in New York. And no one will ever know where he got the idea. Remember, we've stopped Jane's photograph from being taken."

"But *I* know," Mary Louisa said, sounding heartbroken, "and my parents know. I wish I'd never seen that photograph!"

"Me too," said Julia, finally registering her sister's distress. "It was stupid."

"You're right," Victoria said. "It *was* stupid—and wrong! But—as much as I hate to say this, considering it was Clifford Graham who took it—from an artistic point of view, it was a good photograph. I mean, it was perfectly composed. A friend of mine, an artist, says Sargent needed that fallen strap to balance the lines of his composition."

"That's no excuse," Mary Louisa said stubbornly.

"I know. But, remember, Sargent's portraits can be disturbing. Think of how he painted Jane and Florence."

"But he had to paint them like that," Mary Louisa said. "It's what he saw."

Precisely, Victoria thought. Sargent saw that the older Boit girls were troubled and he painted their secret pain by cloaking them in shadow. That mystery was what had drawn Victoria to the painting in the first place—that, and Mary Louisa's face, a face from her dreams.

Victoria believed that Sargent was also painting what he saw when he painted Madame Gautreau with her strap falling down. The woman was elegant, to be sure, but she was also vain and irritating and careless. Victoria remembered her own mother's word, "sordid" when describing *Madame X*. Madame Gautreau was sordid in some of the same ways as Clifford Graham. They both took advantage of people for their own selfish ends. Maybe, Victoria thought, when Mary Louisa is older, she might come to see this for herself—someday when Jane's photograph no longer haunts her and her misgivings about Sargent are replaced with kinder thoughts.

"Here," Victoria said, reaching for the calendar. "Let me write something in it." She rummaged in the breast pocket of her jacket and found the ballpoint pen she always carried there.

Carefully, she wrote inside the front cover: "To my friends Julia and Mary Louisa. I will never forget you. Love, Victoria." She wished she could think of something more original, but it was all that came to mind. If only she'd thought to bring a photograph of herself to give them. She handed the calendar back to Julia.

"Before you go," Mary Louisa said, rousing herself from her dark mood, "tell us something about Boston—the Boston you know. In the year—" she referred to the front of the calendar, "1963. I've been wanting to ask you."

"Well," Victoria said, "we have lots of things you've probably never heard of like cars and airplanes and televisions."

"What's a television?" Julia said.

Victoria did her best to explain some of the more astonishing twentieth century inventions, but decided not to mention space travel or the atom bomb. She told the girls about the vaccines and medicines that had helped wipe out most of the major childhood diseases. "Babies have a much better chance of surviving," she said, "and mothers, too, because doctors have learned how to take care of them when they get pregnant and give birth."

Julia's eyes filled with tears when she heard this. "You mean the new medicine could have saved baby Elliot?" she said.

"It's possible," Victoria said. "It's kind of a miracle how many things can be cured with antibiotics."

"It sounds like everything is better in your time," Mary Louisa said wistfully.

"Not everything," Victoria said. "Most men still think women are only good for doing housework and raising children."

"I'm going to be an artist," Julia said. "A real artist like Mr. Sargent."

Mary Louisa looked dubious. "Women almost never get to be artists."

"But if anyone can do it," Victoria said, giving Julia's arm an encouraging squeeze, "it will be you, Julia." She, of course, knew that Julia's dream would come true. Both girls would lead unconventional lives. Their father would never "give them away" in marriage, but would continue to support them so that they could pursue their own hopes and dreams as independent women.

"What else isn't better than now?" Mary Louisa asked.

"Well, Black people are still treated horribly," Victoria said.

"You mean the people from Africa, the slaves?" Mary Louisa said. "I thought the Civil War freed the slaves."

Victoria was pleased to hear Mary Louisa knew at least this much about American history. "That's true. But being set free didn't solve the problem. Many people still think Negroes are inferior." She told them about Martin Luther King Jr. and what he hoped to accomplish with his civil rights movement.

Julia was getting squirmy. "I wish we had a present for you," she said, fingering the little calendar.

"So you'll remember us," added Mary Louisa.

"I have the painting, don't forget. I can go to the museum in Boston and visit you any day I want."

Both girls smiled. It was getting late. By silent agreement, the three of them got out of bed and stood to give each other hugs.

"Don't go," Julia said, her eyes filling with tears.

"Thank you for everything," said Mary Louisa, struggling to keep her face composed.

"I'll miss you—so much!" Victoria answered, hearing the tears in her own voice. "Goodbye."

She wasn't sure what would happen next. She'd never had control over her own return—it had always simply happened to her—and it might not happen now. But she closed her eyes and, without knowing quite how, slipped back into her own time.

When she opened her eyes, she was in the museum, standing before the painting. Mary Louisa was there, and Julia. And, though they weren't smiling, they appeared, for the moment, content. She wished she could say the same for Jane, but if anything, she looked slightly more bewildered than ever. Victoria knew that Jane's actual mental state would soon become apparent to everyone, not just Sargent. She supposed that by exposing Clifford Graham, she had spared Jane some humiliation, but she wondered if any of it would have even registered in Jane's scrambled brain. *Hers was a sad fate*, Victoria thought, *and nothing I did could change it.*

Chapter Thirteen

Disruptions

June/July, 1963, Boston

When Victoria and her mother got home from the museum, Victoria went straight to her room and got into bed, the better to savor her last moments spent under the quilt with Mary Louisa and Julia. She knew she was going to miss them terribly. Though she'd held back the tears when she was with them, she cried freely now and didn't know if she'd ever be able to stop.

It wasn't just leaving the Boit girls—it was everything: all the stress and worry of the last weeks, the on-again, off-again friendship with Hillary, the excitement and eventual disappointment of her fledgling attraction to James, the struggles with her mother—all of it coming down on her in one thunderous deluge.

To top it all off, when she went into the bathroom an hour later, she noticed blood on her underwear. Her period had started at last. She'd imagined feeling elated, but instead she felt only heaviness and dread. Her childhood was over, she realized, and today of all days she didn't feel ready for the next stage.

She found the bulky pads her mother had bought for her and

managed to attach one to the sanitary belt without too much difficulty. Walking, however, was a different matter. It felt like she had a folded *New York Times* between her legs. She waddled back to bed, a fresh wash of tears seeping down her face.

When her mother knocked on her door a couple of hours later, Victoria had recovered somewhat, but was still feeling very tender. She lay on her stomach, her face buried in a book so her mother wouldn't see her puffy eyes and reddened cheeks.

"Dinner's ready, dear," her mother said. She crossed the room and kissed Victoria lightly on top of her head. Surprised by this unexpected display of affection, Victoria almost started crying again. She wanted to tell her mother about getting her period but couldn't form the words.

Victoria splashed water on her face, then headed downstairs. She was stopped in her tracks by a photograph she'd never seen before that was hanging in the hall outside the dining room. It had to be one of her father's pictures, blown up to gallery size and showing Victoria's mother in much the same pose as in the Clifford Graham photograph. But in this picture she looked completely different—older, of course, but also smiling and relaxed.

Just then, she heard a soft melody coming from the dining room. It was her mother singing, "Summertime, when the living is easy," in a slow, almost sultry voice that Victoria hardly recognized. She'd never heard her mother sing before and was amazed to discover she had a lovely voice. Victoria turned to her father, who had just arrived home from a Saturday golf game, to see if he was having a similar reaction. He smiled at his wife as the two of them entered the dining room together, but appeared unsurprised. Puzzled, Victoria studied her mother's face during dinner. The lines of strain Victoria had seen there the last few days were gone.

Victoria couldn't muster much appetite and retreated to her

bedroom right after the meal. Besides missing the Boit girls and feeling achy and tired because of her period, she couldn't stop fretting about Sargent and his decision to copy Jane's drooping strap in his portrait of Amelie Gautreau. It wasn't like Sargent to be so insensitive. She worried that Mary Louisa would never forgive him.

She got out her Sargent biography and reread the description of the disastrous day at the Paris Salon, when *Madame X* first went on display. She read until she fell asleep, the book still open on her chest, the light on.

Victoria woke up late the next morning. Her abdomen felt puffy and sore, and it was all she could do to drag herself out of bed. She decided to skip putting on her brace that morning and not tell her mom.

"You're looking down in the dumps," her mother said, when she made it to breakfast. "Why don't you invite Hillary over today?"

It seemed like a good idea since Hillary would be dying to hear what had happened in Paris. Victoria called her right away.

Hillary said she'd be over as soon as her dad could give her a ride.

Victoria's mother was still at the breakfast table reading the Sunday paper when Victoria returned to the dining room. "All good?" she asked. Victoria nodded, then accepted Rose's offer of a cup of cocoa and sat down. Her father was most likely already at work on his legal papers in his study, but her mother didn't seem as irritated about this as she usually did on a Sunday morning.

"I'm going to start painting again," her mother said, looking pleased. "I bought six canvases and a new set of oil paints."

"That's great, Mom," Victoria said, with as much enthusiasm as she could muster. She'd always admired the paintings her mother had done in college.

"Maybe I can get something ready for the Summer Arts Festival, if I work really hard," her mother said, sounding excited by the prospect. Victoria raised her mug of cocoa to take a sip, then set it down, wincing as a cramp seized her belly. "What's wrong, Victoria?" her mother asked. "Is your back bothering you?"

"I got my period yesterday," Victoria said, with a little quaver in her voice.

"But, that's wonderful, dear," her mom said. She looked happy, but concerned. "I was just about your age when it happened to me. Later than my friends by a mile, but my sisters were the same." She reached across the table and took her daughter's hand. "Do you have all your supplies? Can I get you anything?"

"No, I'm all set."

"How are you feeling?"

"A few cramps. Nothing bad."

"Good," her mother said, picking up her plate and standing. "But, take it easy today. It's a big day!" She came around the table to give Victoria a hug. "And don't look so glum. You'll feel better soon," she said, then headed for the kitchen

Victoria stayed where she was, too moved by her mother's kindness to get up right away. Her abdomen still hurt, but she felt much better than she had moments ago. She heard her father come into the kitchen and a low murmur of voices. Then he stuck his head around the door of the dining room and smiled broadly at her.

"I hear you're to be congratulated," he said.

Victoria ducked her head in embarrassment. Her mother must have told him what had happened.

"You probably think it's none of my business," her father went on, "but as your mother says, it's a rite of passage and needs to be celebrated."

Victoria nodded, unable to look at him.

"That's all," her dad said and turned to go.

"Thanks, Dad," Victoria called, just loud enough for him to hear.

When Hillary got there, the two girls went up to Victoria's room.

"Tell me everything!" Hillary said. She kicked off her shoes and sank onto the bed.

Victoria sat carefully beside her, feeling self-conscious about the lumpy pad in her underwear. As she related the story, from her arrival in the entry hall to her confrontation with Clifford Graham to showing Mary Louisa and Julia the calendar and saying goodbye to them for what she believed was the last time, Hillary's eyes never left her face.

"You must have been terrified," Hillary said, when Victoria finished, "not knowing if the Boits would believe Mary Louisa's story."

"I was," Victoria said, "when we were waiting for Graham to show up, I was so scared I thought I might pass out."

"I would have lost it for sure. " Hillary's brow wrinkled. "But it's weird. Do you think Mary Louisa's right? That Sargent put the fallen strap into his painting of *Madame X* because of seeing Jane's photograph?"

"Very weird," Victoria said, "Why would he do that?"

"Maybe it was unconscious," Hillary said, but she sounded dubious.

"Maybe," Victoria said. "Wait! I've got to show you what I found in this book." She opened the Sargent biography she'd been reading and pointed out the passage that had so interested her the night before.

A letter by Sargent's good friend, Ralph Curtis, was quoted in the text, describing his visit to the Paris Salon on opening day in 1884.

    Walked up the Champs-Elysées, chestnuts
    in full flower and a dense mob of "tout

Paris" in pretty clothes, gesticulating
and laughing, slowly going into the Ark of
Art. In 15 minutes I saw no end of acquain-
tances and strangers and heard everybody
say, "Ou est le portrait Gautreau?"

Too impatient to let Hillary continue reading, Victoria jumped in to summarize. "He goes on to say he was disappointed when Sargent met him and took him to see *Madame X*, writing that he thought the woman looked 'decomposed.' Curtis went home with Sargent that day, since Sargent was really upset after seeing the crowd's reaction to his portrait. According to Curtis, Sargent left—get this—to visit the Boits, returning later to find Madame Gautreau and her mother at his house 'bathed in tears' and begging Sargent to remove the portrait from the exhibition. Sargent said he couldn't, it was against the rules. He defended himself by saying he'd painted Amelie exactly as she appeared to him." Victoria paused to take a breath. "So, why did he go see the Boits in the middle of all that?"

"To apologize?" Hillary mused. "Even if Mr. and Mrs. Boit hadn't seen the painting yet, they would hear about it and make the connection to Jane's photograph."

"What do you think he said to them?" Victoria asked.

"Maybe he told them he would repaint the strap," Hillary guessed, "as soon as he could get the portrait back from the Salon—which he did."

"But, was that enough?" Victoria said.

"Well, they did remain friends for many years after that," Hillary countered. "Maybe the Boits were mad for a while and then got over it."

"That makes sense," Victoria agreed. "Mr. and Mrs. Boit forgave him—and I'm sure Mary Louisa did, too." She sighed. "I wish I could ask her. Or Julia." She paused, deep in thought.

"I keep thinking Julia's still alive. I never found a death date for her, but if she was four in 1882, she'd be eighty-one by now."

"What would you do if you found out she was still alive?" Hillary said. "Write her a letter?"

"I wish it was that easy," Victoria said. "I don't begin to know how to find her. I can't very well hire a private detective to go to Paris and track her down."

"Maybe she's not even living in Paris anymore," Hillary said. "And, if she's still alive, she might be senile."

"I know," Victoria said. "It's maddening not knowing what became of her." She shrugged.

"Does the book say anything about what happened to *Madame X* after the Paris Salon?" Hillary asked.

"Yeah," Victoria said, putting aside her thoughts about Julia. "After the Salon, Sargent repainted the strap, then kept the painting hidden away in his studio for years and years, exhibiting it only rarely. He sold it to the Metropolitan Museum of Art in 1916, a few months after Amelie Gautreau died."

"When did the Boit parents die?" Hillary asked. "Do you remember?"

"I'm not sure," Victoria said. "I remember reading that Mrs. Boit died when Mary Louisa was just twenty, but Mr. Boit lived a long time after that, even remarried and had more kids." She consulted the index of her book and turned to the page listed for "Edward Darley Boit, death of."

"It says 1915," Victoria said, reading from the text. "The same year as Amelie!"

"Wait a minute," Hillary said, sitting up. "That means Sargent waited to sell the painting till both of them were gone. He really did feel bad about the strap thing!"

"You're right," said Victoria slowly. "What other reason would he have to wait so long?"

"The picture in the Met is the repainted version, but no one who knows anything about the painting will ever forget that fallen strap," Hillary insisted.

"So, if all the people who would hate having it on permanent display were dead—" Victoria said.

"He'd have no reason not to sell," Hillary concluded. "Wait, was Jane still alive?"

"Yes, but she's described as being mentally ill for most of her life. I don't think she would have objected." Victoria said. "Besides," she added, remembering, "she never saw the photograph!"

"That's right," Hillary said. "It never got taken!"

"The only other Boits who saw the photograph, besides the parents, were Mary Louisa and Julia. Maybe Sargent figured they were both too young to remember anything about it."

"I doubt that," Victoria said. "Mary Louisa would remember for sure. But I bet she was ready to put it behind her after so many years."

"Don't forget you and me," Hillary said. "We saw Jane's photograph."

"Yeah," Victoria said, laughing, "but we weren't even born!" She shook her head at the strangeness of it all. If Hillary hadn't believed her, she might not believe it herself. "Sargent sold all his paintings as soon as he could," Victoria continued, still turning it over in her mind. "He needed the money. So why else would he keep one that was worth so much? He said—wait, let me find it." She turned a page in the book and read aloud. "At the time of the sale to the Met, Sargent was quoted as saying, 'I suppose it is the best thing I have done.'"

"It *is* the best thing he ever painted," Hillary said.

"He saw something in Amelie—what? Vanity? Selfishness? A desperate need to be admired? I still think the fallen strap was his way to paint what he saw."

"I agree," said Hillary, "even if it did hurt her social standing, it was who she was. And, maybe that was mean, maybe

Sargent was a flawed human being, but after all, none of us are perfect."

"Speaking of flawed human beings," Victoria said, suddenly mortified. "I forgot to ask you about James! I'm sorry! Did you ever talk to him?"

"I did talk to him," Hillary said, looking relieved to be asked. "It was hard—he was angry at first. Really angry. He accused me of snooping. But later, I think he was glad to have someone to talk to. No one knows besides me—except Alec, of course. James said he's felt really alone."

Victoria thanked her lucky stars that she'd never confessed to Hillary about having a crush on James. It made the conversation they were having now so much easier.

"What's he going to do?" Victoria asked, rolling gingerly onto her stomach on the bed.

"Nothing, for now. When he gets to college, he figures he'll have time to think things over and decide how to tell the family."

"What will your parents say?"

"They'll be upset," Hillary said. "They're good Catholics and the Church considers homosexuality a sin, at least if you act on it. Just lusting after someone of the same sex is not so bad. But if you do anything about it, look out!"

"So do your parents do everything the Church tells them to do?" Victoria said.

"No!" Hillary retorted. "I know for a fact that my mother uses birth control—I mean, now she does—not when she was having all us kids. She even showed me her diaphragm."

"So, maybe they'll come around eventually?"

Hillary shrugged uncomfortably. "It's tricky. They've pinned so many hopes on James. He was an altar boy when he was younger, and they dreamed he'd become a priest. But homosexuals can't even be Catholic anymore."

"They'll kick him out of the church?" Victoria said, unable to keep the outrage out of her voice.

"First the priests will try to talk him out of liking boys."

"You're kidding."

"I'm not. And if he can't change he won't be able to be a Catholic."

Victoria stared at her friend. "That's terrible."

Hillary nodded. "James is devastated. Being Catholic is a huge part his life." Hillary fell silent and her shoulders slumped.

Victoria waited, not sure what to say.

Finally, Hillary gave herself a little shake and continued. "I'm pretty sure if my parents think that being with a guy is the only way James can be happy, they'll come around. It'll take time, but they love him; they want him to be happy." Hillary was trying to sound positive, but Victoria could tell by the way her hands had clenched into fists that she was far from certain.

"Does James agree?" Victoria asked.

"He's not sure. What he's really afraid of is that our parents will think it's just a phase or something."

"But, he's sure?"

"He says he's known for as long as he can remember."

A wicked cramp took Victoria's breath away and a little groan escaped her lips.

"Are you okay?" Hillary asked, looking concerned. "Is it your back?"

Victoria clutched her middle. "I just started my period yesterday," she said, giving Hillary a sheepish look. "It hurts!"

"I know," Hillary said. "I got mine last month."

"You never said!"

"I wanted to," Hillary said, raising her eyebrows and looking pointedly at her friend, "but—"

"Oh, right," Victoria said and shrugged apologetically. "I was—otherwise occupied."

"But, you're here now," Hillary said. "I hope for good."

It wasn't easy for Victoria to put aside her preoccupation with the Boits. When she was alone, especially falling asleep at night, she cried when she realized that her brief experience of having little sisters was over for good. Did they miss her as much as she missed them? Or had they forgotten her the minute Violet arrived? Over the next couple of weeks, her sadness drove her to stand in front of their portrait every chance she got. Each time she waited to see if the picture would open up to her, but it never did.

One day, the Black guard came to stand beside her. "You really love this painting, don't you?" he asked.

Victoria glanced at him. "I do," she said simply. "The girls . . ." Her voice trailed away.

"I love it, too," said the guard. "Not sure why."

They stood quietly together staring at the painting. Remembering her manners, Victoria turned to face the man. "I'm Victoria," she said.

"And I'm Clarence," he said, giving her his hand to shake. "It's a pleasure to know you."

From then on, Clarence, when he was on duty, would often come to stand with her in front of the painting. This made her feel better for a time, but beyond that, Hillary was her only comfort. Hillary never seemed to get sick of hearing Victoria relive the events of that last day. In comparison to her adventures in Paris, Victoria's everyday life felt dull.

On their way out of the classroom, after their last art class, Victoria told Hillary, as she always did, that she wanted to visit the Boit girls' portrait before she went home.

Hillary put a restraining hand on her arm. "Don't," she said. "You need to stop."

"What do you mean?"

"I mean you've got to move on," Hillary said, using an unusually stern voice. "You're never going to see the Boits again."

"So?" Victoria said. "Does that mean I have to stop visiting their portrait as well?" She was confused; Hillary had been so understanding up until now.

Hillary crossed her arms over her chest. "It makes you depressed," she said. "You should feel happy you were able to help them, but instead you just mope around all the time."

"I am happy," Victoria said, but she could hear the flatness in her tone. "I can't explain it. I feel—I don't know—let down." Tears welled in her eyes and she shook her head in frustration. What she wasn't telling Hillary was about the strong pang of jealousy she felt whenever she thought of Sargent's sister Violet taking her place. It made her ashamed. Why would she begrudge the Boit girls a friend when they obviously needed one? "I miss Mary Louisa and Julia—" she said miserably. "I feel like they've deserted me."

"Good grief—they didn't desert you!" Hillary said, flinging out her arms. "You're the one who left. Remember what you told them—you have to live in your own time." Hillary's face was turning red. She looked angrier than Victoria had ever seen her. "You need to stop feeling sorry for yourself!"

Victoria felt attacked. "It takes getting used to," she said defensively. She hesitated, then tried again. "Walking into a painting was the best thing that ever happened to me. I can't just pretend it didn't happen."

Hillary wouldn't look at her.

"Mary Louisa and Julia felt like my sisters—like they belonged to me and I belonged to them!" Victoria said. "You *have* sisters. I don't." Even to herself she sounded pathetic.

Hillary looked up at that, but her stubborn expression barely softened. "But you have me!" she said. "The Boits are part of the past. *I'm* part of now."

Looking at her friend's closed expression, Victoria felt something give way inside her chest. She understood that Hillary was feeling jealous, too. She was experiencing the same kind of jealousy toward Mary Louisa and Julia that Victoria felt toward Violet.

"Oh, Hillary, you've been such a good friend," Victoria said, feeling like an idiot. She reached out timidly and touched her friend's arm. "I don't know what I would have done without you."

"Okay, okay," Hillary said.

"Wait, let me finish," Victoria said. "I need to start being a good friend back."

"That," Hillary said blushing, but forcing out a grudging smile, "would be grand."

"I mean it," Victoria said, giving Hillary's arm a little squeeze.

"All right then," Hillary said, laying on a thick Irish accent in her embarrassment. "This is me, going now."

Victoria watched Hillary walk away, her heavy braid making its usual rhythmic swing with each step. She decided to heed Hillary's advice and *not* visit the painting. But since she had some time to kill before meeting her mother, she decided to walk the two short blocks to the Gardner on her own. Hillary was right—she needed to shake the Boits' hold on her, but she wanted to see Jane's photograph one more time. She wasn't sure it would help, but perhaps seeing the photograph one last time would allow her to put the whole business behind her once and for all.

When Victoria arrived, she asked permission at the front desk to go up to the fourth floor to visit Martha. Martha came down to meet her and took her up. "Help yourself," she said, showing Victoria into the archives, then excusing herself to return to the adjoining office. Victoria went straight to the drawer of Victorian photographs and flipped to the folder where she'd found the original photograph of Jane in its hiding place behind the larger print.

There was nothing there.

"Martha," Victoria called, "have any of the photographs been removed?"

"No," Martha said. "No one has been near those photographs since you were here last."

Victoria looked feverishly through the rest of the folder, then in the folders that came before and after it in the file drawer. The photograph was nowhere to be found. After calling a quick goodbye and thanks to Martha, Victoria rushed back to the Museum of Fine Arts to meet her mother, her mind spinning.

As soon as she got home, Victoria ran upstairs and rummaged in her desk drawer for the snapshots that she'd taken of Clifford Graham's photograph of Jane.

She could hardly believe her eyes. They too had disappeared. The envelope containing the prints and negatives was there, but both the photographs and the negatives were blank. Victoria stared at their fogged surfaces and felt a strange disorientation. Next, she looked for the Clifford Graham photograph of her mother at age fourteen, but search as she might, it was missing as well.

What is going on? Victoria wondered. Had she imagined the whole thing after all? With the photographs gone, she had no proof. She had only Hillary as witness that the photograph of Jane had existed—and her mother! She ran downstairs and found her mother watering plants. "Mom, do you remember the photograph I showed you of the girl in the slip?"

"Of course I do," her mother said, pinching a yellow leaf off a begonia. "That sad picture of the girl with the drooping strap?"

Relief flooded Victoria. "Yes, that one," she said.

"Why do you ask?" said her mother, looking up.

Victoria stared at her mother. Her reaction was bewildering. Was this the same woman who had broken down in her room a mere three weeks ago? If so, her reaction was bewildering. "No reason," she said hesitantly. "And the picture of you, when you were fourteen—from the attic?"

Her mother looked blank. "I don't. Maybe you should show it to me again."

"Are you sure?" Victoria said.

"Yes, I'm sure," said her mother laughing. "I would remember a picture of me as a teenager!" She turned back to her begonias, as if the only thing on her mind was the health of her plants, as if she had no memory of her own involvement with Clifford Graham, no memory of telling Victoria about her wretched past.

And in that moment, Victoria understood.

She hurried back upstairs.

Why didn't I see it before? she thought. *The photograph of Jane and the copies I made are gone, because the original was never taken.* She'd stopped Clifford Graham's career in its tracks and by doing that, stopped him from tormenting her mother as well!

If Victoria had prevented Graham from becoming a portrait photographer of the rich and famous, Victoria's grandparents would never have hired him to photograph their daughters. In which case, none of her family would ever have met Clifford Graham, the nude pictures of her mother were never taken, and Margaret was never abused. And this was why her mother was acting like a different person. The shadow hanging over her life had vanished!

Victoria sank down on the bed, her knees too weak to hold her upright. The implications of her discovery were just starting to sink in. She remembered her mother's shock at seeing Jane's photograph—that sense of panic, the horrified reliving of her past humiliation, her inability to forgive herself for not protecting her younger sisters. Victoria understood all too well from her mother's behavior that once abuse happens it never entirely goes away; it stays inside you. You might be able to manage it—her mother had tried—but you could never really get rid of it.

The only thing you could do to get rid of it entirely was to stop it before it happened.

Because of Victoria's actions in Paris in 1882, her mother, having never known Clifford Graham, was now a different person, and had been ever since Victoria's last trip to Paris. She was happier and less fearful than she'd been before. Victoria had been too caught up in her own unhappiness to piece it all together, but the signs were everywhere. Her mother was painting again and getting out more; she didn't hover over Victoria as she had in the past and was generally so much more relaxed. There was even that photograph of herself she'd hung in the hallway, something she never would have allowed previously. It seemed like Victoria was the only one on the planet who knew what her mother used to be like and why.

It was the only thing that made sense. Everyone else— Victoria's father, Rose, Aunt Margaret, Aunt Constance— *everyone* but Victoria would recognize this calm, affectionate Bernadette Hubbard as the one they'd always known. Victoria had traveled through time and disrupted the future—she was the only one who could see the *before* and the *after*. So, it was her secret, and hers alone. No one else would ever know, unless she told them. And she couldn't imagine ever wanting to share such a sordid, unbelievable tale, not even with Hillary who knew about the changes Victoria had wrought in the Boit sisters' lives, but nothing about her mother's involvement in Clifford Graham's schemes.

It meant, Victoria realized, that she'd accomplished far more than she'd set out to accomplish. What had happened to her mother in her alternate past, could easily have happened to Jane. Worse, what happened to Aunt Margaret could have happened to Julia. By stopping Clifford Graham, Victoria had protected Jane and Julia—and saved her mother and Aunt Margaret, too. It was almost too much to take in, but she was beginning to see that her relationship with her mother would be completely different from now on.

One Saturday evening in early July, Victoria was at Hillary's house, sitting in the window seat in Hillary and Peg's room, listening to the rumble of Bob Dylan's *Baby Let Me Follow You Down* coming from James' bedroom. Since school had let out, Victoria had changed her mind about Dylan's gravelly voice. James had persuaded her to give him another chance. The two of them had listened to Dylan's album in the evening, up in James' room, with the lights turned low. A few weeks before, Victoria would have thought it romantic; instead, it was just companionable.

Victoria still found James attractive, but it was a comfortable feeling—it didn't make her palms sweat. They were becoming friends. He'd be leaving for college soon, and she was determined to enjoy his company for as long as he was around.

As though her thoughts had conjured him, James appeared in the doorway of Hillary's room and asked, "Hey, are you spending the night?"

"I think so," Victoria said. "I seem to have a standing invitation."

"Well, let's listen to some music later," James said, pushing his glasses down to peer at Victoria over the rim. "Alec loaned me the new Pete Seeger album."

"Great," Victoria said. On James's last weekend before leaving home for college, he and Alec and the entire O'Brien family planned to travel to Washington D. C. and join Martin Luther King's March on Washington. They'd invited Victoria to come along—and her parents had said yes. It would be her very first protest march. She couldn't wait.

Hillary was down in the kitchen getting them some lemonade. While Victoria waited for her to return, she looked out the window and saw Hillary's sisters, Erin and Peg, walk out into the lawn with their father. As she watched, Mr. O'Brien lit a couple of Fourth of July sparklers for the little girls. Laughing, they danced around the tiny yard, making wide sweeps with their arms, sending colored sparks flying up into the darkening sky.

The scene reminded Victoria of something and, after a second, she knew what it was. She went to Hillary's bookshelf and pulled out a book of Sargent prints, turning to his painting called *Carnation, Lily, Lily, Rose.*

In the picture, two little girls in white ruffled frocks were lighting paper lanterns in a garden. The dark background suggested twilight on a summer evening, and the lilies, roses, and carnations in the foreground glowed with an otherworldly luminescence. As the girls in the painting looked down at the lighted tapers in their hands, the flame from the candles turned their cheeks a warm pink. The picture captured all the effortless grace of a happily absorbed child and made Victoria smile.

As she read the description next to the print, something about the picture nagged at her. Sargent had begun the project a year after the *Madame X* debacle, when he'd moved to England and was spending time with friends at their country home. He could paint in many moods—flamboyant, mysterious, provocative—but the mood of this painting was one of pure delight. The painting was described as "so transcendent in its loveliness" that it had reestablished Sargent's popularity as a portrait painter and brought him many new commissions in both England and America.

"Hillary, look at this!" she said, when Hillary returned carrying two glasses of lemonade. "Look at the date."

Hillary peered at the text. "1885."

Victoria looked at her expectantly. Hillary was usually very good at making connections, but she looked blank.

"This book says the painting was begun a year after the *Madame X* scandal and that Sargent painted it to erase the memory of that picture from the public's mind," Victoria said.

Hillary nodded. "So, what's your point?"

"I just think he may have had another reason. Maybe he was thinking of something besides *Madame X*. This painting is about the innocence of the children."

Hillary's face finally lit up. "You mean, maybe he wanted to paint a picture of happy children—very different than his picture of the Boits?"

"Yes, but I wasn't thinking of the painting of the Boits."

"What then?"

"Not a painting," Victoria said.

"Oh! The photograph of Jane!"

Hillary handed Victoria her glass of lemonade and sat down beside her on the window seat. She was wearing a pair of ghastly plaid shorts that she might have borrowed from James. It always amazed Victoria—Hillary had such a finely tuned appreciation of beauty in art, it seemed a shame she couldn't see the possibilities for beauty in her own appearance.

But it didn't matter what Hillary looked like, what she wore or how she did her hair, Victoria reminded herself. She was a friend for keeps. If anyone ever made fun of her, Victoria would scratch their eyes out.

As the two of them looked out at the night sky, Victoria felt herself relaxing in a way she hadn't for a long time, maybe ever. She and her mother were at peace and the friendship with Hillary felt solid, one that would last a long time.

Whatever happens, she vowed, *I'll never stop being a Sargent fan.* Sargent knew that kids were vulnerable and painted that vulnerability in so many of his child portraits, especially in his painting of the Boits. Thanks to that unsettling portrait, Victoria's eyes were open and she'd always be grateful to him for that.

She hoped that, if she went ahead with her plan to be a child psychologist, she could find ways to protect children from monsters like Clifford Graham—not by keeping them ignorant of danger, as her mother had tried to do, but by teaching them ways to protect themselves. Maybe, just maybe, she could help the ones who were abused to find some measure of peace, at the very least, to stop blaming themselves. *All* abused or neglected or misunderstood children, rich or poor, needed that kind of help. And you never knew from where —or when—that help might come.

Hillary nudged her arm. "Hey," she said. "Where'd you go? Don't disappear on me again."

"I won't," Victoria replied.

Epilogue

September, 1986, Boston

Victoria checks the waiting room and is surprised to find it empty. Her next patient, Samantha, a five-year-old, who stopped speaking at age four, is late. The light on the answering machine is throbbing insistently—on-off, on-off—and Victoria sees there are three messages.

The first is from her mother. "Victoria, call me. It's important."

The second is from Samantha's mother. "Sorry for the late notice, but Sam is running a fever. We won't be able to make it today."

Victoria sighs. In her previous therapy session, the girl had finally started to relax. Victoria hopes this won't mean a setback.

The third is her mother again. "I couldn't wait to tell you! The vases—the Boit's vases! They've been loaned to the museum. They're on display with the Boit girls' portrait. You must see them. They're magnificent."

A chill runs down Victoria's spine. She checks her watch and her appointment book. If she skips lunch, she's got just under two hours. She can make it. Pulling off her heels, she grabs her comfortable walking shoes from the closet and runs down the front steps of her office. She hurries up Boylston, hoping there'll be a cab waiting in front of the Lenox Hotel. She's in luck.

As the cab backtracks along one-way streets and turns into Copley Square, they pass the Boston Public Library. Victoria thinks of the hundreds of hours she spent there as a girl, one of them the most fateful of her life. She stares at the library's beautiful Beaux-Arts façade as if seeing it for the first time, admiring the broad stone steps with the long line of gracefully arched windows above.

Then they're pulling up to the imposing front entrance of the Museum of Fine Arts and Victoria steps out. Inside, a docent tries to hand her a museum map, but she rushes past him. She knows exactly where she's going.

This is how she finds herself standing, once again, in front of her favorite painting, *The Daughters of Edward Darley Boit*. It's been years since she's seen it, but it still has the power to stun her.

And here are the vases, the actual vases, not just their painted images, standing sentry beside the painting. They're as overwhelming as ever, so huge, yet so delicate in their painted detail. The ceramic seems to glisten oddly, and she realizes she has tears in her eyes—this is hitting her harder than she imagined it would. Blinking, Victoria steps closer to admire the tiny cracks in the ceramic surface of the nearest vase. The contrast between the finely painted birds and flowers on the real vases and the blurry, impressionistic rendering of the same birds and flowers in Sargent's painting is startling.

There is a sign describing the objects that were discovered inside the vases when the museum staff was preparing them for display, and Victoria steels herself to read it. The objects include: a cigar stub, a paper airplane, a pink ribbon, a tennis ball, sheets of geography lessons, a letter about the repeal of Prohibition, an Arrow shirt collar, an old doughnut, an admission card to a dance at the Eastern Yacht Club in Marblehead, three badminton shuttlecocks (*Yes! I remember the shuttlecocks!*), many coins, and a feather.

She was quite sure Jane's photograph wouldn't be here—inside one of the vases—but she wasn't able to stop feeling anxious, all the same. Relief floods through her as she reads the list once more and comes to the firm conclusion that the final piece of damning evidence is, without a doubt, gone for good.

She lets her mind wander back to the first time she saw the actual vases, not just their painted images. And the girls—their faces, so alive, so present, even after all these years. Their lives are inextricably bound to hers, and though Victoria thinks she understands why, when it began it seemed like an accident, one that changed her life in ways she's still trying to comprehend.

Before finding the girls, she felt alone and shut off from the real world; afterward, she felt connected—to people, to history, to the whole messy, imperfect carnival of life. But that happened over time; in the beginning, when she was only fifteen, it was all about finding a friend.

In two months, Victoria realizes with a shock, her own daughter, Lucy, will be as old as she was then. She hopes she'll find the courage to tell her daughter what happened to her when she turned fifteen. Perhaps Lucy, already so worldly wise, is ready to hear it now. *Who knows?* Victoria muses, *maybe she'll believe me, just as Hillary did all those years ago.*

Afterword

The 1960s was a hair-raising time to be a teenager, and the year 1963, when this story takes place, was a pivotal year. Many of the over 250,000 people who were lucky enough to be in Washington on August 28, 1963, to hear Martin Luther King Jr.'s "I Have a Dream" speech went on to become dedicated civil rights advocates.

Life in Boston, and in the entire country, changed for everyone after President Kennedy was assassinated a few months later, in November of 1963. But it was young people in particular who felt a new sense of urgency and a strong desire for change. The passage of the Civil Rights Act in 1964, which outlawed discrimination based on race, color, religion, sex, or national origin, was a significant step in the movement toward change.

The assassinations of Martin Luther King and Bobby Kennedy in 1968, coupled with the escalation of the war in Vietnam and the wholesale draft of young college-age men, left everyone, young and old, shaken. There seemed to be no choice but to take to the streets in protest.

Julia Boit lived long enough to see this turbulent period of history unfold. She died in February 1969 in Newport, Rhode Island, where she had lived with her sister Mary Louisa since 1939. Mary Louisa died at age seventy-one in 1945, but her younger sister lived to be ninety-one. Julia was still painting at the time of her death and her watercolors were frequently exhibited at the Newport Art Association. She stayed in touch with her many young nieces and nephews, who were at her side when she died. These were the children of her half-brothers, born after Edward Darley Boit remarried following the death of Mary Louisa Cushing Boit, his first wife and mother of the four girls.

Florence Boit died in 1919, shortly after suffering a mental breakdown, and Jane Boit in 1955, after a long life spent struggling with serious physical and psychological problems. Neddie, the unacknowledged Boit son, died at his institution in 1888 at the age of twenty-three. Judging by the evidence, there is some basis for the notion of an inherited strain of mental illness in the Boit family.

Sargent lived a rewarding life as a much-acclaimed painter and died in England in 1925, at the age of sixty-nine. He remained close with his sisters Emily and Violet throughout his life and was a fond uncle to Violet's children, though he never had children of his own.

As a time-travel story, this novel dwells in the realm of magical realism, but all of the details about John Singer Sargent are based, as much as possible, on events that actually occurred in his life. The information about Sargent's paintings is taken from various books of art history, including Trevor Fairbrother's book *John Singer Sargent* (Harry H. Abrams, Inc. 1994). Historical details about the Boit family are likewise based in fact. I am indebted to Dr. Erica E. Hirshler, Croll Senior Curator of Paintings, Art of the Americas, at the Boston Museum of Fine

Afterword

Arts, who wrote her exhaustive *Sargent's Daughters: The Biography of a Painting* (MFA Publications, 2009), which provided much valuable insight into the painting and the lives of both Sargent and the Boits.

The photographer, Clifford Graham, is an imaginary person, though he is based, in part, on other photographers of the time. Lewis Carroll's shocking photographs of Evelyn Hatch and Irene MacDonald do exist and can be seen online. The idea that Clifford Graham's photograph of Jane Boit may have influenced Sargent's painting of *Madame X* is pure fiction.

Many of the Sargent paintings described may be visited at the Museum of Fine Arts and the Isabella Stewart Gardner Museum in Boston. The Boits' Japanese vases are now owned by the Museum of Fine Arts and are on display alongside the Boit girls' portrait. *Madame X* is, of course, at the Metropolitan Museum of Art in New York. The portrait of *Dr. Samuel Jean Pozzi at Home*, Sargent's painting of the infamous "Dr. Love," is owned by the Armand Hammer Museum in Los Angeles. The beloved painting *Carnation, Lily, Lily, Rose* is at the Tate Gallery in London. Julia Overing Boit's watercolors may be viewed at the Newport Art Museum in Rhode Island.

All of the paintings and photographs mentioned can be viewed online or at the author's website, saraloyster.com.

There is some question about whether Sargent painted his large seven-by-seven-foot canvas of the Boit girls in the Boits' home or in his studio, but for the sake of this novel, an authorial decision was made in favor of the Boits' apartment.

The quote which begins this story is from "The Pupil," a story by Henry James that is said to have been inspired by Sargent's experience as a young American boy growing up in Europe.

Acknowledgments

Thank you to my early readers: Mary Ann, Julia (you are both still with me), Suzanne, Cynnie, Annie, Ann L., Jessica, Linda L., Ann C., and Bob; and many of the later ones: Linda C., David, Claudia, Elizabeth, Armin, Martha, Lucy, Ella, Jan, Beth, and my oldest friends John and Freya. Thank you for plowing through those unpolished drafts and thank you for all your helpful suggestions and words of encouragement. It takes a village, I believe.

To my endlessly enthusiastic and highly skilled editors Kate Brubeck and S. Baer Lederman, thank you. And thank you to my agent, Joelle DelBourgo, who suggested I try She Writes Press and told me my publisher Brooke Warner was brilliant, which is true. Thanks also to Samantha Strom, my indomitable Project Manager at She Writes Press and to Linda Paulson, proofreader extraordinaire.

My family deserves the deepest gratitude. My mother Eugenia was my biggest champion, prodding me forward when life threatened to derail the project. My sister Karen was always ready to read the latest version and sisters Jenny and Gretchen, niece Sara, and cousin Beth all said bravo.

Special thanks to my son Daniel Hennen who gave me a time travel tutorial and suggested a plot twist that was devious in its cleverness and my daughter Clara McFadden, a writer/ librarian like me, who supplied valuable advice and editing throughout. Granddaughter Saia McFadden helped with the teen perspective. And last, but certainly not least, thanks to Geoff Van Lienden, my dear husband, who read every word of every draft and happily tramped with me through many, many museums in this country and abroad in search of Sargent's art.

About the Author

Photo credit: Karl Siefert

Sara Loyster is a writer and a librarian with forty years' experience working in public libraries. She has a B.A. in English and Creative Writing from the University of Wisconsin in Madison and an M.L.S. from the University of California in Berkeley. She lives in Berkeley and Point Reyes Station with her musician husband. They have four grown children and nine grandchildren. This is her debut novel.

SELECTED TITLES FROM SHE WRITES PRESS

She Writes Press is an independent publishing
company founded to serve women writers everywhere.
Visit us at www.shewritespress.com.

Chasing North Star by Heidi McCrary. $16.95, 978-1-63152-757-9.
With help from a worn leather journal, a young girl learns the story
of another girl who escaped war-torn Germany for a better life in
America—except her life didn't turn out as expected. The stories of
these two girls intertwine and eventually collide one Christmas night
when a long-buried secret finally comes to life.

The Lines Between Us by Rebecca D'Harlingue. $16.95, 978-1-63152-
743-2. A young girl flees seventeenth-century Madrid, in fear for her
life. Three centuries later and a continent away, a woman comes across
old papers long hidden away, and in them discovers the reason for the
flight so long ago, and for her own mother's enigmatic dying words.

The Black Velvet Coat by Jill G. Hall. $16.95, 978-1-63152-009-9.
When the current owner of a black velvet coat—a San Francisco artist in search of inspiration—and the original owner, a 1960s heiress
who fled her affluent life fifty years earlier, cross paths, their lives are
forever changed . . . for the better.

The Pelton Papers by Mari Coates, $16.95, 978-1-63152-687-9. A richly
imagined novel based on the life of artist Agnes Pelton, *The Pelton
Papers* covers everything from her shrouded Brooklyn childhood to her
early success in the Armory Show of 1913, subsequent retreat to a con-
templative life, and, ultimately, the flowering of her deeply spiritual art.

Shrug by Lisa Braver Moss, $16.95, 978-1-63152-638-1. It's the 1960s,
and teenager Martha Goldenthal just wants to do well at Berkeley
High and apply to college—but how can she when her father is a
raging batterer who disdains academia, and her mother is arguably
worse? When her mother abandons the family, Martha must stand up
to her father to fulfill her vision of going to college.